a hint of

HITCHCOCK

stories inspired by the master of suspense

OTHER TITLES FROM BLACK BEACON BOOKS

Anthologies:

Murder and Machinery
The Black Beacon Book of Mystery
Shelter from the Storm
Lighthouses
Subtropical Suspense

Books by Cameron Trost:

Oscar Tremont, Investigator of the Strange and Inexplicable
The Animal Inside
Letterbox
Hoffman's Creeper and Other Disturbing Tales
The Tunnel Runner

www.blackbeaconbooks.com

a hint of
HITCHCOCK

Black Beacon Books

A Hint of Hitchcock
Published by Black Beacon Books
Edited by Cameron Trost
Cover design by Cameron Trost
Copyright © Black Beacon Books, 2022

Photograph by Nikola Johnny Mirkovic
https://unsplash.com/@thejohnnyme

Better Not Look Down © Josh Pachter
First appeared in Mickey Finn: 21st Century Noir, Vol. 1,
Down and Out Books, 2020
Golden Curls © Rebecca A. Demarest
More Than Suspicion © Joseph S. Walker
Paranoia © Paulene Turner
The Suitcase © Jason Fischer
Rebecca Redux © Elizabeth Elwood
Highwayman's Hitch © Cameron Trost
Relish © David Carroll
First appeared in Southern Blood, Sandglass Enterprises, 2003
Karma is a Thief in the Night © Roger Johns
Scallion's Head © H.K. Stubbs
Closed Circuit © Mark Blackham
Vault © Andy Rausch

Black Beacon Books
blackbeaconbooks.com

ISBN: 978-0-6452471-0-7

Alfred Hitchcock—the name that springs to mind whenever you think about suspense films or legendary directors—and if you're like me, that's on a regular basis. His films never cease to be cited in lists of the seventh art's masterpieces, crediting him for ground-breaking camera work in *Vertigo* or the ability to build edge-of-your-seat suspense with a wheelchair-bound James Stewart in *Rear Window*.

Many of his films, including the two mentioned above, were inspired by novels and short stories, and in turn, he put his hand to producing books with his thrilling anthologies. Is it not surprising then that there are so few anthologies dedicated to the master of suspense? With *A Hint of Hitchcock*, my aim is to fill that gap, and to give modern authors a chance to send a chill up our spines the way Hitchcock did—to subtly pay homage to his legacy but without forsaking originality.

Each story in this anthology is inspired by one or more of Hitchcock's films, with one exception which is based on a classic short story Hitchcock wanted to develop into a film but never got the chance to. When I first began putting this anthology together, I planned to include the title of the film upon which each story is based, because the link isn't always obvious, but on second thoughts, I decided against it. Letting the reader work it out adds a dash of suspense in itself. Consider it a test—how well do you know Hitchcock's opus?

Now, do you dare read on? Are you ready? Great! Go ahead and turn the page. Let the suspense begin!

Cameron Trost, editor

Author Biographies

Better Not Look Down

Josh Pachter

As I stand here on the narrow ledge on the outside of the Bradbury Building, five flights above the rumble and honk of the midtown L.A. traffic, a line from an old B.B. King song floats across my mind.

Better not look down, if you want to keep on flyin', put the hammer down and keep it full speed ahead.

My eyes are squeezed tightly shut, so there's no danger I'll look down, B.B., no need to worry about that.

Instead, I look *back*, twenty-four hours into the past, to a time when all I had to worry about was whether or not I wanted another cup of coffee with my breakfast…

#

Millie stood on the other side of the counter with the carafe in her hand, her face a vision of Hollywood loveliness, her scarlet fingernails tapping on the glass. The nails were carefully manicured, much too nice for a waitress in Jerry's Diner, and they distracted me from the question of coffee.

Millie snapped her gum, and I blinked out of my reverie.

'You was sure out there somewhere, Mr. Taylor,' she said, the New York not yet bleached out of her voice by her years in La La Land. Her lips were the exact same red as her nails, their bold color contrasting attractively with the pastel pink of her uniform. 'You want a refill or not?'

'Sure, hit me again,' I said. 'But cut me off after this cup. I

9

don't want to show up for work with too *much of a buzz.'*

She topped off my coffee, and as she turned away to replace the pot on its burner I scanned the sleekness of her afterdeck. Then she swiveled back to face me, and once again I admired the warm curves of her superstructure.

'What are you doing in a dump like this, Millie?' I asked her, not for the first time. 'With your looks, you ought to—'

'I ought to be in pictures, I know,' she completed our daily ritual. 'Just like a million other girls in this town. If only you was a producer, Mr. Taylor, maybe you could do something about it.'

'I'm working on it.' I smiled. 'I might be just a crummy claims adjuster today, but I'm making headway on my script, and someday I'll—'

'Someday, yeah. You and a million other guys in this town. Except by then I'll be too old to play anything but grammas.'

She went off to take an order from an elderly couple who'd just settled into a booth, and I shoveled the last of my Western omelet down the hatch and chased the eggs with a swallow of hot java.

I was sliding my check from beneath my saucer and reaching for my wallet when she called 'Adam and Eve on a raft, whiskey down, and flop two with a brick' through the pass-through into the kitchen, then came back to where I was sitting. 'Hey, Mr. Taylor,' she said, frowning slightly, 'maybe you could help me out with something, after all?'

'If I can,' I said, wondering how in the world a schlub like me could possibly be of assistance to a knockout like her. 'What's on your mind?'

#

As I balance precariously on the ledge, B.B. King goes on singing that damn song inside my head.

An old girl friend of mine showed up the other day. That girl

10

had lived in *love and* for *love and* over *love and* under *love all her life.*

My fingertips and the right side of my face are pressed tightly against the Bradbury's rough exterior brickwork. My toes are beginning to cramp. I ease my eyes open a crack. About eight feet to my left, a uniformed cop is leaning out my manager's office window, forcing a friendly smile, waving encouragingly for me to come on back inside.

I swivel my head and look the other way. Eight feet to my right, a boulder in a cheap suit leans out *my* window, his ugly mug wearing an expression that is neither friendly nor a smile.

'What do you think you're doing out there, asshole?' the boulder growls. 'Get the fuck back in here and take what you got coming.'

I lick my lips. My throat is bone dry. It's maybe a quarter past nine and the sun is hidden behind a bank of gray clouds, but the day is already hot, and inside my jacket and tie I'm sweating like a pig.

Better not look back, B.B. sings, *or you might just wind up crying.*

Ignoring his advice, I look back, back thirteen hours, though it seems like it all happened years ago…

#

Just after eight pm, Millie and I strolled into Barney's Beanery on Santa Monica and managed to snag a booth by the window. This was the first time I'd ever seen her out of uniform, and she looked even more shipshape in a sheer white blouse and short sea-green skirt than in her waitress outfit.

At the diner this morning, she'd explained that she'd been dating some guy named Terry d'Agosto for a couple of months. He was a decent young man, but it wasn't serious between them, at least not as far as Millie was concerned. He was more a friend than a boyfriend, someone to catch a movie with, go to

11

the Zoo on a Saturday afternoon, drive up to Griffith Observatory and gaze out at the view.

Then, two weeks ago, Terry'd invited her to Sunday dinner at his parents' house in Reseda. That seemed a little premature to Millie, but she didn't have any other plans for the day, so she agreed to go. Mom and Pop were pleasant folks, but Terry's brother Tony showed up halfway through the meal and put a damper on things. He was a thug, a creep, 'sort of, I don't know, Godfather-y, you know what I mean?'

And that tore it for Millie. In Terry's car on the way back downtown, she told him she was uncomfortable about his brother, and she thought it would be best if the two of them didn't see each other any more. Terry was disappointed, but he seemed to take it well enough, and when he dropped her off at her place in Central-Alameda they shook hands and parted, she thought, on friendly terms.

Except that wasn't the end of it. Terry started sending her emails and texts, calling her at home and at work, begging her to get back with him, and nothing she said seemed to penetrate his dogged determination.

Which is where I came in. Once Terry saw she'd moved on to another guy, she explained, he'd have to get the message and leave her alone. She hated to put me out, but would I be willing to?

Barney's Beanery was pretty much a busman's holiday for Millie, but it was a place she knew Terry and his pals frequented, so there was a good chance either he'd see us himself or someone else would and would pass the word along that she'd found herself a new beau.

We'd both already eaten supper and neither one of us was hungry, but for the sake of appearances we ordered a plate of Irish nachos and a chocolate milkshake with two straws. We nibbled nachos and took turns sipping the shake and talked. Somewhere along the line, I convinced her it was okay to drop the 'Mr. Taylor' and call me Al.

12

Right at nine, they dimmed the lights for some reason, and it took a few seconds for my eyes to adjust to the different illumination…

#

The sun comes out from behind the clouds, and my eyes adjust to the sudden glare.

'We can work this out, Al,' a voice says, and I turn back to my left and see my boss, Ira Steinmetz, leaning over the cop's shoulder. 'Whatever this is, it can't be as bad as you're thinking. Come back in, and we'll figure it out, I promise.'

'Butt out, shitheel,' the boulder on my right rumbles. 'You got no fuckin' *idea* what kind of trouble this dick is in.'

I keep my attention focused on Mr. Steinmetz and the cop, so the boulder jacks up the volume. His voice pounds inside my skull.

'I'll give you exactly thirty seconds to haul your sorry ass back in here, Taylor. Don't *make* me come out there and get you.'

If the arrows from Cupid's bow that had passed through her heart had been sticking out of her body, B.B. sings inside my head, drowning out the angry howl, *she would have looked like a porcupine.*

I force myself not to think about the boulder or Mr. Steinmetz or my situation. Instead, I cast my thoughts back eleven hours into the past…

#

It was about ten pm by the time Millie and I came back out of Barney's onto Santa Monica. I'd left my car on the upper deck of the Kings Road Municipal Parking Structure, and while we waited for the light at North Olive to change she put her arm through mine. I glanced down, surprised. 'Just in case

13

he's watching,' she whispered, and I half relaxed but felt a twinge of regret that the physical contact was just an act. I think by then I was beginning to believe the whole story of Terry d'Agosto and his hoodlum brother was just a story, an excuse to give Millie and me some time to get to know each other as something more than merely waitress and customer.

There's a narrow alley halfway between Olive and Kings, and as we walked past it a hand shot out and grabbed my collar and hauled me into the darkness. Millie, her arm still linked through mine, staggered in on my heels.

'So this *is the scumbag you dumped me for?' a reedy voice spat. I was confused for a second, since the voice was a good six feet away, too far to go with the hand still clamped on my collar.*

'Terry!' Millie gasped. 'What do you think you're—?'

A cellphone flashlight blinked on and lit up a sliver of the alley, revealing two guys I'd never seen before. The scrawny one holding up the phone, six feet away, was apparently Terry d'Agosto.

And the gorilla who had me tight in his grip was apparently his brother, Tony.

#

The hulk to my right disappears from my office window, and for just a second I feel relief wash over me.

Then a weathered brown brogan comes into sight, and I realize the guy is about to do exactly what he warned me would happen next: he's coming out to get me.

I shuffle a careful step to my left, lengthening the distance between me and the boulder but bringing me that much closer to the cop hanging out Mr. Steinmetz's window.

What difference does it make which way I go? They've got me surrounded.

Inside my head, B.B. King sings, *Do you think I've lived my life all wrong? And I said, 'The only advice I have to pass along is concealed in the chorus of this song.'*

This is too goddamn much for me to handle, so I disconnect from the present moment and let my thoughts go back…

#

'Here's how this is going to work,' Tony d'Agosto growled. 'You,' he nodded at Millie, 'are gonna get back with my brother. And you'—he shook me like a maraca to make sure I was paying attention—'are gonna go on about your business and forget you ever met this young lady.'

'Are you crazy?' Millie exploded. 'What makes you think you can order us around like that?'

Tony's free hand slipped inside his jacket and came out holding the biggest gun I have ever seen in my life.

'This does,' he said.

#

As I inch further to my left, away from the boulder and closer to the uniformed cop hanging out my boss's window, I see that the forced smile is gone from his face and he's holding a matte-black gun in his hand. It might be a pistol, a revolver, a Glock, a Sig Sauer, I don't know anything about guns. I'm not sure I ever *saw* one in real life before last night.

I've been around, and I've seen some things, B.B. King sings inside my head. *People moving faster than the speed of sound, faster than a speeding bullet.*

Right here, right now, my thoughts are moving faster than I can process, so I let my mind drift back to that alley between Olive and Kings Road…

#

I am not a man of action. I'm a claims adjuster, for God's sake! I haven't been in a fight since I was ten years old, and I lost that one, wound up with broken glasses and a bloody nose.

But at the sight of Tony d'Agosto's gun some primal instinct kicked in, and I grabbed for it with both hands. If Terry's brother had been thinking rationally, he would have backhanded me the hell out of the way, but I guess my sudden shift onto the offensive sent him into instinct mode, too, and before I knew what was happening I was wrestling him for control of the weapon, so focused on the moment I barely heard Millie's screams and Terry's shouts in the background.

And then an enormous blast knocked me on my ass and the air was heavy with the stink of gunpowder and the world went completely silent.

It took a while for my hearing to come back, and all I heard when it did was a horrified whimpering. I looked around and saw Terry's iPhone lying in the dirt, the flashlight still on, its harsh glow leaking from around the edges of the case. I managed to crawl over to it and pick it up and pan it around the alley.

All four of us were on the ground. Millie was shaking convulsively and sobbing. Terry had a hole the size of a baseball ripped out of his chest.

'Jesus God,' Millie was whispering, over and over again. 'Jesus! Jesus God!'

The gun lay in the dirt at Tony's side. His head was covered with blood, and he wasn't moving. The recoil from the gunshot had apparently flung him backwards, hard enough to smash his skull against the brick wall of the building that ran along the side of the alley.

#

I stare at the gun in the cop's hand. It's pointing downward, not at me, and B.B. King reminds me *You can keep it moving,*

16

if you don't look down.

But where else is there to look? I've got an armed cop to my left, a raging boulder coming at me from my right. Where else *is* there?

So I press my forehead against the Bradbury's brick wall and look back, of course, back ten hours in time…

#

Millie and I sat there in the dirt, holding hands, expecting at any moment to hear the wail of approaching sirens.

But there were no sirens. No one seemed to have heard the gunshot but us, and after a while her weeping tapered off and she wiped her runny nose with a tissue from her purse and we had to decide what to do.

'It was an accident,' she said. 'And it was their fault, Al, not ours. We have to call the police.'

'No way,' I said. 'We're sitting here with two dead bodies for company, there's no way the police don't arrest us. Me, at least, and maybe you, too.'

'Then what*?' she said, and I could see fear growing in her eyes.*

I thought furiously. 'Nobody knows a thing about this except us,' I said at last. 'You got any more of those tissues?'

She handed me the packet, and I picked up Tony's gun and wiped it clean, then worked it back into his lifeless hand and pressed his index finger against the trigger to leave a print.

#

The imprint of the rough brick wall on my forehead brings me back to the present. I'm looking left, at the cop, but to my right I can hear the scuffle of the boulder's shoes on the ledge, coming inexorably closer. Who does this guy think he is, a superhero?

17

People living like Superman, B.B. King sings inside my head, *all day and all night. And I won't say if it's wrong, and I won't say if it's right.*

Time's getting short, I know. Another minute or two at most, and one or the other of them's going to grab me.

I used to be a claims adjuster, I think. How the *hell* did I get from there to here?

#

An hour ago, I was sitting at my desk, trying to concentrate on a claim form. Act normal, Millie and I had decided, go to work, live your life, pretend it never happened, there's nothing to tie either one of us to two dead bodies in a Los Angeles alley.

Except then my phone rang, and when I picked it up a terrified Millie was on the line.

'Mr. Taylor,' she whispered fiercely, and then she caught herself and said, 'Al! He's not dead!'

I thought I must have misunderstood her. 'Who?' I demanded. 'Terry? He had a hole the size of a—'

'Not Terry, Tony! When the gun went off last night, it kicked him back into the wall and knocked him out. He was bleeding and unconscious, but he wasn't dead!'

'How do you—?'

'He came to the diner! Just now! He grabbed me and pulled me outside and—I'm sorry, Al, I didn't want to, but he hurt me. He made me tell him who you are and where you work! He says you killed his brother, and he's on his way to your office right now! And there's something else—'

#

Maybe there's something else I can do to protect Millie and me, to keep us both safe, but I can't for the life of me think fast enough to figure out what it is.

18

I'm pretty fast myself, B.B. King sings inside my head, but I know I'm not fast enough to find a way out of this mess.

The boulder named Tony d'Agosto is closing in on me, only a couple of feet away. He's not shouting any more, just muttering under his breath, and, honestly, I think that's worse.

I sneak a glance to my right. The back of his head is bandaged from where he crashed into the alley's brick wall, and there is murder in his black eyes.

I turn back to my left, clinging to one last shred of hope, but I know the uniformed cop won't do anything to help me, thanks to that 'something else' Millie told me on the phone, an hour ago…

#

'There's something else,' Millie said urgently. 'Tony's not a gangster, Al—he's a policeman, a homicide detective. He's got you dead to rights for Terry's murder, he says, and the court will throw the book at you, not just for shooting Terry but for trying to frame Tony for the killing. You've got to get out of there, Al! He's on his way!'

I should have taken off, like Millie said. I should have gone straight to the bank and cleaned out my accounts and run. I don't know why I didn't. Instead, though, I just sat there at my desk and stared blindly at that stupid claim form until I heard the commotion out in the lobby, and then I panicked. My office has just the one door, which opens right out into the lobby, so I couldn't go that way. But the Bradbury—L.A.'s oldest landmarked building—is old enough it's still got windows that open, so I threw open my fifth-floor window and, like an idiot, climbed out onto the ledge.

#

Like an idiot, I close my eyes again, hoping against hope

19

that dangers I can't see will somehow, miraculously, disappear.

Idiot, I scold myself, and I open my eyes. I'm facing the Bradbury's historic brick wall. I look to my left and see the uniformed cop, gun in hand, scowling, all trace of friendliness gone. I look to my right and see Tony d'Agosto inching closer.

Better not look down, B.B. King warns me, but at this point, what do I have to lose?

I look down.

There's a crowd gathered on the sidewalk, peering up at the show, a line of cops holding them back. I'm too high up to know for sure, but I think Millie might be down there in her pink uniform, her soft hands cupped around her red lips, shouting words that don't quite reach up to my perch.

A cop to my left, waiting to arrest me for murder. Detective d'Agosto to my right, coming to arrest me or beat the shit out of me or both. And five stories of nothing but air beneath me, with a cement sidewalk carpeting the bottom.

A fire truck screeches around the corner of South Los Angeles onto East 3rd. It will pull up in front of the Bradbury within seconds and disgorge men with a big trampoline-like net, ready to catch me if I fall.

Oh, B.B., Riley B. King sings inside my head, *sometimes it's so hard to pull things together. Could you tell me what you think I ought to do?*

Maybe a jury will believe Millie over Tony at my trial, and they'll let me go.

Maybe a good lawyer might get me off on a technicality.

Yeah, sure, I think, or maybe I can fly—up, up, and away, like Superman, faster than a speeding bullet.

Probably not, but what the fuck?

I look at Tony d'Agosto and say, 'Sorry about your brother.'

I look at the uniformed cop and say, 'Sorry to disappoint you, pal.'

I look down and mouth the words, 'Sorry, Millie. Honest to God.'

And then I raise my hands from the bricks and lean back and fly away, full speed ahead.

Golden Curls

Rebecca A. Demarest

'Mother! You'll never guess who is wearing the centrepiece in the next dress show at the shop.' I slipped out of my coat and hung it from the hook in the mudroom before continuing into the kitchen.

'Daisy, a delight as always.'

I skidded to a halt as Joe Chandler, still in his copper's uniform, rose from our table. 'Mr. Chandler, how are you?'

Joe took my hand in both of his. 'You know you can call me Joe, and I am the better for seeing you. I'm sorry you had to cancel tea last week. You said something about work?'

My mother—the traitor—smiled into her tea cup; I bet she had invited him in for a cuppa this afternoon precisely because I was due home. No matter how many times I told her I was *not* interested in the policeman who lived down the street, she kept insisting. I 'just had to give it time' or 'get to know him'. As if time would temper his overbearing personality or familiarity blunt his tendency to run roughshod over me in conversation.

I let him hold my hand exactly long enough to be polite before I gently pulled it from his grasp. 'Yes. We have a dress show in a few weeks and they needed all us mannequins to come by for fittings.'

He laughed, too loud for the small space of the kitchen and I winced. 'I do wish they'd stop using that outdated term for you. It makes me think you're made of wax! Apparently in New York they're calling your kind of work "modelling" now.'

I went to the stove and poured myself a cup of tea, adding a generous dollop of cream. 'Yes, I had heard that, but the girls and I prefer the French term. It is more elegant. Did you have a reason for stopping by today?'

Mother let her cup clink hard against the saucer. 'Tosh now, girl, does a man need a reason to stop by a lady's house?'

I raised an eyebrow at her, trying to communicate just how much I'd prefer to hurry him out the door. 'Not as such, but he usually does.'

Joe laughed, raising his hands in surrender. 'Guilty as charged. I did have news I wanted to share with you. Another girl was found murdered this evening.'

Stirring my tea, I frowned. 'What is that, two?'

'Three now. All with blonde curly hair.' This last he addressed to my mother and I could see his argument coming from a mile out.

Mother obliged, gasping in horror, her hand to her chest. 'Just like my baby. Oh, Daisy, won't you let Joe escort you to and from work? It would make me feel ever so much better.'

I disguised my instinctive wrinkled nose response by taking a long sip of my tea. 'You know perfectly well how safe I am. I walk home with Betty and Marcy, they only live a few doors away from us. I wouldn't want to be a bother. Joe must have a very busy dance card, being a policeman.'

'Really, it would be my honour to walk beside you, and keep you safe from the scourge of this killer who is stalking our streets.' Joe pulled out a chair for me, but I ignored it, unwilling to get closer than I needed to.

'I need to put some toast on,' I demurred. I turned to rummage in the bread box, hoping to light on an argument that might make him give up this preposterous line of inquiry when a smart rapping at the front door drew my attention. 'I'll get it.'

Leaving the kitchen before either Mother or Joe could complain, I made my way to the front of the house and unlocked the front door. A gentleman stood on the stoop, looking out into the gray drizzly evening, his overcoat fine quality wool, if a little worn, and his hat in his hand. At the sound of the door opening, he turned, and the hallway lamps caught the brilliant green of his eyes and shined on his dark, rain-damp hair.

'Mr. Bunting told me you still have rooms to let?' he inquired.

'Pardon?' I asked, half my head back in the conversation with Joe, the other half admiring how his frame filled out his jacket.

The man twisted his hat in his hands. 'I met Mr. Bunting at an associate's house and he implied he had rooms to let?'

I smiled as my thoughts caught up. 'Oh! Yes. Yes we do. We're a little empty at the moment, seeing as the college is out for the term. Come in.'

'Thank you.' He shook the rain from his coat before entering the hall and I shut the door, being careful to re-lock it. Just because I was not willing to suffer Joe's company every day did not mean I wasn't taking the killer in our city seriously.

Gesturing into the morning room, I smiled. 'Wait right here, if you please.'

The man took a look around the room, noting the copious amount of crochet doilies and walls crowded with paintings of family members, before turning to the divan to take a seat. 'As you wish.'

I smiled again, and scurried back to the kitchen.

'Who was that, dear?' Mother inquired.

'New lodger. Says father met him at the manor.' I picked up my cup of tea again, but grimaced to find it had gone cold. 'I put him in the morning room for the moment.'

Mother groaned as she stood, stiff in her joints after sitting still too long. 'Lovely! Joe, dear, do excuse me.'

He nodded and watched her leave before turning to me again. 'I really think you'd be safer—'

'Look,' I interrupted him, 'I'm safe as houses already,

please don't make a big fuss out of this. You know what my father is like when he gets worked up.'

Joe scowled, chewing on the inside of his cheek, a sign I was coming to know well since I made it a point to frustrate his affections whenever possible. After a moment, he stood. 'I see. If you'll excuse me. I should get back to work.'

I laid a hand on his arm as he made his way past me to the back door. Better to mitigate that temper now than deal with the petulance later. 'I appreciate the offer, I really do. But I will be fine.'

He didn't meet my eyes, but did lay a hand on top of mine. 'I just worry, is all. Is that so bad?' Patting my hand, he continued out the door, closing it gently behind himself. Finally.

The murmur of conversation from the front of the house drew me back to the morning room.

'Ah, Daisy, you must have felt your ears burning. This is my daughter, Daisy.' Mother gestured for me to come closer and I was happy to oblige. 'This is Mr. Sleuth, he will be staying in the Green Room, I think. Closer to the privy,' she confided to the man. Mr. Sleuth, I reminded myself.

'Pleased to meet you, Mr. Sleuth.' I offered my hand and to my delight, he gripped it in a firm handshake instead of that limp cupping most men apply to a woman's hand. 'What brings you to London?'

'Is it that clear that I'm from out of town?' He smiled and his cheek dimpled on the right, giving him an asymmetrical, wry expression whether he intended it or not.

I nodded at his hat. 'Your top, sir. It's fashioned in the Italian style, regardless of your British accent. Not common around these parts.'

Mr. Sleuth laughed. 'You have me there. I've just returned from my travels, but the coach seems to have lost most of my luggage on the way here. You have an eye for fashion, Daisy. Do you have any recommendations for shops near here that could accommodate my sudden need for a new wardrobe?'

'Depends on your purse,' I replied.

Heavy! mouthed Mother behind his turned back.

'I'm sure I have enough to cover the stores around here. I can always make a trip to the bank, however, if I find myself in need of additional funds.' Mr. Sleuth smiled at me and I almost melted into my bar shoes.

'Tomorrow, then. I have the morning free, I can take you around if you'd like.'

'I'd like that very much, thank you.' He turned to my mother. 'If you do not mind, it's been a long day of travel and I'd like to make my toilet and retire.'

'Of course, Mr. Sleuth, right this way.' Mother led the way out of the room, and the new lodger followed, murmuring a good night as he passed.

#

The next morning, I made my way to the kitchen to help Mother with breakfast to find Father already ensconced with his tea and the paper. It was sitting front page up on the table and they were whispering to each other, agitated, when I walked in. They immediately stopped, but it was obvious what they were talking about.

The headline screamed from the page in large font: 3RD BLONDE DEAD! NO LEADS.

I snorted on my way to the stove. 'No leads, my arse. If they'd look a little harder at the gentry, I'm sure it'd be solved in two shakes.'

'Language!' Mother scolded me.

I snagged a piece of toast from the stove and sat at the table, juggling it until it cooled enough that it wouldn't burn. 'It's appropriate in this instance. You mean to tell me that three young, blonde women have died and the police have no clue? Poppycock.'

26

Father harrumphed, and gave Mother a meaningful look. She nodded and turned to me, ignoring the eggs on the stove for the moment. 'Daisy. Darling. We think it would be best if you let Joe walk you to and from work, at the very least. Especially when you are coming home late at night.'

'For the last time, no. I don't want to encourage him. He's bad enough as it is and I'll never accept a ring from him, so it's probably best if *you* stop encouraging him as well.' I buttered my toast and took a large bite.

'I respect your wishes in regards to marriage, but look, see?' Father spread out the map on the second page of the newspaper, showing where the bodies were found. 'This lunatic is getting closer by the minute. A straight line, pointed right at our neighbourhood. You need *some* sort of protection when you're out walking late at night. You know it can't be me, I'm needed at the manor for work at that time.'

'I could accompany Miss Bunting.' The three of us turned at the sound of our new lodger in the doorway. To be honest, I think the three of us had forgotten he had moved in last night, it'd been so long since we had one. 'The eggs, Mrs. Bunting?'

'What? Oh!' Mother whirled to the stove and snatched the pan off the stove in a vain attempt to keep them from scorching. 'Drat. Let me start over, it'll just be a moment.'

The tall man gave an abbreviated bow. 'Please, don't worry on my account, I was planning on stopping for tea on my way to the stores this morning. Miss Bunting, I believe you might have some suggestions on the shopping, given your knowledge of Italian hats?'

I struggled to swallow the last large bite of toast and hastily wiped my mouth with one of the napkins at the table. 'Just Daisy, please. And I'd be happy to show you the worthwhile clothiers in the area.' I popped up from the table. 'Mother, Father, I'll see you this evening after work!'

Counting on them not making a fuss in front of the new lodger, I dodged their weak protests and snagged my coat and bag from beside the door. Mr. Sleuth was on my heels and I spun when I hit the sidewalk, walking backwards to talk to him face to face as he caught up.

'So, Mr. Sleuth, are you in the market for high-end clothing? Midrange? Used? How fashionable do you like to be? Avant garde? Fresh out of Paris? Staid standards?' I stumbled a bit on an uneven cobble and the lodger darted forward to steady my arm until I found my footing. Laughing at my own clumsiness, I turned to face forward again. He let go just as soon as he could be sure I wasn't tumbling down.

'Good, quality clothes that will last several seasons. I'm not one for flashy fabric nor expensive for the sake of the expense. And please, call me Randall.' He clasped his hands behind his back as he walked, giving him the appearance of a large, drably coloured stork stalking at my side.

'Randall it is. Come now, let's start at Rosie's Tea Room. She makes the most divine cakes.' I pulled him down a side street and we were off.

The day passed quickly as we darted from shop to shop, gathering everything Randall needed to expand his now respectable wardrobe. I stuck to the shops I knew had good deals and quality clothes, and by lunch he was kitted out. We were finishing up at a café not too far from my evening job at the club when Joe strode past.

'Daisy! Hullo, this is a pleasant surprise. And who is this?' My perennial suitor eyed Randall, measuring him with a policeman's keen eye.

'Mr. Sleuth, this is Joe Chandler, of the City Police. Joe, this is Randall Sleuth, our new lodger. I was showing him the best places to repurchase his lost wardrobe.' I took a sip from my lemonade, watching Joe preen and Randall...not care? Interesting.

'Pleased to make your acquaintance.' Randall offered his hand and after a hesitation, Joe shook.

'Any friend of the Buntings is a friend of mine. Daisy,' Joe turned back to me, effectively dismissing Randall. 'I stopped at your house to pick you up for your shift at the club tonight, but your parents said you were out. I'm glad I ran into you, as I'm sure Mr. Sleuth here should be heading homeward with his packages.'

I rolled my eyes, not caring if it hurt his feelings. 'I'm fine, really, Joe. Randall offered to accompany me to work to stop Mother and Father from fretting, but I am an adult, and it's still daylight!' I stood up, tossing my napkin on the table. 'Would you be so kind as to help Randall carry all his purchases back to the house? I will head, *alone*, to the club.' I flounced away, not looking back when Joe called my name.

#

When my shift was done, I exited the club with my fellow waitresses into the foggy London night. I'd changed back into my more comfortable shoes, but even still, my dogs were barking and I was ready to collapse into bed. Marcy, Betty, and I waved goodnight to the girls headed in the opposite direction and we linked arms, hobbling down the street, complaining about our feet, the scanty tips, our manager, all of it. Granted, dressing in a skimpy flapper dress and serving drinks to wealthy men definitely had its advantages, but it was still a job.

It didn't take us long to reach our street, but Marcy and Betty hesitated at their house. Marcy shared a glance with Betty before turning to me. 'Maybe we should go all the way down to your house first, Daisy.'

I laughed, waving them off. 'Oh, so just because I'm blonde, you think I'll get lost?'

Betty grimaced. 'No, we're afraid you'll get dead. Lookit the hair on you!'

I started walking backwards down the block. 'I'll be fine. Good night, girls. Sweet dreams!' I turned and strode off, pretending the shadows in the alley weren't causing unease. I heard a whispered conversation behind me, followed by their door opening and closing and I headed down the lane.

I hadn't passed the next house when I heard the echo of footsteps behind me, obvious now in the absence of chatter. I paused, but heard nothing more. Sometimes, the fog was like that, playing tricks. I took another step, but hesitated, and in the space where my heel would have impacted the sidewalk, I heard someone stutter to a halt behind me again.

I broke for the house, hiking up my skirts and taking the long strides the neighbourhood boys used to tease me about. A moment later, I was at my front door, fumbling to find the keys in my purse. The sound of steps closed in behind me and I swung out with my purse, hollered, 'I'll gut you, you gormless wretch!'

My purse missed but I finally got the key in the lock, opened the door, and slammed it closed again, slapping the locking mechanism till it caught. I caught my breath for a moment, but when there wasn't any other noise from the front walk, I peered out the morning room window onto an empty street. Whoever it was, they were long gone.

'Daisy? Is that you?' Mother called from the kitchen. 'Everything alright?'

'Fine, Mother.' I wiped my face, realizing for the first time that I was crying. 'I'm going to go take a bath, alright?'

'Of course, sweet dreams, love.'

'You, too.' I climbed the stairs to the washroom slowly. There wasn't any noise from Randall's room and I wondered if he'd gone to bed early, but that was neither here nor there. I ran the water into the tub, and while I waited for it to fill, I stripped in front of the small mirror. As I stared at myself, I wondered if I should tell my Mother what had just happened, but I couldn't be sure if anything *had* happened. What if I had just scared myself with the dark and the fog? I groaned and realized that if Joe heard about this, real or not, he would be glued to my side. No, I was fine, I was home, and who knows, maybe it was just my imagination. Better to leave it alone.

I sank into the tub, making sure my curly bob stayed well above the water line. I dabbled in the water with my feet, stretching out my sore muscles. Before too long, I was much calmer and decided that I was just being silly; no one had been following me. I sighed and sank further into the water.

I had nearly fallen asleep in the tub when I heard the front door open and close and I sat up with a slosh, listening to the stairs. I didn't know Randall all that well yet, so I wasn't sure who it was until he knocked on the door and asked, 'Daisy?'

'Hi, Randall. Out late, were we?' I stepped out of the bath, towelling off vigorously to keep the chill of the house at bay.

'Yes, I had an appointment. I wanted to be sure you made it home safe before I went to bed.'

'Well, question answered. I'll be done momentarily, if you need the washroom.' I shrugged into my shift and dress again and unlatched the door. Randall stood in the hall, hands once more clasped behind him.

'Yes, thank you, but I hope you didn't rush on my account.' His smile was slow and shy.

'No, I was about to fall asleep and drown myself from exhaustion, so, really, you did me a favour.' I slipped past him into the hall, but he didn't retreat to the washroom quite yet.

He met my eyes, and it took him less effort to keep his eyes off my damp décolletage than most of the men I served during the evening. 'If you need a chaperone at any point, I am happy to be of service again. I begin my posting next week, but if you need me in the meantime, I'm at your disposal.'

I smiled, blushing a little at his earnestness. 'I appreciate it, thank you, Randall. I'll let you know. Goodnight.'

'Goodnight, Daisy.'

#

For all that I took a fright that evening, I slept soundly and without dreams. One of the few benefits of hard work. I joined my parents for breakfast and found Randall already there. The three of them stopped speaking when I entered the room, and I sighed before fixing my tea.

'I begin to think there's a conspiracy with all the sudden silences. What is it this morning?'

'Perhaps it's best if you sit, love.' Mother approached me as if I would collapse at any moment.

'Perhaps it's best if you just tell me. What's going on?' I looked for the newspaper, but my father was holding it folded under his arm so it offered no clues.

Finally, he spoke up. 'Betty was killed last night.'

I set the teacup down with a clatter. 'What? No, that's impossible, I…they were inside before I was even down the block. What do you mean she was killed?'

Mother took my hands. 'Apparently, she was waiting for her beau to come by for a nightcap and when someone knocked on their door, she opened it. James found her not ten minutes later.'

I looked at Randall, the only one not speaking in this tableau, but he kept his eyes on the table. Fair enough, he didn't know Betty, or who she was to me. To him, she must have been just another girl with golden curls. Just like me.

Oh, God, what if it had almost *been* me? She was alive and at home when I bolted from those footsteps last night. And if he couldn't have me, then…

I sat abruptly at the table, and I could hear Mother talking to me, but I wasn't listening all that well. Instead, I was replaying the scene from last night over and over in my head. I blinked and Joe was crouching in front of me. When did he get here?

'Daisy? Daisy, I'm so sorry, I know she was your friend. Did you witness anything last night? Was there anyone else on the street?' He took my hands, and I didn't pull them back like usual. The warmth felt good on my too-cold skin.

My voice started out too quiet around the lump in my throat.

'Someone followed me.' I cleared my throat and tried again. 'After Betty and Marcy went into their lodgings, I believe someone followed me down the block. I thought it was just my imagination, but...'

Joe cursed and Mother reprimanded him, but I thought he had the right of it. 'This! This, right here, is why I want someone walking with you every evening, Daisy. That's it, I'm meeting you after work every evening so you get home safe and sound.'

I didn't bother protesting, knowing that tone of voice. Joe was done playing. It reminded me of when we were kids; once he started losing, he'd call the game dull or declare it was over, and there was no arguing with him after that. Especially when Mother and Father were nodding along with him. I looked over his shoulder at Randall, studiously ignoring the scene in front of him but not touching breakfast.

'Thanks, Joe. But I should go see Marcy now, she must be a wreck.' I stood, straightening my dress out of habit, reinforcing a small moment of normality.

'I'll take you over because I've officially been moved onto the case of these murders and I have to meet back up with the Captain.' Joe offered me his arm but I shook my head.

'I'll meet you at the front door, Joe, must fetch my purse, is all.' I waited for him to head down the hall and turned to Randall and my parents still in the kitchen. 'I'll be alright, and I'll be safe. Don't fret.'

Mother gave me a hug, Father, too, for all that he normally wouldn't be caught dead. I took my leave and headed out the door with Joe. He paused when we reached the front walk and turned to me, gently holding me by my arms.

'I just want you to know that when we are married, you'll never have to worry about a thing like this again. I'll keep you safe.' Furious, I opened my mouth to reply, but he held a finger to my lips. 'I know you're undecided, but, for now, just think about it, alright? Your parents are in favor of us together, and what better match are there than the two of us?'

My anger left me in a gust and I gave him the smile like I knew he wanted, but didn't respond, too caught up in the bruised feeling of my heart. I didn't have it in me to argue this morning. Not after what happened to Betty. Arguing with Joe just took too much energy.

Marcy was distraught, out of clean handkerchiefs, and the bloodstains were still on the front stoop when we arrived. I sat with her as the bobbies came and asked us the same questions Joe did, over and over, until I declared enough and ushered Marcy upstairs to her bed.

Fortunately, I had something to take my mind off matters: the Winter Dress Show was today and I was finally wearing the centrepiece dress. It was a glittery, flowing flapper dress that I could never afford in several lifetimes, but at least I got to wear it for a few minutes today. I hurried out of the house and ran into Randall in the street.

'Oh! You startled me.' I braced myself against his chest to keep myself from falling down the stairs and he gently put me back on my feet.

'That was rather the opposite of my intentions. I thought your policeman might be busy here and you'd like an escort back to the house.' Now that there was no danger of me falling over, he adjusted the front of his suit and offered me his arm.

I sighed, out of any ability to argue. 'Not you, too.'

Slowly, he lowered his arm. 'I assure you, it is simply because I thought you might like company after the death of your friend.'

Randall looked so earnest, his hands once more clasped behind his back, that I couldn't help but smile. 'I appreciate it, truly, but I must get down to the dress shop, I'm needed for the afternoon show.'

'Of course. I intended to head downtown myself for an appointment, if you don't mind the company?'

'That would be lovely. And he isn't mine, you know.' I

started off down the street and Randall sprang into movement at my side.

'Who isn't what now?' At least he wasn't out of breath keeping up with my long stride.

'Joe. He's not *my* policeman, no matter how much he thinks he is. Or my parents think he should be.' It was an effort not to grind my teeth in frustration at their absolute obtuseness.

'I see,' was all the answer I got before he changed topics to the fashions we were displaying this afternoon. When we reached the door to the dress shop, he hesitated at the doorway. 'My meeting isn't for another couple hours and I was planning to spend it at a teahouse reading, but perhaps I'll come watch the show? That is, if you don't mind.'

I beamed. 'No, not at all. I hardly ever have anyone watch my mannequin. Mother and Father are always busy working and Joe never showed an interest, saying it wouldn't matter after we were married. It would be pleasant to have a face I know in the crowd for once.'

'It's settled then. I'll sit up front and centre.' He held the door open for me and I thanked him, peering up through my eyelashes, trying the coy look the girls and I practiced all the time for just such occasions.

After pointing Randall towards the area of the shop where the show would take place, I hurried into the back dressing rooms, already later than I liked. There was a whirlwind of makeup and hair product already in movement and I fit myself into the cacophony, chatting with the girls and helping each other into the shapewear that management insisted we wear.

I was used to being early in the show and I was not used to the nervousness that accompanied needing to wait till the very end. The dress I wore was heavy with beading, long fringes of glass beads swaying as I shifted, waiting for my entrance. Finally, it was my turn. I took a deep breath, plastered a dazzling smile on my face, and swayed out onto the stage.

The audible gasps and murmurs of appreciation in the

audience were enough to make my head spin with pride. I knew their appreciation was for the dress and not me, but it was my job to show it off in the best light possible. Even the most gorgeous frocks could be ugly if worn haphazardly and without care. I turned and posed, turned and posed, all the way down the runway. When I reached the end, Randall was exactly where he promised to be, offering a genial smile and a subtle, quiet clapping. I preened a little more, gave an extra twirl, and then retreated back behind the curtains.

I feigned collapsing onto one of the divans in the dressing room and the other girls laughed and clapped, except for Gertrude, who had been passed over for the spotlight. Grinning, I rose and curtsied to them all and then remembered about this morning and the grin melted off my face.

Shimmying out of the dress, I took care to hang it back up properly. I slipped back into my street clothes and went out to find Randall browsing the luggage near the entrance to the green room.

'How was it?' I inquired, sidling up to him as he examined an attaché.

He started, not having noticed me until just then. 'Excellent. You are quite graceful on the stage.' Randall turned and there was mischief glinting in his eyes. 'It's a shame you're not as surefooted when you're walking on the street.'

'Oh, you.' I gave him a playful little shove and laughed, despite the gloominess. 'I have an hour before I need to be at the café, would you like to take tea with me before I go?'

Glancing at his watch, he nodded. 'I have some time left, and tea is the most important meal of the day.'

'It's settled, then. Let's go.'

#

We chattered away down the few blocks to my favourite tea room, partaking of some lovely cakes and tarts while talking about books and travelling. I'd always wanted to go across to the continent and Randall was happy to regale me with stories from India and Asia where he had travelled for work. He was a magnificent storyteller and I could almost feel the dry heat of deserts, the mugginess of monsoon season. I'd only ever been as far as Leatherhead before, visiting an ailing aunt.

'One of these days, I am going to get off this rock and go someplace warm and sunny.' The tea was getting cold and I signalled a waitress to refresh the water.

'Warm and sunny gets tiring, too, after a while and all you want is for the clouds to come back so you can stop squinting all the time.' Randall stirred in cream, sugar and a squeeze of lemon at the end. 'Some days, it feels like my ancestors were mole people.'

'Vampires, then, or ghouls!' I leaned forward and smiled, resting one hand on his while we both chuckled at our absurdity. Maybe Randall could be presented to my parents as a viable alternative, at least long enough for Joe to move on and find someone new.

'Here you have me chattering away and it's almost time for your shift.' He pulled out a napkin and folded the tea cakes we hadn't finished into a bag and handed them to me. 'For later.'

I laughed. 'Thanks. I appreciate it. Here…since you bought last time…' Rooting in my purse, looking for my coin pouch, I missed him sliding out the appropriate bills and handing them to the waitress.

'Taken care of. Now, would you like an escort, or should I leave you to your own devices?'

Thinking for a moment, I finally replied, 'You know, I think I'll take you up on that offer. After last night…'

'Say no more,' Randall said, correctly interpreting my trailing sentence as an opening to dismiss the thoughts about last night. 'You're safe as houses with me.'

'That's what I'm worried about,' I quipped with a giggle, before retrieving my purse and standing. The walk to the café was quiet, broken by the sound of children playing, and the sounds of people's footsteps along the sidewalk. We continued our discussions about nothing in particular until we reached the back door.

'Here we are.' I hesitated, then grabbed Randall for an embrace, needing to feel someone solid and present to offset the mourning that was only just now settling in. Betty wouldn't be here tonight, nor any other night again.

Randall returned my embrace after a second, holding it only as long as was appropriate. 'Do you need an escort home?'

'No. I'm sure Joe will turn up. The less I want him around, the more I see him, it seems.' I squeezed his hands and turned to the back door of the café, bracing myself for work.

As Randall made his way out of the alley again, he stepped around Marcie, who was just coming towards the door.

'Marcie, what are you doing here? You should be home.' I embraced her, keeping hold of her hands when we stepped back.

'I couldn't bear it after I spent all afternoon scrubbing the blood off the stoop. It just wasn't coming up. I need something to distract me.' Marcie wasn't crying, but her eyes were red as though she had just stopped.

'I can certainly understand that sentiment. Come on, then.' I led her inside and we swapped our street clothes for our uniforms. We were doing up each other's hair when Maude, the house manager, came bustling back.

'What are you two ducks doing here today? Grievin' as you are.' She enveloped us in a hug that nearly swept us off our feet.

'Marcie thought it would be good to keep her mind off things,' I gasped out. 'Me as well.'

Maude set us back on our feet and set her hands on her hips. 'That just won't do. Not least because such sad faces will send the patrons hurrying out before their second drink. Now, take these coins and go to the pictures. And don't worry about today's wages, you'll find them in your packet at the end of the

38

week, same as always.'

We knew from experience not to fight Maude when she was being motherly, so we thanked her profusely, changed back into our street clothes and hurried off into the afternoon.

'You up for a picture?' I asked Marcie. 'Because I could go either way.'

'A picture would be nice.' She let out a wet chuckle. 'Betty kept going on about this one. I'm not even sure what it's about.'

'It's settled. Let's go.' I took her arm, and we made our way to the cinema, trading our extra coin for tickets. We were just in time and settled in the back of the full house.

The lights had gone down as the newsreel started when I heard the door open and turned instinctively to see who had entered. To my surprise, the flickering lights lit up Randall's face. This was his appointment? I almost opened my mouth to call out to him, but he definitely had a seat already in mind. He slipped into the final row across from us without noticing me at all, and kissed the person already sitting in that row.

Just what I needed to top a bloody awful day. No wonder he seemed immune to my charm, he was already spoken for. I couldn't see the person on his other side, but it was clear they were holding hands as the main picture started. What the picture was, I'm not at all sure, as I was distracted sneaking glances over at Randall and his mystery lover throughout the showing.

Finally the lights came up and I turned to look once more over to see if I knew the woman he was seated with, only to see Randall hastily letting go of the hand of another man. Not just any man, either, but Lord Bletchly, Father's employer. The world tilted on its side as I reeled and it took my thoughts a moment to catch up with my eyes as at first I wondered where the woman had gone, but then...oh. Oh! I could tell I was blushing furiously as Randall finally noticed my presence.

At first he was puzzled, then the blood drained from his face and he made a hasty exit from the cinema.

'Meet me in front of concessions?' I grabbed my coat and purse, not waiting for Marcie's response, and hurried after Randall. Damn, but his legs were long. I had to catch him before he left, before he told the Lord I had seen them and let him know I was no threat to him. I've never judged love before, and I wasn't about to start. He was almost outside by the time I caught up with him.

'Randall! What a surprise! I didn't know you were planning an evening at the cinema.' I caught his sleeve and pulled him to the side of the flow of traffic leaving the building.

'Daisy, I—' he began, but I cut him off.

'It's lovely to have bumped into you. Perhaps you could escort Marcie and I back to our street? It is dark, after all.' I could see he was torn between bolting and making sure we were safe, and in the end, our safety won out.

He sighed. 'Yes, of course.'

'Good. Oh, here's Marcie now. Look who I found!' As Marcie dug through her purse for something, I leaned over to Randall to whisper, 'It's okay, your secret is safe with me. You're not the first I've known, and I'm sure you won't be the last.'

Randall relaxed, marginally, and nodded. 'I do have another stop I need to make this evening, would you mind terribly if I put the two of you into a cab to make sure you got home safe?'

'Oh, you don't need to do that,' I protested, but he insisted and Marcie was thrilled with the convenience, so I gave in. 'I'll see you back at the house?'

'Yes, I just need to have a quick conversation with a friend.' Randall tipped his hat to us and flagged us a cab.

Before he could wave us off, and while Marcie settled into the cab, I grabbed Randall's hand. 'I just want to make sure you know I meant what I said before. Marcie and Betty, they were in the same predicament. I never spilled their secrets and I won't yours either. And not just because you're in love with

40

my father's employer.'

He finally smiled, his quiet, reserved flash of good humour. 'That is a relief to know. Now please excuse me while I make sure the Lord is also put at ease. I'm afraid I rather bolted on him.'

I squeezed his hand in farewell and swung into the cab, settling beside Marcie, watching Randall stride into the night.

'He's a nice sort, and handsome,' Marcie observed as I watched Randall fade into the night.

'He is that, but I'm afraid his heart is already spoken for.' I sighed and leaned back into my seat. 'Why is it that all the good-looking, kind men are already taken?'

'Because they're good looking and kind,' was Marcie's prompt response.

We laughed all the way to our street and the cabby insisted on dropping us each at our doors and waiting for us to get inside before moving on. I watched Marcie hesitate, but after a moment she cleared the stairs and went inside. As her door closed, I breathed a sigh of relief.

My parents were surprised to see me home early, but when I explained why, Mother fixed me up a warm supper and sent me off to dine in peace. I contented myself to sitting in the parlour and reading by the fire, happy to be safe inside. It was only an hour after I had settled in that Randall opened the front door, chased by the tendrils of fog that was already taking over the streets.

'Everything alright?' I inquired, raising an eyebrow.

He grinned, ducking his head. 'He understood. I think the…arrangement is still on.'

'Glad to hear it. Wouldn't want to jeopardize your business prospects, after all.' I patted the sofa beside me. He sat, more comfortable than he had been before. I kept my voice low. 'I won't ever sell you out, you know.'

'Thank you. I think I may actually believe that,' he murmured back.

A hammering knock made us both jump and I made to hurry for the door, but Randall shook his head. 'Not after last night. Let me.' He peered out the window and then opened the door. 'Officer Joe Chandler.'

'Where's Daisy? What have you done with her?' Joe's voice was thick and angry.

I stood. 'Joe? I'm right here. What on Earth—?'

'I went to bring you home tonight, and you weren't there. I was so worried something happened to you.' My erstwhile pursuer grabbed my hands, kissing my fingers.

'I'm fine,' I assured him, and when he didn't cease, I pulled my fingers away from his hands. 'I said, I'm fine. Why are you so worked up? Maude gave Marcie and I the evening off.'

'There was another murder a block away this evening. I was so afraid when the call came in that it might have been you.' He touched my hair, the ringlets falling out after the long day.

I stepped back, just a little. 'Well, it wasn't. You can see I am just fine.'

Joe turned to Randall. 'And where were you this evening?'

Blinking in confusion, I interjected. 'Why, Joe, what does that matter?'

'Because he's new in town, has a thing for blondes apparently, and the murders are swirling around this very street. That's why.' Joe puffed himself up, trying to look down his nose at the man who was several inches taller.

'Well, I was…I was out this evening. Business.' I could see Randall fumbling and I made a quick decision. Maybe I could take care of two problems at once.

'He was with me, Joe. We went to the pictures since I did not have to work.' I took Randall's arm, and, to his credit, he adapted immediately.

'Yes, we have our ticket stubs if that would be helpful.' Randall dug in his pocket and produced his.

'*The Pleasure Garden*?' Joe's voice was scandalized. 'What sort of picture is that to take a lady to?'

'Oh, it wasn't like that. Don't be that way.' I gave Randall's arm a little pat. 'It was a suspense movie, wasn't it? Something about two couples. Well, I wasn't paying much attention, were you?'

'By a new director, Hitchcock, I believe his name was. Frankly, I didn't find it terribly well put together.'

I looked back at Joe and it was like watching a tea kettle heat. You could practically see the steam coming from his ears. 'Fine,' he snapped and crumpled the movie ticket before he stalked out of the house, slamming the door behind him.

Mother finally turned up. 'Did I hear Joe?'

'Yes, but I think he's gone now.' When she turned to leave, I added under my breath, 'Finally.'

'Thank you.'

I turned back to Randall and smiled. 'Like I said, I won't let your secrets get out.'

#

I slept fitfully, but was glad to wake to a quiet house. The nightmares were going to get me even if I did survive the killer stalking our streets. I took a few deep breaths, before climbing out of bed and heading downstairs. It was my one day a week that I had no other obligations than helping Mother clean the house, and I was glad of the excuse to stay home.

We filled the day with sweeping and dusting and mopping, laughing over the work as we always did. I did not see much of Randall except as he was headed out for the day, though he smiled at me, shy, on his way out.

'I think you've made another conquest with that one.' Mother nudged me.

'No, his heart is already taken,' I sighed.

She tutted but let it go. At least she was starting to be willing to entertain prospects other than Joe.

We had just sat down to supper that evening when there was

43

a ferocious banging on the front door, again. When would Joe ever learn to knock like a gentleman instead of a copper? Father opened the door and I gaped at the crowd of policemen, in uniform, who entered the house. They shut the door behind them and Joe sent several upstairs, and a few more downstairs.

'Joe, this is outrageous, what are you doing?' Mother shrieked.

One of the policemen upstairs shook his head at Joe who was still in the lobby. 'Where is Randall Sleuth?' Joe asked me.

I crossed my arms, defiant. 'He was out all day. I haven't seen him.'

'Did Mr. Sleuth do something?' Father was nervous, fidgeting with his pipe. This was his worst dream come true; the police were hunting one of his lodgers.

Joe stared at me, ignoring Father. 'You never went to the cinema with him last night, you went with Marcie. I asked Maude and verified it with Marcie.'

'He absolutely was there! Marcie saw him after the picture!'

'Which gave him ample time to kill and then use you as an alibi. What I can't understand is why you'd lie to me like that.' Joe became gentle, holding my shoulders. The quick change from angry to conciliatory was hard to keep up with.

I finally broke, yelling, 'Because I wanted you to leave me alone!'

Joe gaped at me, for a moment his expression nothing but shock. Then, his mouth snapped shut and his eyes began to narrow, his mouth twisting. I don't know what he would have done or said, because Randall came home at that same moment.

Joe was closest to the door, and he spun as it opened, moving faster than I thought he could and pinned Randall to the door before spinning him around, one hand was wrenched behind his back. 'Randall Sleuth, you are under arrest for murder.' Leaning in, he hissed, 'Give me an excuse, and I'll beat the bloody hell out of you.'

Randall stood frozen against the door, shocked and confused.

'No, Joe, you've got it all wrong!' I grabbed his arm before he shrugged me off.

'Unless you want to join him in the cells, Daisy, let me do my job.' Joe slapped his handcuffs around Randall's wrists and shoved him over to a couple of policemen. 'Take him.' As they hauled Randall out to the wagon, the foyer became uncomfortably quiet. After a moment, Joe turned to me, once again calm, conciliatory, condescending. 'I'm sorry you had to see that. You have a good heart and believe the best in people. Let's you and I go for a walk. I have something I want to talk to you about.'

I started to shake my head, but Mother interrupted. 'That sounds splendid.' She winked at me and mouthed, *this is it!*

I bit my lip. Maybe if I went with Joe I could convince him of Randall's innocence, that they had the wrong man. It was worth a shot, and if I had to play into Joe's fantasy just a little bit longer to save an innocent man, I would.

'I could use some air, thank you.' We stepped outside in time to see the wagon head down the street. 'You don't need to take Randall in yourself?'

Joe smiled at my concern. 'The men know what they're about and I had promised myself that once I solved this case, I would finally ask you a question.'

'Let's walk,' I interrupted, wanting to forestall him as long as possible.

Joe agreed and he steered us down towards a park that we used to play in when we were children. 'I really admire you, Daisy, your kindness for people, even when they are obviously guilty, your tenacity, your work hard, your beauty.'

'Thank you. It's kind of you to say.' We reached the park, and I steered us to the nearest benches, empty in the late evening fog. The benches were illuminated by a solitary lamp, creating an oasis of light. We sat, but Joe did not let go of my arm, keeping me close.

'Solving this case will secure my promotion at City Police. I can afford a wife, and I was hoping, Daisy, that you would do me the honour of becoming my wife.' Joe took my hands, earnest now, and confident already in my answer. 'I'll keep you safe. You won't have to work ever again on my salary, you can stay home and raise our children.'

'I…I'm touched, really, but might I have some time to give you my answer?' I couldn't meet his eyes, but I could feel his grasp tightening on my hands. 'It's just, I'm not sure I'm ready. I enjoy my work, too. Must I give it up?' His grip kept tightening until it was crushing my fingers. 'Ow, Joe, you're hurting me!'

'I'm hurting *you*? You. Do you know the lengths I've gone to, to make this happen? What you made me do?' Joe wouldn't drop my hands, even though I was tugging now, trying to free myself from the vice-like grip. 'All I've ever done is love you. Our whole lives! I've loved you, and you kept pushing me away! I had to make you see you *needed* me, the same way I need you!'

Joe tried to kiss me, but I managed to free a hand and slap him. The crack was muffled by the fog surrounding us, and I held my breath, terrified of how he would respond. I didn't have long to wait.

Once Joe snapped out of the shock of the slap, he backhanded me off the bench. 'Ungrateful bitch!' He stood over me, panting in anger. My heart was racing, my face hurting, and there was blood on my lips. Joe's fists were clenching as he wrestled for control of himself. 'Once we're married, you'll see, you'll understand that I did all this for you. And we will be married.' He reached down to grab me and I didn't think, I just lashed out with my heel and drilled him with a solid kick in the shin. He yelped and I scrambled up, darting away from him and deeper into the park. If I could just find a place to hide—

'Get back here, Daisy! Don't make me hunt you down like all the others!' I could hear his footsteps crunching on the gravel behind me and I hurriedly stepped off the path and onto the dead grass, darting for a pavilion in the centre of the park. My frantic thoughts latched finally onto what he had been saying and I finally realized, oh God, *Joe* was the one killing all the women. I picked up my pace as best I could, wearing heels in the dirt. I stumbled up the stairs onto the pavilion platform and paused to look behind me.

I didn't hear his footsteps anymore, but I doubt I could if he'd followed me onto the grass. I couldn't see more than a few yards into the park because of the fog and hunched behind a pillar, straining to see into the dark. A soft step on the brick behind me was the only indication I had before Joe's hand grabbed my hair and I shrieked, scrabbling at his fingers. He dragged me backwards, my feet trying to find purchase on the slick brickwork. He threw me against the fencing ringing the pavilion and crouched beside me, a wickedly long knife in one hand.

'It didn't have to go like this. You should have said yes. Why didn't you say yes?' Tears filled Joe's eyes. 'You're just the same as all the other girls out there, aren't you? Just the same spoiled whores. I'll just have to teach you a lesson, like all the other lessons.'

The knife swung towards me, slicing across the arm I raised to protect myself, once, twice. The pain brought a clarity to my thoughts that had been clouded by the sudden reveal of the depth of Joe's depravity and I realized I did not want to die like this. Not here, not under the knife of the bully from my childhood, the constant irritant in my life who always wanted everything his way and to hell what I wanted. Screaming, half in rage, half in fear, I grabbed his arm, wrestling for control of the blade. I twisted, bracing myself on the ground, using whatever leverage I could find. I brought my knee up, aiming for his groin, and he twisted so I hit his thigh instead. It wasn't enough to get him off me, but it was enough of a distraction that I could grapple his arm and sink my teeth in. He yelped, flinching away for a moment and I used all my strength to shove his arm away from me.

The knife slipped in, slick through his flesh, and he stiffened. It had been enough, just enough of a distraction, for me to turn the blade away from me, though I had not intended to stick him with it. I watched as his blood ran freely down the hilt of the knife still grasped in his hand, my hands over top of his.

I panted, waiting for him to move, but I must have gotten lucky. Lucky, right, so lucky I was pinned under a dead or dying man, his blood hot and sticky on my hands. I tried to shove him off, crying, not sure if they were tears of fear, rage, or relief. Maybe all three. After a few moments of struggling, I managed to worm my way out from under Joe and backed away until I felt my back hit the other side of the pavilion where I slumped, gasping for air, trying to wipe the blood off my hands onto my saturated dress. I couldn't look at the other side of the pavilion, at the spreading pool of red so dark it looked black in the night.

I wasn't sure how much time had passed, but the blood on me was cold and tacky when I heard someone walking by. 'Help!' I called, my voice a pale echo of usual. I tried again. 'Please, someone, help!'

The footsteps hurried towards me and I finally saw three young men come out of the fog, stopping short at the sight in the pavilion.

'Please, please, help me,' I sobbed, all the terror of the evening ebbing out of me as I shook, huddled in the corner.

One of the men took off into the night, presumably to summon the police, while one of the other men wrapped his coat around me. I looked over to where I had left Joe's body, but he wasn't there. I sobbed even harder and the men hurried to reassure me, awkwardly due to lack of practice with hysterical women, I presume, but they didn't understand the cause of my terror. Where had he gone?

That rest of that night was a whirlwind. There were doctors

and policemen, and the same questions over and over. Randall was released from prison, the Lord having arrived to vouch for his whereabouts during several of the crimes. Mother and Father hovered over me, Mother not even letting me bathe by myself as I washed off Joe's blood. Maybe now she would listen when I told her I wasn't interested in someone. Hope springs eternal.

Finally, everyone left the house in the wee hours of the morning, leaving the four of us sitting in the kitchen, tea detritus on every flat surface from the multitude of people who had been in and out.

'The doctor left you something to help you sleep, Daisy. You should take some and head to bed.' Mother offered me the dropper bottle and I shook my head, still worrying at the edge of the bandages wrapped around my forearms. I didn't want to sleep yet, maybe not ever, the threat of Joe still out there, somewhere, looming ever present.

'How about a game of chess?' Randall offered. 'I know I could use something to take my mind off this evening.'

I nodded, not really up to talking anymore, my voice sore from screaming and crying and explaining endlessly. My parents both hugged me and headed to their beds to get at least a little sleep before the day began, leaving Randall and I to our own devices. We made our way to the morning room and Randall set up the board while I poured us each a stiff drink.

'Thank you, again,' Randall was still placing the pieces into their opening positions, not looking at me while he talked. 'You could have just told the police what you saw at the cinema and you didn't.'

I gave him a small, sad smile when I handed him his drink. 'Not my secret to tell. And it might have gotten you killed faster than a noose. Love is…'

'Complicated?' Randall finished for me.

'That's a good word for it.' My voice was more bitter than I had intended and I took a deep draft of the scotch in my glass.

49

He laughed, softly, the sound just as harsh as my own voice. 'Your turn.'

I picked up the white pawn and turned it over in my hand. 'Is it?'

More Than Suspicion

Joseph S. Walker

Hannah shrank more deeply into the corner of the closet, pulling Darlene's few hanging clothes tightly against her. With the power gone, the bedroom was as dark as the closet. Peering with one eye over the shoulders of the dresses, she could make out only the rectangle of the window, curtains pale with light gathered from street lamps outside. She could see nothing of the bed Darlene had crawled under.

She bit the inside of her cheek to kill a surge of laughter that threatened to burst out. Darlene under the bed, her in the closet, like children playing hide and seek. Maybe Gerald would yell, 'Come out, come out, wherever you are,' and they'd reveal themselves, giggling.

Footsteps in the hallway. A man's heavy tread on the scarred wooden floor.

And now a voice, but not the booming threat she expected. 'Darlene, honey. I know you're here. Won't you come out? I miss your pretty face.' Gerald's voice was soft, conciliatory, concerned. Hannah wasn't fooled. Darlene wouldn't be, either.

The footsteps came into the bedroom.

Hannah had never seen Gerald. In her mind's eye, it was Cary Grant whose steps she heard, Cary Grant bearing a tray with a glass of milk that glowed with menace. She first saw Darlene in the light of that image. Darlene in the front row, Hannah in the projection booth, waiting to see if Cary was really going to poison his wife. Hannah thought what she felt, watching the movie, was real fear. She knew better now.

51

Ten days earlier

The woman in the blue coat always sat in the front row, her petite frame dwarfed by the stars on the screen. Hannah would have noticed anyone coming to the same movie, *Suspicion*, several nights in a row, but with only a few people in the audience, she stood out all the more. Most folks had little appetite for entertainment. They preferred huddling in their living rooms, listening to the news, waiting for the next disaster. Since the attack at Pearl Harbor, the country seemed to be holding its breath, preparing for the plunge into some abyss.

One night, the woman emerged from the women's lounge just as Hannah came down from the projection booth. 'You must love this movie,' Hannah said. 'You've seen it almost as many times as I have.'

The woman in the blue coat started, staring at Hannah. She seemed shocked someone had spoken to her. The wide eyes behind her thick eyeglasses were brown, and a few blond curls escaped from the edges of a red hat that clashed badly with her coat.

'I'm Hannah Albright,' Hannah went on. 'Projectionist and, well, manager, for the moment anyway. I usually stop on the way home for a cup of coffee. Would you like to join me?'

The woman edged toward the exit, never taking her eyes off Hannah. 'No,' she said. Her voice was barely more than a whisper. 'No, thank you.' She pushed through the door, letting biting December air into the lobby. Hannah watched through the box office window as the woman hurried across the street and around the corner, looking back two or three times, as though afraid of being followed.

Jimmy was wiping the counter of the concession booth, the left sleeve of his usher uniform pinned neatly to his side. 'What did I say wrong?' Hannah asked him.

Jimmy barely looked up. 'Some folks just want to be left

alone.'

When Hannah came down from the booth the next night, the woman was in the middle of the lobby floor, shifting her weight from foot to foot and holding her purse in front of her like a shield. Hannah shot a questioning look at Jimmy, who shrugged.

As soon as she saw Hannah, the woman stepped forward. 'I'm afraid I was very rude last night.' Her voice was halting, uncertain.

'Not at all,' Hannah said. 'I startled you, that's all.'

'Well.' The woman bit her lip. 'You were being kind.'

'Also curious,' Hannah said. 'I don't often see people come to the same movie so many times.' She put out her hand. 'Let's start again. I'm Hannah.'

The woman hesitated only a moment before shaking hands. 'Darlene.'

'Hello, Darlene. My offer still stands if you'd like to come to Abbott's.'

Again, the delicate bite on the lower lip. 'All right.'

#

Abbott's Diner was between the theater and Hannah's apartment, and two blocks off the main highway. As usual at this time of night it was almost empty, with only one produce truck in the parking lot, its driver at the counter eating a plate of meatloaf and potatoes. Hannah led Darlene to her usual booth, the farthest from the door.

'I like to sit back here,' she said. 'You don't get that nasty cold air every time the door opens.'

Darlene was looking around as though she'd never seen a diner before and suspected it might be a trap. She sank into the seat across from Hannah as Betty approached, already carrying Hannah's cup of coffee.

'Same for you?' the waitress asked Darlene.

'Oh, no,' she said. 'I couldn't possibly drink coffee this late, or I'd never get to sleep. Just water, please.'

'No problem, hon,' Betty said. 'Say, Hannah, are you going to keep lighting up your marquee every night? Lew is thinking about getting blackout curtains for the windows here.'

'Good heavens, why?'

'He's got that sister in L.A., you know. She wrote they're having blackout orders at night.'

'We're a thousand miles from the coast, Betty. I don't think Holcomb, Colorado, is on the list of Japanese targets.'

'He says they might come up through Mexico.' Betty shrugged and walked away.

Hannah sipped at her coffee. 'Lew Abbott is a fool. I wonder where he got that nonsense about Mexico.'

'People are afraid,' Darlene said. She moved her purse from her lap to the chair beside her. 'When you're frightened, you feel desperate. You want to do something. And you'll believe anything.'

'I suppose so.' It was nice sitting here with someone across the table, for once. Hannah felt the warmth radiating from the kitchen on one side of her face, a touch of bitter cold from the windows on the other. 'Believe anything or do anything. Take Cal Roberts, the man who owns the movie theater. I've worked for him for six years. The quietest, most gentle man you'd ever hope to meet. Two days after the attack he told me that he was going to Denver to enlist, and I would be in charge of the theater. Well, I thought he was joking at first. To just up and take off like that.'

Betty set a glass of ice water in front of Darlene, who nodded her thanks. 'He wasn't joking,' she said, after the waitress walked away.

'No, he wasn't. And he took all three of his sons to join up with him. I'll have to hire some people after the holidays, if I can. For now, it's just me and Jimmy running the place.'

'The one-armed man,' Darlene said. 'Does he ever come for

coffee with you?'

'Not once. He lost the arm in France, in the last war, and I think he lost something else, too. Something inside. He never says a word he doesn't have to, and he doesn't socialize.'

'The poor man. There are damaged people everywhere.'

'We'll all be damaged by the time it's over,' Hannah said. 'My father always told me there would never be another war, that mankind was all done with that.'

'What does he say now?'

Hannah looked at the cup between her hands and told the lie that was starting to come too easily. 'I lost both my folks in a car accident two years ago.' Better to say this than to picture the house where she was no longer welcome.

'I'm so sorry.' Darlene's hand twitched as though she wanted to reach across the table, but she didn't.

Hannah made herself smile. 'Like you say, we're all damaged.' Or had she said that herself? She was out of practice at talking to people. 'What about you? You must be new in town. I don't think I ever saw you before a couple of weeks ago, and now I see you every night.'

Darlene pulled her hands back against her chest. 'Yes. I got off the bus because it looked like a quiet little town. I don't know how long I'll stay.'

'Oh, Holcomb's a nice enough place. Not much happens here. A lot of the younger people have left for Denver or California.'

'I've been spending most of my time at the library. And at night I go to the movie.'

'*Suspicion*,' Hannah said. 'I'd like to tell you that I'll have something new to show soon, but I really don't know. Everything is upside down. I can't get anyone on the telephone at our distributor who knows when we'll get a print of something else. Probably they're all off enlisting too.'

'That's all right. I'm not tired of *Suspicion*.'

'I suppose I'm not, either.' Hannah drank the last of her

coffee. 'What is it you like about it?'

Darlene put her hands in her lap and looked at them, her face pale. When she didn't say anything, Hannah went on, speaking brightly.

'I'll tell you my favorite thing, shall I? It's Phil.'

Darlene looked up, a line between her eyebrows. 'Phil?'

'She's toward the end of the picture.' Hannah leaned forward. 'They go to dinner at Isobel's house, remember?'

'Yes.'

'It's the two of them, and Isobel, and Isobel's brother, the doctor. And Phil. Maybe it's Phyllis, but Isobel calls her Phil, and Phil calls her Izzy.'

'You mean the woman in the suit?'

'That's right! She's wearing a man's suit, with a very thin tie, and she has short hair with a stiff kind of wave to it. And there's this moment, this very specific moment, where Isobel says, 'Do the wine, will you, Phil?' and Phil gets up and pours everyone more wine while they're talking about poisons and getting away with murder.'

'And that's your favorite part of the movie?'

'Oh, the rest is good, too.' Hannah forced herself to lean back, to stop speaking with such urgency. 'I can't explain it, not the way it is in my head. It's something to do with the fact that she's there, but not explained. Did you notice she's not even in the cast list? She's just in that one scene, and we're not told why, or why she's dressed that way, or anything about her, or even who plays her. She's like a lost piece of some other world.' She held her hands up in front of her, groping for the words she needed. 'It just gives me a kind of little thrill. The way they call each other Phil and Izzy. It makes me feel like what I really want is a movie about them.'

She was talking too much. She dropped her hands and gave an unconvincing little laugh. 'I suppose what you like most is Cary Grant. He's almost too good-looking, isn't he?'

Darlene had been watching Hannah intently, but now she

56

lowered her eyes again. 'I like the movie because it's true,' she said, seeming to drag the words out. 'It's the truest thing ever. How some men are one way in the world and another way at home, and how scary that is.'

'But it all comes out right in the end. They drive away happy together.'

'Oh, no.' Darlene looked up, straight into Hannah's eyes, and her voice, for the first time, was clear and certain. 'The end is the only part that's a lie. A pretty lie, but still. He kills her. Of course he kills her.'

#

Darlene wasn't at the theater the next night. Hannah thought she might come to Abbott's afterwards, but she wasn't there, either. Hannah drank her coffee quickly, aware in an entirely new way of the emptiness of the rest of the table.

The emptiness of her cramped apartment, when she reached it, was much the same. The sour stillness of a room nobody has been in for many hours. She sat in the dark for a while, looking out at the empty street. What an idiot she had been, going on and on about Phil and Izzy. Darlene had probably been on the next bus out of town.

Nothing moved outside the window. She could turn on the radio, but only a few stations were still broadcasting at this time of night. Classical music, or perhaps a preacher decrying the evils of the day. There were plenty to decry. It was nothing worth turning the dial for.

'Do the wine, will you, Phil?' Hannah said out loud. Then she went to bed.

The night after that, she looked down from the projection booth and saw the familiar blue shoulders under the unfortunate red hat. After the show, Darlene was waiting in the lobby. They ran together to Abbott's through the bone-numbing wind that had been punishing Holcomb all day, rolling down off the snowy mountains fifty miles to the west to scour the middle of the continent. They stopped inside the doors to breathe deeply and rub their raw, red cheeks.

'I found the book in the library,' Darlene said, once they were sitting with their drinks. Tonight, she asked for hot chocolate. 'The novel *Suspicion* is based on.' She took the book from her purse and set it on the table.

Before the Fact, by Francis Iles. Hannah flipped through the book curiously. 'Did you read it?'

Darlene nodded. 'That's why I wasn't at the movie last night. It's completely different. In the book, Johnnie *does* kill Beaky, and he kills Lina's father, too.'

'Does he kill Lina?'

'The book ends with him bringing her the drink she thinks is poison, and she drinks it, and then it just ends.'

'Why does she drink it?'

'Because she's given up,' Darlene said. 'She knows it's the only way the story can end.'

'But it's not. We just saw it end differently, twenty minutes ago.'

'That's just Hollywood. They have to make it come out that way. They have to make it that the woman was stupid for ever being suspicious, and that the man was all right the whole time.' Darlene stopped. 'I'm sorry. I'm getting too upset.'

'No,' Hannah said. 'Really, no.'

Darlene put her hands around the warm mug. 'You asked why I see this movie over and over. I'll tell you the truth. It's because that last scene makes me so angry. It's so absurd, the way it tries to make Johnny a nice guy, and Lina just paranoid. I get mad every time, and that anger...it's important. It makes me feel that I did the right thing when I got on that bus.'

Now it was Hannah who wanted to reach across the table, but didn't. After a moment, she said quietly, 'Do you want to talk about before the bus?'

'No,' Darlene said. She pushed her glasses up her nose and

58

straightened herself in her chair, and her smile seemed almost genuine. 'Let's talk about other things. Tell me something about working in a movie theater. Tell me...oh, tell me your favorite of the movies you've shown.'

'You'll laugh.'

'I won't.'

'*The Wizard of Oz.*'

Darlene laughed, and immediately clapped her hand over her mouth. 'I'm so sorry! Honestly, I loved it too. It had such wonderful songs.'

'Hardly anyone came. There aren't many children in this town.'

'That's a shame.'

'I will say that I didn't like the ending, kind of like the end of *Suspicion* makes you mad.' Hannah waved her arm at the window. 'Kansas is just down the road, that direction. It's flat and dull. Why couldn't the poor girl stay in Oz, in all that beautiful color?'

Darlene smiled. The conversation fell into an easier path, Hannah scrupulously avoiding anything that might sound prying. Before she knew it, an hour and a half had passed, and it was getting more and more difficult to ignore the significant looks Betty was trying to give her.

Every night afterwards, Darlene waited in the lobby, studiously ignoring Jimmy studiously ignoring her, while Hannah shut down the projector and put everything in place for the next day. The women dashed to Abbott's, making a game of running as fast as they could through the frigid air. Betty had coffee and hot chocolate ready. They talked, at first of movies and books, then more and more of the frightening events in the world beyond Holcomb. Every day's newspaper brought grim tidings: enemies advancing, ships sinking, Europe falling. It all felt distant but inescapable, a black tide of misery closing in from every direction. They tried to end their talks on hopeful notes. This was still America. Impossible that the tide could not be driven back. It seemed obvious that one way or another, victory must be ahead.

'Of course,' Darlene said, 'we only think so because that's how it would be in a movie. Wouldn't it?'

She never said a word about her life before she got on the bus. Hannah didn't ask.

#

Two nights before Christmas, Hannah fell behind on their run to Abbott's, slowed by a pebble that snuck into her shoe. There were three or four big delivery trucks in the lot, a substantial crowd by the diner's standards. A dozen feet ahead of Hannah, Darlene opened the door and went in. Hannah had just reached the door herself when it exploded back outwards and Darlene pushed past her, moving fast, her face tucked as deeply as possible into the lapels of her coat. Without a word to Hannah, she dashed around the nearest corner.

'Darlene?' Hannah looked in the diner, seeing nothing to cause immediate alarm, just Betty bringing plates to four men gathered at a table. She went in the direction Darlene had taken and found her just around the corner, pressed up against the wall, her teeth sunk into her bottom lip and her whole body trembling.

Before Hannah could say anything, Darlene seized her arm. 'Did anyone follow me?'

'What?' Hannah looked back at the corner. 'Just me, I think.'

'Go look,' Darlene hissed. 'Peek around. See if anyone's come out. Please. Quick, quick.'

Her panic was contagious. Hannah stayed pressed against the wall as she eased back to the corner and peered back toward the diner and the parked trucks. 'No. Nobody's coming.'

Darlene sagged in relief. 'I have to go home. Will you walk

60

with me? I'd rather not go by myself right now.'

'Of course.' Though Hannah hadn't been there, she knew Darlene was renting a small house a few blocks away. Darlene set a brisk pace but paused frequently, looking back over her shoulder and staring down side streets they passed. She avoided pools of light from street lamps. After two blocks, she stretched out her gloved hand wordlessly, and Hannah seized it and held it the rest of the way.

Darlene's house was even smaller than Hannah had expected, not much larger than her own apartment. There was only a sliver of a moon, making the tiny structure little more than a gray outline in the darkness, set well back from the street. Darlene unlocked the front door and pulled Hannah inside, closing the door firmly behind them and slipping on a chain. She held Hannah's arm and stood with her back against the door. 'Let's not turn on any lights,' she said. 'For a little bit, anyway.'

'All right,' Hannah said.

They stood, listening to each other breathe. The house made the little sounds wood makes as it shifts and settles in the cold. The world was otherwise silent.

'You haven't asked me any questions,' Darlene said.

'You'll tell me what you want to.'

'Oh, God.' Darlene slid down the doorway, sitting on the floor with her forehead against her knees. Hannah sank down beside her and sat quietly on the chill wooden floor.

'There was a man at the diner,' Darlene said. 'His name is Pete. I don't know his last name. He works for my husband.'

'Did he see you?'

'I don't think so. I don't know. I don't think he followed us.'

'Nobody followed us,' Hannah said. 'Will you tell me about him now? Your husband?'

Darlene put her head back against the door. 'He's not a good man,' she said.

Hannah waited.

'He runs a trucking company in St. Louis,' Darlene finally said. 'I'm pretty sure it's crooked. A front for something. Or maybe smuggling. He hints, but he never says anything straight about it, and he comes home with envelopes stuffed with cash. And some of the men he spends time with frighten me. When they come to the house there are armed men with them who sit in the driveway or on the porch.'

This sounded like a movie. For a moment Hannah wondered if Darlene was entirely stable.

'Everybody loves Gerald.' Darlene had dropped her voice almost to a whisper. 'Always buying rounds at the bar. Slapping people's backs, giving his workers tickets to the ball game. But none of them have to go home with him.' She was quiet so long that Hannah thought she had finished. 'He's different at home.'

'So you ran away,' Hannah said.

'One day he went to work, and I took three of his envelopes full of cash and got on the first bus leaving town.' It came in a rush. 'I didn't know I was going to do it until I found myself doing it. I've been terrified ever since. He'll find me, Hannah. I know he'll find me.'

'He doesn't have to.'

'He's not Cary Grant,' Darlene said, as if she hadn't heard. 'He won't turn out to be a nice guy. Especially not since I took his money.'

'I don't think that man saw you.'

'I didn't go far enough. I have to leave. I'll take another bus tomorrow.'

'Tomorrow? But that's Christmas Eve! I won't be working.' Holcomb town ordinances strictly banned secular public entertainments from five o'clock on Christmas Eve until the 26th. 'I was going to invite you to my apartment for a Christmas dinner.' She'd spent much of the day cleaning, imagining the places Darlene was most likely to sit, the pictures or books she would comment on.

'Oh,' Darlene said. 'That's nice of you.'

'Just wait a couple of days,' Hannah said. 'Nothing will happen on Christmas, surely. We can plan together, figure out where you should go. What about your folks?'

'I married Gerald to get away from them. My parents had eleven children, and they should have never had any. There are some people who shouldn't. If I went there, they'd send me back to him.'

'We'll think of something,' Hannah said. 'Do say you'll come.'

She held her breath for a moment as Darlene sat quiet. 'I'll wait until after Christmas,' Darlene finally said. 'But could we have the dinner here? I have a sick feeling since I saw Pete. I want to stay inside tomorrow.'

'Of course,' Hannah said. 'I can bring everything here. Say seven?'

'Yes,' Darlene said. 'But please, don't leave yet. Keep me company a little longer.'

'As long as you want.'

Darlene pushed herself up to stand. 'You haven't had your coffee. We can probably risk a little light in the kitchen.' Hannah tried to protest, but Darlene led her to the back of the house and sat her at a small table with two wobbly chairs. She turned on a light and pointed at a big metal coffee urn on the kitchen counter. 'That was here when I took the place. It's about time I got some use from it.'

'Probably too heavy to move,' Hannah said.

Darlene took off her coat and hat, hanging them by the back door. It was the first time Hannah had seen her without the coat on. The dress underneath was a simple black, the hems of the sleeves a bit ragged. Her shoes were simple flats, her stockings clean but worn. Everything about her was modest, contained. *Held down*, Hannah thought.

'Where will you go?' She spoke quietly. Something about

63

being in the small lighted kitchen, the rest of the house looming dark beyond the doorway and the cold world outside, made her feel that they were being naughty, sneaking a forbidden treat in the middle of the night.

Darlene didn't look at her. 'California, I suppose. I can't go back east.'

'And of course Mexico is about to be overrun by the Japanese.'

Darlene's mouth twitched briefly upward. 'Of course. I read a newspaper article at the library a few days ago. It said there would be lots of work in California, for women too.'

'I've never been to California,' Hannah said. 'I've never been out of Colorado. Oh, Darlene!'

Darlene had stopped working. She stood with her back to Hannah, her body tense, her hands fists against the counter. 'He'll find me, Hannah,' she said. 'It doesn't matter where I go. Gerald will find me.'

'He won't.' Hannah stood and put her arms around her friend. At first Darlene was rigid, but then she almost collapsed, clinging to Hannah's arm. 'He won't,' Hannah repeated.

It was well past midnight when Hannah closed Darlene's door softly and walked briskly off in the direction of her apartment. Had there been any snow on the ground, she might have seen heavy, booted tracks coming partway up Darlene's walk before turning back to the street. Cold as it was, though, Holcomb wasn't having a white Christmas, and Hannah's steps clicked lightly along on the clean, dry sidewalk.

#

Hannah was superb at blocking things out when she had to. Going out the next morning to shop, she put the thought of Darlene leaving Holcomb behind a door and locked it. She would think only of the coming twenty-four hours. She bought enough food for four, traveling dishes to keep everything warm,

64

and a bottle of red wine. By noon she was home, cooking. Everything fit neatly into the old picnic basket she hadn't used in years. To the side of the food, wrapped in a twist of green tissue paper, she put the new hat she had found a few days before, the blue one. It would go beautifully with Darlene's coat.

The wine was a good thought. She would pull it out and hand it to Darlene and say 'Do the wine, will you, Phil?'

At the last minute she remembered to add cutlery, glasses and a corkscrew. There was no telling what a kitchen in a rented house might be deficient in.

#

Darlene was subdued and listless when Hannah arrived, but at least she was no longer sitting in the darkness. Every light in the house was on, and she was wearing a red and green checked frock that was probably the most colorful piece of clothing she owned. Hannah couldn't decide if Darlene was making her own effort to ignore her looming departure, or if a day of hiding in isolation had left her unwilling to face the dark.

She made Darlene sit at the kitchen table to watch as she produced her wonders from the basket, Darlene protesting all the while at the trouble and expense. She left the wine and the hat in the basket, out of sight, as she put several dishes in the oven to be warmed and spread napkins and silverware on the table.

'Really, Hannah, this is all too much,' Darlene said. She touched the corkscrew. 'I don't even have any wine, I'm afraid.'

'Ah,' Hannah said. 'Let the spirit of Christmas provide.' She took the bottle from the basket and held it up for inspection, the word *do* already starting on her lips.

That's when the lights went out.

Darlene leaped to her feet with a high-pitched squeal,

jostling the table and sending most of Hannah's place settings bouncing across the floor. Hannah reached out blindly, trying to find her friend's arm. 'It's all right,' she said. 'It's just a line down. It happens in the cold.'

'No,' Darlene said. Her voice was flat. 'It's him. It's Gerald.'

Before Hannah could reply, the back door, only a few feet away, shuddered under a barrage of heavy, fast knocking. 'Darlene,' a deep voice said. It might have sounded concerned, if not for the edge of mockery it carried. 'It's time to go home, honey.'

Just enough light filtered in through the windows for Hannah to make out the shadow that was Darlene sinking in despair toward the floor. 'No,' Hannah hissed. Stepping forward, she pulled Darlene to her feet and pulled her toward the front door. 'Out the front. *Run*. Fast as you can for the place next door.'

The house shook with the impact of something heavy against the back door. 'No use,' Darlene moaned.

'Nonsense,' Hannah snapped. She pulled fiercely at the knob of the front door. It came toward her and jerked to a stop, with such force that Hannah almost fell over backwards. She yanked again, meeting the same resistance. The door would only open a little more than an inch. Putting her eye to the crack, Hannah could just make out a chain, looped around the outside knob and running off somewhere.

The house shook again.

Hannah pushed the door shut and turned back into the house, taking Darlene's arm once more. The short hallway ahead ran back into the kitchen. A door to the left led to a compact bathroom, the two on the right to the front room and the bedroom. 'Bedroom window,' she said. 'Hurry.'

Darlene came along with no resistance, but no real will of her own. They were at the bedroom door when an echoing sound of tearing wood came from the kitchen and there was a rush of cold air. Darlene shook violently and fell to the floor. No chance of getting through the window now. Crouching, Hannah pushed at Darlene, urging her under the bed. '*Hide, hide,*' she hissed. Darlene began to crawl. There'd be no room for two. Hannah spun away from the door and pushed into the closet, into the corner behind the clothes.

She could hear him. His tread was heavy and slow on the bare wooden floor.

'Darlene, honey. I know you're here. Won't you come out? I miss your pretty face.'

His show of concern almost sounded sincere now, but Hannah wasn't imagining the edge of menace Gerald couldn't entirely mask. The steps came into the bedroom and stopped. Hannah closed her eyes for a moment and listened, hearing the change in Gerald's breath as he stooped to reach down. 'Got you, girl,' he said. His voice was now a growl. There was the start of a scream from under the bed.

Hannah came out of the closet. The dim bulk of him was silhouetted against the doorway and she jumped onto his back, wrapping her legs around his midriff and one arm around his throat. Gerald stumbled from the sudden weight, grunting, then snapped upright and clamped his hands on her arm, trying to pry it away from his windpipe.

'Out the back!' Hannah shouted. 'Run! Run!'

Gerald spun into the hallway, bouncing Hannah painfully off the doorframe. His balance failed and he went over, backwards, falling through the doorway into the kitchen. His full weight came down on Hannah's chest and stomach, knocking the air roughly out of her. Her grip weakened, and in a heartbeat Gerald had rolled and had his hands on her throat, squeezing hard. Hannah kicked at him, her hands scrambling madly, but his grip only got tighter. There was a flutter at the edge of her vision. Darlene breaking for the back door? Hannah renewed her wild flailing. The longer she could last, the more time Darlene would have.

The fingers of her right hand fell on something they recognized. She seized it and, without thought, drove it up as hard as she could into Gerald's side.

It was the corkscrew. With a curse, Gerald reared up on his knees, releasing her to grope for the thing tearing a hole in him.

'Run!' Hannah yelled, her voice a rasp. She tried to scramble backwards, but he was grabbing at her, trying to get to her throat again.

'I'll kill you,' Gerald grunted. Then there was a noise, like the tolling of a very deep, very dull bell, and Gerald went limp and collapsed across her.

At the edge of the slanting light from the broken back door, Darlene stood over her husband. The heavy steel coffee urn held in both her hands carried a sizable new dent in its side.

Hannah kicked and levered her way out from under him and rolled against the nearest wall. Her whole torso ached, every breath causing sharp new pains that made lights swim in front of her eyes. She wondered if Gerald had broken some of her ribs, coming down on her with such force.

Darlene's voice came out of the confused shadows at the other end of the room. 'Did I kill him?'

'I don't know.' Hannah was still fighting for air. 'Give me a minute.'

The urn fell to the floor with a crash. Darlene turned her fallen chair upright and sat, her movements slow and weary. 'I figured it out,' she said. 'The end of *Suspicion*. Johnny pushes Lina out of the car, over the cliff. The whole scene where they make up and everything is all right is in her mind. Her hallucination before she hits the rocks.'

Hannah was getting her breath, but the pain was still intense. Moving carefully, ready to jump back, she got to her knees and held her hand in front of Gerald's mouth, feeling a bare flutter of air. She touched the back of his head and, repulsed, pulled her fingers away from a mat of bloody hair, the head beneath softer than it should be. She moved the hand to Gerald's chest

68

and had to concentrate to feel it moving with shallow, irregular breaths.

'He's not dead,' she said.

'It doesn't really matter,' Darlene said. She sounded like she might drift into sleep at any minute. 'If he's alive, he'll come for me again. If he's not, the police will take me.'

'You only did it to save me.'

'They won't care, Hannah. They'll just see a bad wife who ran away and then killed her husband. Anyway, there are the people Gerald works for. They won't just let somebody get away with killing one of theirs.'

Sounding like a movie again, like they needed to worry about Jimmy Cagney turning up with a tommy gun. But then, Hannah had thought that yesterday, and Gerald was very real, as was the blood oozing from his head and the memory of his fingers on her throat.

'It's all over,' Darlene said.

'It's not.' Hannah crawled over to push the door shut against the freezing air, though the frame was broken and it wouldn't close properly. The path forward was in her mind, as perfect and sure as if it had always been there. She knew what they needed to do. 'Think for me, Darlene. Gerald came here from St. Louis, right? How would he make that trip? Bus? Train?'

'He drove,' Darlene sad. 'He loves driving. It's another way to show off. A bus would be beneath his dignity.'

The note of mockery there was a good sign, Hannah thought, but no time to dwell on it. 'Well, now it's beneath yours, too. We need to go through his pockets and find the car key.'

'You mean, take his car?'

'Fastest way I know to get to California.'

'Hannah, I don't know how to drive.'

'I do.'

'What?'

Hannah's eyes were getting used to the dark kitchen. She saw Darlene's head come up. She stood and walked across the room to put her hand on Darlene's shoulder. 'I'm coming with you.'

'Hannah, no. Your life is here.'

'Do you have candles?'

'Candles?' The change of topic threw her for a moment. 'Of course.'

'We don't have time to find where he cut the power line. Light a candle and pack your things, quick as you can. While you do that, I'll go find the car.'

'I can't let you do this.' But her hand came down on Hannah's and tightened.

'We'll have to stop by my place. I can have everything I care about in a suitcase in ten minutes. We'll drive three or four hours and then find a hotel room for the rest of the night. Probably near Denver.'

'Your home is here,' Darlene said again.

'My home is with you. You can pretend you don't already know that and waste a lot of time arguing, or start packing. I'm going to find that key.' She crouched over the fallen man, starting with the pockets of his jacket.

Ten seconds went by before she heard the rustle of Darlene rising and going into the other room. Then there was a hint of golden candlelight, and the rattle of hangers being moved.

#

The key in Gerald's pocket fit a big black Ford parked on the next block. While Darlene was putting her suitcases in it, Hannah went back inside the house, saying she didn't want to leave the basket.

Gerald was still stretched across the floor in the same position. Hannah knelt, bringing her head down close to his, and listened. Thin, gasping breaths, with long pauses in between. She didn't think he would live, but she couldn't be sure. She began to sweep things up from the floor and put them

70

in the basket. The hat, inside its paper, seemed intact, and the bottle of wine was unbroken. She found spoons and forks and the good linen napkins she'd taken when she left home, knowing they would be missed, wanting to know some absence, at least, would be felt. She found rolls and cookies that could be eaten easily on the road. She found the heavy carving knife with the ivory handle.

Darlene shivered on the passenger side of the front seat as Hannah put the basket in the back and got behind the wheel. 'Here we go,' she said. She reached for Darlene's hand and gave it a squeeze. The answering squeeze, before Hannah reclaimed her hand to steer, was weak, but it was there. Later, she could tell Darlene that she would neither have to worry about Gerald again nor feel responsible for his death. Later, in some hotel room somewhere, she could produce the bottle. *Do the wine, will you, Phil.* Later she could give Darlene the hat, and tell her about watching her from the projection booth. They had plenty of later. For right now, they could just be a pair of Dorothies, ripped out of the middle of the country, finding their way through an America at war.

Paranoia

Paulene Turner

'Emotion.'

Griffin Chance spoke the word like it was the answer to life's biggest questions (which it probably was). Rocking back in his chair, hands behind his head, he hoped he cut a casually brilliant figure. 'Emotion was the key to Hitchcock's work as a film-maker. He wanted to make you *feel* something. Fear, usually.'

The English film director struggled not to smile as Phoebe, his Australian mentee, wrote it all down. Her thick golden hair hung over the page as her pen flew back and forth, capturing every word. While he waited, he gazed about their Australia park location, with its forest of paperbark gum trees—so called because the trunk's layers peeled off like sheets of paper. It reminded him of decaying zombie flesh of his student film days.

'Hitchcock moves the camera as if it's a character—witnessing events. In this way, he draws the audience into the story, so they feel the same emotions the characters feel.'

When she'd done, Phoebe looked up at Griffin, pen poised, her sapphire eyes wide, eager for more.

Ooh! Wouldn't I like to give her more, right now? But no! He'd never be one of those old dudes using power to get sexual favours; he was totally onboard with the #metoo movement. Thankfully, at 38, he didn't need to coerce anyone. Slim, with spiky dark hair and "to-die-for" eyebrows, he had enough attractions for most of the women he fancied, without needing to leverage his position.

'That's all really interesting.' Phoebe's face flushed with exertion.

When his assistant phoned a few days earlier saying she needed a week off to care for a sick relative, Griffin was irritated. He'd just broken her in, got her doing things the way he liked. But a few hours after the call, Phoebe showed up on set—an Australian film school graduate looking for work experience. She'd slipped into the girl's shoes, as though she'd worn them all her life.

Almost too good to be true.

'And you wrote the screenplay for the film we're shooting?' she asked.

'Yes, I did.' Griffin smiled. *Time Out* had called him a "double threat". *Should I mention that?*

'What inspired you to write that story?' Phoebe asked.

Behind her, Griffin saw the crew assembled, waiting for him. He should stop things here, get through the shot list for the day. But having a hot film student hanging on every word was just too much fun. They could wait a few more minutes.

'I got the idea one night in the shower,' he said. 'Warm water running all over me, steam rising. When I dried off, I went straight to my computer and stayed there till dawn.'

'All in one shower?' Phoebe shook her head, awestruck. 'A man who drives women to commit suicide and then steals their fortunes. It's a very Hitchcockian plot, if you don't mind me saying.'

Griffin did not mind one bit.

If I wasn't so scrupulous, I could take her, behind that tree.

But, tasty as the girl was, he wouldn't make any moves just now. She was too valuable as his go-fer. And, anyway, to do his director's job well, he needed a good night's sleep and a clear head in the morning—something an all-night sex-fest would not provide. This was his first feature film. It had to be the best. The girl would keep until they'd wrapped.

'Didn't I hear that some woman claimed she'd written the script, not you?' Phoebe asked.

'Err, yes, that claim was made,' Griffin said. 'But thankfully, I registered my early drafts with the Writer's Guild, so I had proof mine pre-dated hers.'

Always register scripts, Phoebe noted. With three exclamation marks.

'What happened to her?'

Griffin licked his dry lips and cleared his throat. 'I believe she died. In a road accident.'

'Ohmigod!'

But was it an accident, Griffin wondered, or had she thrown herself under the car intentionally after her conflict with him?

Griffin stood up, ready to work.

'One last thing,' Phoebe said. 'How did you decide on the title—*Paranoia*?'

'Alfred Hitchcock made *Suspicion* and *Vertigo*. *Paranoia* seemed to fit with them. It's my homage to a director who's influenced me more than any other.'

Phoebe worked at the page with the gravity of a student sitting an exam, the tip of her pink tongue peaking out of crimson lips. 'But you know what they say?' she called after him. 'Paranoia will destroy ya.'

Her words sent a ripple of fear through him. To cover up, he became all business. 'Okay, positions guys!' he shouted. 'Energy up! Let's do this!'

#

At thirty-eight, Griffin Chance had made *Time Out*'s list of *Film-makers to Watch*. He'd done TV and worked as AD on some big films. Now, he was directing his first feature—in Australia! In a beach town north of Sydney. It was a dream location with blue skies, golden sands, cicadas singing as sausages sizzled on the all-famous Aussie barbecue. And—

74

most importantly—lots of good cappuccino.

He had a decent budget, a pretty good crew—mostly Aussie. And as writer/director, he'd get double credit, double payment. *Double bubble.*

He was on the crest of a powerful wave and he liked the view from here. And he'd do whatever it took to ensure it was a long, smooth ride.

#

Griffin made gun fingers with both hands, paired them together as a frame, and closed one eye to peer through them at the scene that Pierre, the cinematographer, had set up for him.

'Yep, that's what I want,' he told Pierre. 'With a creepy pan to the left, as if a head was slowly turning.'

'Gotcha, boss,' said Pierre, in a broad Aussie accent.

Griffin turned to the lead actors—Josh Churchill, forties, well-made with a hint of silver fox, and Roxanne Rose, late thirties, ice-cool blonde, one of the most in-demand actresses on the planet.

'Ready, guys?'

They nodded.

'Scene 15, Take 1…mark it,' yelled Ben, the 2nd Assistant Camera.

The clapperboard snapped.

'And…action!' Griffin shouted.

They went into the scene, with Griffin nodding. But quite soon he was biting his lip, brow furrowed. 'Cut!'

'Err, Roxy.' He curled his finger to call her over.

'Roxanne, if you don't mind,' the actress said.

'I thought we'd discussed the tone.'

'Was I too shrill?'

'A bit.'

Roxanne was aghast. 'But I thought—'

'You were great in that last horror film you did,' he said.

'But this is a psychological thriller. It's more subtle. For grown-ups, not teenagers on a first date looking for an excuse to grope each other in the dark.'

'Of course, that's what I was going for.'

'The tension needs to be there, in your movements, in the way you say things. But restrained. This is not theatre.'

'I know that, of course.'

'Positions everyone.'

'Err, could we take five?' Roxanne's voice was high-pitched and child-like. 'I just need a little more clarification about my motivations?'

'Can't it wait till we've completed the shot list?' Griffin glanced at his watch. 'We're already behind schedule.' He was fobbing her off and she knew it.

'Scene 15, Take 2...' Ben yelled.

'And...action!'

Roxanne Rose stumbled through the next take visibly unsettled. Though she tried to hide it, her unease was there in the wrinkling of her normally smooth brow, the pouty fullness of her usually smiling lips.

'Cut.'

'But Griffin, can we just have a word...?' she began.

'Take 3...' Ben shouted over her. 'Take 4...Take 5...' And so it went on.

'Excuse me, Griffin,' Phoebe whispered. 'I think Roxanne's trying to get your attention.'

The director smiled and decided to let his pretty disciple in on a secret. 'This is something Hitchcock did, in *The Man Who Knew Too Much*,' he whispered.

'The film with Doris Day and James Stewart?'

He nodded. 'In that film, Doris Day played a character who was on edge and, well, Hitchcock "helped" her with her motivation by not interacting with her on set and refusing all her requests for a private meeting. The result was a performance quite different to her usual fare.'

76

'Oh, so…'

'If it's good enough for Hitchcock…'

Phoebe glanced over at the actress. 'It seems to be working. Roxanne's close to tears now.'

'They say you have to suffer for your art.' Griffin smiled. 'Sure, Roxanne's suffering now. But she'll be happy with the results.'

It would give them an interesting talking point during pre-screening publicity, Griffin thought. And confirm his reputation as the new Hitchcock on the scene.

'Take 9!'

The clapperboard's snap made Roxanne flinch, as if she'd been struck. For the rest of the day, Griffin watched the world's most famous actress delivering her lines with a quivering lip.

'And cut!' he shouted. 'Excellent work. That's our slate for the day. See you all bright and early tomorrow!'

TAKE 1

The five-bedroom lakefront house, behind Avoca beach the producers had rented for Griffin was like a paradise. Light-filled rooms, lots of glass to take in the water view and an ever-present scent of the sea. For someone who'd spent too many years in a dumpy Clapham flat, with crummy furniture and a loo that never flushed properly, Griffin was elated.

The first thing he did when he got back in the evenings was have a swim in his private pool. It was summer in Australia, staying light till after eight pm. Slipping into the icy water seemed to revive every cell in his body. He floated on his back, watching the clouds scud across the sky. *Delightful.*

After a shower, he'd pour a glass of sauvignon blanc and take it out onto the deck, by the lake. And just breathe.

He hadn't done a lot of that lately. In London, there never

seemed to be enough air. Especially since *that night*.

#

He'd arranged to meet Juliette McKenzie late, on Primrose Hill, to discuss their "issues"—namely, she said she'd written the script, he claimed he had.

It was a bleak evening, cold and windy, so the park was deserted. And the meeting did nothing to warm either of them.

'The Guild ruled in my favour,' Griffin reminded Juliette. 'I registered my script a year before yours which means I had the idea first.'

'That's impossible,' she said. 'Someone must have backdated your submission.'

He couldn't see her very well in the dark. Her skin looked smooth and young with clumps of black hair poking out from beneath a dirt-brown beanie. She was average height, slightly built, but that was as much as he could tell in the bulky coat and scarf. And when he looked for her profile pic on social media, later, all he found was the eye of a film camera.

'You're a liar and soon the world will know,' Juliette said.

'If you make that claim in public, I'll sue you,' Griffin warned. 'No-one will take your word over mine. And I'll make sure you never work in the industry again.'

He was glad to get back into his car and switch on the heating. As he drove along the road by the park, it began to rain. Water streaked down his windscreen, like tears. Inside, the glass fogged up.

And then, suddenly, a woman in a brown beanie was on the road in front of him. He braked, inches from her. She thumped the hood of the car and screamed, 'Plagiarist!' The headlights revealed droplets of spittle flying from her horror film mouth.

When he tried to swerve around her, she jumped in front of the car. So he jammed it into reverse and backed away.

It all happened so fast. One minute, she was jogging

78

alongside him, hitting the windows. The next—*thump*. He'd never forget that sound or the feeling as he drove over a bump on the road. He moved the vehicle forward a bit, then stopped and looked back. Light reflected on the wet streets, like a film noir image, revealing the silhouette of a body on the road— Juliette's presumably. Unmoving.

For seconds stretched by terror, he considered getting out to help. But his hand seemed frozen; he couldn't make it clasp the door handle. The next thing he knew, he'd taken off, wheels spinning on the wet road as he accelerated away.

In the morning, his first thought was that it had been a nightmare. But then cold reality settled on him, like threads of ice tightening around his chest, his throat. Had he…hit and run? No. It was her who hit his car, not the other way around. Though he had run afterwards.

Did anyone see? From the surrounding flats or somewhere along the road?

For the next few days, he expected police to storm his home at every moment. When nothing happened, he scanned the news for a story about the accident. *Police seek witnesses to Hit and Run*. Or some such. But there was nothing.

A few weeks later, he came across a paragraph in a trade journal, in the *In Memorium* column. *Juliette McKenzie, emerging screenwriter, dies at twenty-four*. There was no mention of how she'd died, just details of a Crematorium service. For two heartbeats, he thought about attending. But he'd seen too many cop shows to make that mistake. Police always checked out funeral attendees, in case the villain couldn't resist a peek at their handiwork.

In the first few weeks after the accident, he thought about that awful night a lot and tried to slow down the frames of his mind to work out if it had been an accident, or if Juliette had thrown herself under the car deliberately. If it was the latter, was she motivated by distress? Or revenge? To make him 'pay' as she'd threatened to do?

79

I guess I'll never know.

It wasn't till he arrived here, in Avoca beach, that he finally felt free. Gazing at the lake, reflecting the olives and golds of the gum trees along its banks, Griffin raised his wine glass to the darkening sky. 'Here's to screenplays in heaven, Juliette. I'm not sure whether you were punishing yourself or me, but…no hard feelings?'

By candlelight, he began flicking through the notes and storyboards to prep for the next day's beach shoot. A loud buzzing distracted him. *A mosquito? A very big one?* Something was flying towards him, through the trees—not an insect, but a drone emitting a high-pitched sound.

A squawk followed, so shrill, it hurt his ears to listen, as a bird zoomed by.

'What the—?'

Within minutes, the sound had increased five-fold as more of the creatures swooped in, from left and right, flying fast, barely missing each other. One flew at the balcony's wooden railing, nicking it, before taking off. Another set down on the railing and tipped its head to study him. *Creepy.*

'What are you looking at?' Griffin demanded.

It was a big bird, with feathers as white as fresh snow, a parrot's curved beak and a Mohawk of buttery yellow—a sulphur-crested cockatoo. A dozen of them moved through the trees—like streaks of white paint slashed across a dark canvas.

One shrieked and flew straight at the director, jabbing him on the forehead with its beak.

'Ah!' Griffin cried out. He touched his head and his fingers came away, bloody. 'Fucking bird!'

The drone's noise climbed an octave and another half dozen birds joined the fray. In a storm of frenzied flapping and other-worldly screeching, straight out of a horror film, they attacked the balcony rail, sending woodchips flying. Then, one after another, they came at the director, sending him racing for the doors. *Bang!*—one hit the glass in front of him. *Wham!* A second did the same. *Could they actually break through?* Another bird hit the back of his head before he slid the door open and hurtled inside, locking up behind him. *Bang, bang, bang*...three more birds struck the glass. Griffin backed away, scanning the room for a place to hide if they broke through.

Then one, two, three...seven of the creatures set down quietly on the wooden rail. The silence as they tilted their heads, trying to see him through the glass was more chilling than the noise, Griffin considered.

A few minutes later, they'd gone. All was quiet again, but for the whooshing of the nearby ocean. And the creak of the ghost gums in the breeze.

What the Hell was that?

Griffin grabbed some paper towels to sop up the blood and stood nervously by the backdoor for a while. When no more birds appeared, he slipped out to grab his work. It was only then he noticed half a dozen shiny spots along the railing—birdseed mixed with something sticky and sweet. That must have been what the birds were after. *The people who lived here must feed them, and they were angry no fresh seed had been put out.*

Whatever. He'd had enough of the outdoors for tonight. He'd finish his work inside.

Sinking into the sofa, he slurped down the last of his wine. And did a double take at a framed poster on the wall—Alfred Hitchcock's *The Birds*.

Was that there before?

TAKE 2

The terrors of the evening faded away the next morning, as Griffin watched Phoebe hurrying across the sand to him with a bucket size cappuccino. *Just what I need. A tasty treat with a tasty treat.* He took the cup and slurped.

'Is everything okay, Mr. Chance?' Phoebe asked, studying the gash on his forehead.

'I had a rough night, but I'm fine. And, please, call me Griffin. Mr. Chance is my father.' He gave her a cheeky I'm-only-your-age smile.

While the crew set up for the first shot, the director recounted his ordeal with the birds the previous night. 'And then, this morning, I woke at some God-awful hour to this chorus of jeery laughter outside my window. For a moment, I thought it was the Joker, come to life in stereo—'

'Kookaburras, mate!' Nick the prop's assistant said. He was in his early twenties, a surfer, with golden brown skin, and hair as crisp as a packaged chip. 'So if you can't handle our birds, have you met any of our spiders yet?'

'Spiders?' Griffin groaned.

'He'll probably meet a few huntsmen, this time of year,' Shane, the prop master, chimed in. Just like Nick only a decade older, Shane had deeply creased blue eyes, and a close-cut blonde beard. 'They like to sit in the corners of the room and keep an eye on things.' He moved his fingers like spider legs, making the director shudder.

'Some are so big, when you look into their eyes, they look right back at you,' Nick added.

Australian wildlife. Now, Griffin remembered why he'd never travelled here before.

'If you see a huntsman, you know what you have to do?' Nick continued.

'What?'

'You have to name it. Harry, maybe,' he said. 'Or Henry. They're harmless. Except they scare the shit out of you.'

'Stop teasing the poor guy!' Phoebe came to Griffin's rescue. 'I hate spiders too. Give me the heebeejeebies.'

'And do you have a pool, mate?' Shane said. 'You gotta watch out for funnel webs. They sit in bubbles underwater. Most deadly spider on earth. And they're called the Northern

Sydney Funnel Web because they're from this area.'

Great. Now, his skin felt clammy. As a cockatoo screeched past, Griffin reeled back, making the crew howl with laughter.

'Okay, okay,' Griffin said. 'Now, let's make a film!'

This morning's shoot was on Terrigal beach, a wide panorama of golden sands, blue sky, and sea, backed by swish houses and rocky hills. They lost the first couple of hours because the light wasn't right and sand got into the dolly. While they waited for the sun to break free from the clouds, they took establishing shots of the beach, and extras bobbing about in the water.

And of Roxanne's body double slipping beneath the waves.

'I didn't know I was getting a double,' Roxanne said, miffed.

'We thought it would save you doing the water work,' Griffin said.

'It's not because you think I'm...' the actress struggled to say it, 'too heavy for a bikini?'

'Of course not,' Griffin said. 'The fans would love to see every inch of you. And the more of you there is to see, the happier they'll be.'

She wasn't sure how to react but sensed an insult buried somewhere.

'How old is the body model?' Roxanne asked.

'Twenty-two,' Griffin shrugged helplessly. 'Audiences have unrealistic expectations.'

'I don't suppose Josh is getting a double.'

'No.'

She stalked off, out of sorts.

Griffin continued to feed Roxanne's discomfort during the morning.

'Bad night last night, was it, Roxanne?'

'No.' The star was confused.

'It's just you look a bit tired today. Make up!' He waved the make-up artist over and pointed to the actress. 'Heavy on the under-eye foundation.'

Roxanne really wanted a word with Griffin after that. But he pretended not to notice. And when she physically pulled his face around to hers, he said he was too busy to 'deal with *that* today.'

'When will we deal with it?' Roxanne demanded. Everyone on the set slowed their movements, awaiting his reply.

'Roxanne, you're a professional, and so are all these people.' He gestured to the boom swinger, focus puller, gaffer. 'We don't want to waste their time. So perhaps you and I should schedule time after hours to talk?'

The star was mortified. 'Fine. I don't want to hold anyone up.'

After that, she went about with a sullen look quite out of character for the bubbly actress.

'The directing technique with Roxanne seems to be working,' Phoebe whispered. 'She's quite miserable now.'

'It might seem cruel,' Griffin said, 'but I've seen the rushes. I think she'll be pleased with the results.'

If she doesn't kill me first.

#

Lunch was a buffet in a waterfront reserve, beneath a sprawling fig tree. They sat at trestle tables with white table cloths as a sea breeze cooled the sweat beading on their faces and necks.

'Has anybody ever told you, you sound like Cary Grant?' Nick, the props assistant, asked Griffin as they lined up for potato bake.

'I've heard that before,' the director said. 'I'm surprised you know who Cary Grant is?'

'Course. Alfred Hitchcock films. Love 'em.'

'Good man.'

'Oh, wait, wait,' Nick continued, unaware Griffin's last comment was meant as a conversation closer. 'What was it

Hitchcock said about suspense versus surprise? Oh yeah! Two people sit in a café talking. Suddenly, *boom*, a bomb under the table goes off. That's surprise. Suspense is when the audience sees the bomb, but the characters don't.'

'Indeed.'

Griffin found the Aussies to be quite confronting. Most seemed clueless about the subtleties of rank, and even the set runner talked to him like he was just another crew member, not director of the production.

Shane, the Props manager, and Nick, his unpaid assistant, were the worst—joking all day long. One look at their white teeth and barbecued skin, and Griffin knew he couldn't trust them with the diamond and emerald necklace, on loan to the production, for Roxanne to wear during the party scene. If the surf was up that day, they'd probably wrap the jewellery in a towel and take a dip anyway, with a 'She'll be right, mate!'

No, Griffin would guard the necklace himself. He'd keep it locked in the safe at the beach house until they needed it on set.

Roxanne tried to sit near Griffin at lunch so they could 'get to know each other'. But the director had briefed the crew to keep her away from him. It was quite amusing to see one of the world's leading actresses being muscled out of the best seats. Eventually, she sat at the opposite end of the table, between the best boy and the continuity assistant.

'So, Griffin,' Josh, the lead actor said. 'Some people have said you write like a woman.'

A piece of chicken wedged in Griffin's throat and he began to choke, until Phoebe thumped him on the back. He took a mouthful of water.

'I think they just mean there's not so many car chases and fight scenes, more psychodrama, mind games,' Josh said.

'Well, it's psychological thriller, not James Bond.'

'You write women very well,' Roxanne said. 'Like you really understand them—how they think, their vulnerabilities.'

'The way I see it,' Griffin said, 'men and women are all just humans with the same insecurities and things that drive them. Love, security, the need for validation.'

Heads bobbed around the table.

'What made you set the story in Australia?' Phoebe asked.

Griffin dabbed the corners of his mouth with his napkin. 'Name me one English director who doesn't want to shoot here, who wouldn't give his—or her—tender parts to do so. Even with the marauding birds and spiders who could devour you in your sleep.'

They cracked up at that. Griffin put on his "good sport" face.

'But the script seemed so spot-on for this location,' Phoebe said, 'right down to this tree we're sitting under? Like you'd actually been here.'

What is this? The inquisition?

'There's this thing called Google.' He tried to keep his tone light. 'Perhaps you've heard of it?'

'Sure, but Google couldn't give you the kind of knowledge you show on the page.'

'You're right. I have an Aussie friend who helped.'

'Did you ever consider calling the film *Gaslighting*?' Phoebe said.

Gaslighting. A script title page flashed up in his mind.

Gaslight Alley
by Juliette McKenzie

'Isn't gaslighting when you make someone doubt their sanity,' Phoebe said, 'which is exactly what happens to the women in this story?'

'I prefer *Paranoia*,' he said. 'Got a problem with that?'

'No, of course not.'

The clinking of cutlery on ceramic plates seemed loud as a dozen cast and crew chewed chicken curry in awkward silence.

'Do people ever send you scripts to read?' Nick asked to break the tension. 'Asking for a friend.'

86

'I get a few.'

'You're a scriptwriter, aren't you, Phoebe?' Nick said. 'Writing anything interesting at the moment?'

'I'm writing a script about someone who steals someone else's script and pretends they wrote it,' Phoebe said. 'A plagiarist.'

'Ooh, is there a part in it for me?' Roxanne leaned forward.

Everyone chuckled. It was always the first question actors asked. But Griffin stood up abruptly, too rattled to join in. 'I need to walk off this lunch.'

He strode away, fast, to avert a full-blown panic attack. *Just breathe. In, out. In, out.* It was just chatter, he told himself. They didn't mean anything by it. *In, out. In, out.*

Behind a roped off area, a crowd had gathered to gawp at the actors. A young woman with dark hair on the end of the row looked familiar. As Griffin got closer, she took off. So he jumped the barrier and chased her into the car park, grabbed her arm and spun her around.

'I wasn't doing anything!' she said, big-eyed with fear. 'I was just looking, like everyone else.'

'Sorry, I thought you were someone I knew,' he said.

This woman looked similar, but it wasn't her. *How could it be? She's dead.*

'Are you one of the crew?' she asked. 'Could you get me Roxanne Rose's autograph?'

#

The director grabbed a coffee and sat back down, slurping. It would be a long afternoon at the beach trying to catch up the two hours they'd lost that morning. He needed to get a grip and fast.

Knock, knock, knock. Everyone looked around but could see no obvious source of the sound.

Knock, knock, knock.

Heads turned towards one end of the table. 'It's coming from the ice box,' Nick said.

The lid flew black suddenly, making them all gasp. And then a groaning began from within.

'What on Earth!' Josh whispered.

No-one moved; they were ever-so-slightly spooked. So Griffin stood and leaned over to peer inside the box. With a sharp intake of breath, he flopped back into his chair, hand on his chest.

'What is it?' Phoebe asked.

The director couldn't speak.

They all crept around to see a woman lying there, her complexion corpse-like, her tongue hanging out, a noose around her neck. Shrieks and hysterical laughter peppered the air as the woman sat up, moaning and moving in jerky zombie style.

'OMG,' Phoebe sank back with relief. 'How long were you in there?'

'I snuck in while you were all getting your desserts,' she said.

'You gave us the fright of our lives,' said Roxanne. 'I think you've scarred our director.'

'I didn't mean to scare you,' said the woman. 'Or, rather, I did, but—'

Griffin drew in a breath. 'Whose idea was this?' He sounded like a schoolteacher searching for a culprit.

'We thought you'd appreciate it, Boss!' Shane sounded nervous. 'A scene from *Rope*, my personal favourite of big Al's films.'

The prop guys. Typical! Griffin tried to summon up his best you-got-me grin when the "undead" extra introduced herself as Miranda.

'I know who to call when I do my next zombie film, Miranda,' he said.

His hand shook as he raised his cup to his lips.

Because Miranda also resembled Juliette.

Would every blacked-haired young woman look like the woman he'd left for dead on a London road?

TAKE 3

It was dark when Griffin got home. A card from the NSW Police sat on his doorstep. 'Burglars about. Ensure doors are locked.' Signed Detectives Feeley and Sedgmore.

The first thing he did was check on the diamond necklace in the safe. *Yup, still there.* Even if the thieves did get in, they'd need the combination to steal the jewels.

He really needed a swim at the end of the Hellish day on set. But when he switched on the pool lights, he saw a spider under the water that looked a lot like a funnel web. *Scotch that.*

Nor could he take his drink out on the balcony, for fear of crazy cockatoos!

And, when he went into his bedroom, there was Harry, the Huntsman, hanging in the corner. He tried hitting it with a broomstick, but that only sent the thing scuttling into hiding. *Well, that's that.* He'd never be able to sleep in that room again.

Griffin settled down on the sofa in the living room, to prep for the following day. Which was when he noticed another poster for an Alfred Hitchcock film—*Rope.*

Weird. How many other Hitchcock posters were there in the house?

Checking all the rooms, he found one more, in a small bedroom. For *Rear Window.*

#

He was just dozing off on the sofa, when he heard raised voices. Through a picture window, he saw a woman running down the grassy slope next door, as if fleeing for her life.

Seconds later, a man barrelled after her.

'Help!' the woman cried. The pair disappeared into the trees.

Digging out the card the police had left, he dialled the number. No answer.

'It's 11:12 pm, and I've just seen a man chasing a woman by the lake. Hurry. She may need help.' He gave his name, address and phone number.

Should he follow them and try to help the woman?

He opened the front door. Moonlight caught strands of a spider's web across the walkway with a small fat insect in the centre. He went back inside and locked the door. After all, what could he do? He'd phoned the police; he'd done as much as he could.

About fifteen minutes later—*thwap*—a woman's face slammed against the window. 'Help me!' It emerged as a squeak as she slid slowly down the glass and out of sight.

Griffin panted, and paced. And burst out the front door, ducking under the web and following the path around the house to where she'd been. But the lady had vanished. He loitered around for a while, dredging his memory for details of what he'd seen. It was dark and hard to be sure. But she looked a lot like Juliette, too. Or Miranda, the "undead" extra in the box.

By the time he'd returned to the house, his front door was wide open. Someone was inside.

Snatching an ornament from the hall table—a glass paperweight with a jellyfish suspended—the director crept down the stairs. Low voices emanated from the dining room. He took a deep breath, then launched around the corner, ready to strike.

A strong hand grabbed his arm before he could crack any skulls.

'You don't want to do that, matey,' said the man. 'Hitting a policeman could land you inside for five years or more.'

The man, mid-forties, introduced himself as Detective Sergeant Ralph Sedgmore. His red-headed partner, thirties, was

Constable Joanna Feeley.

'We're following up on your report of an attack,' said Feeley.

'I'll show you where I last saw the woman,' Griffin said.

He led them to the grassy slope outside the window. 'She was right here.'

They shone their torches around the ground and Feeley squatted down to touch the grass.

'Sir, I see traces of blood here,' Feeley showed Sedgmore the blood on her fingers. 'Fresh.'

They looked around a bit more then trailed back into the house.

'Where were you this evening, Sir?' Sedgmore asked.

Griffin had shot enough police dramas to know what he was really asking. For his alibi.

'I was here, alone. I got home around eight o'clock.'

'Sleeping on the sofa?' Feeley's left eyebrow pinged up.

'There was a spider in my room.'

They pair chortled annoyingly.

'And what is it you do, may I ask?' Sedgmore asked.

'I'm a film director.'

They laughed heartily this time.

'What do you really do?' Sedgmore asked.

'I'm a film director. I'm shooting a film around the central coast, starring Roxanne Rose.'

'Roxanne who?' Sedgmore asked.

Griffin looked to Feeley, who shrugged. *What rock have these guys been hiding under for the past five years?*

The younger detective moved around the flat, like she was looking for something. *Evidence.* 'He has some kind of cartoons here, mounted on board,' she called. 'Maybe he really is a director?'

'I can give you the film's studio number if you don't believe me,' Griffin said. 'But what's that got to with what I saw?'

Feeley squatted down to examine Griffin's shoes. 'I see

drops of blood here.'

'Please remove your shoes, Sir,' Sedgmore said, in a tone Griffin didn't care for. 'We'll need them as evidence.'

'Evidence for what?

'If that turns out to be the victim's blood, you might need to consult a lawyer.'

'Of course, it will be the victim's blood!' Griffin said. 'I went out there to help her. I must have stepped in it.'

They regarded him with blank mistrust.

'This is absolutely ludicrous,' he said. 'You don't have a body. We don't know if there's been a crime at all.'

He watched them bagging up his shoes, in disbelief.

'Do you have a role for a policeman in that film of yours?' Sedgmore grinned. 'Perhaps I might play a small part?'

Griffin didn't know how to reply to that. But he needed to keep the police sweet. 'Well, you could apply to be an extra. Contact Fox and Hounds film production. Mention my name, if you like.'

Feeley wrote a note in her book.

'We'll be in touch,' said Sedgmore.

He followed them to the front door and watched them walking away with his favourite shoes.

'Maybe see you on set!' Feeley said.

As if that wasn't the weirdest experience of my life.

#

Griffin stepped into the shower to wash away the horrors of the day. *A real shit show.*

Flicking on the tap, he closed his eyes and relished the sensation of warm water flowing over him, easing his tense muscles. As the steam rose, he soaped himself up and began the small rotations to wash it off. And that's when he saw it. Another poster—for *Psycho*—with a silhouette of woman in a shower and a bloody knife raised and about to strike.

Now, I know that wasn't there before!

Then he saw words on the fogged-up glass partition. *You know what you did!* His head snapped right and left, checking no-one was lurking in the room. He stepped out of the shower, still soapy.

'Is anyone there?' His voice echoed in the tiled room. 'Come out and show yourself!'

Was someone trying to scare him? Well, they were doing a good job! And now he realised something he'd never considered before. It was possible to have too much Alfred Hitchcock.

He dried off, then checked the house for intruders, every room and cupboard—twice. He triple-checked all the walls and storage areas for any more movie posters. As far as he could see, that was the lot. *The Birds*, *Rope* and *Psycho*.

It took him a long time to fall asleep on the sofa. When he did, he slept like the dead.

Like her.

TAKE 4

He awoke with a stiff neck, to a banging on the front door. It was Nick. 'Just checking you're okay, boss? It's ten o'clock.'

Shit.

He arrived rumpled and late on set for the first time in his career.

'Griffin, a couple of cops were looking for you earlier,' Phoebe said.

Great! Would they arrest him or audition for him? he wondered.

'And,' she kept her voice low, 'there's something you should see.'

She showed him a Tweet from that morning. *English film director falls for Aussie crew's pranks. Griffin Chance looked bluer than the undead extra in a prank recalling Hitchcock's* Rope. *Or had he seen a scary cockatoo in the background?* With it went a photo of Griffin, bug-eyed with shock. And the hashtag *#getasenseofhumourmate.*

It had been posted by Scott Reidel, an industry gossip columnist. But the photo had to have been provided by someone from the set.

'Who gave this reporter the story?' Griffin held up the tweet as he eyeballed the cast and crew. No-one spoke up. 'This is a professional film set, NOT a school yard. What happens on set stays on set. Anyone not happy with that can leave now.'

No-one could meet his eye.

'Now, let's shoot this film!'

They couldn't start immediately, though. Roxanne was refusing to leave her trailer. He'd 'motivated' her too well.

'Time for Plan B,' he whispered to Phoebe. 'I've brought her low. Now I throw her a crumb and she'll be so grateful, she'll be the easiest star I've ever directed.'

As soon as he entered her trailer, Roxanne erupted into tears. She was worried her performance wasn't up to scratch—'the rushes are great,' Griffin said—and that she was behaving like a prima donna—'Not in the least!'—and that the two of them had got off on the wrong foot—'It's my fault, not yours,' Griffin assured her. 'I've been too concerned with the technical aspects of the job. It's me who should apologise.'

By the time he left her, she was ready to do the role any way and with as many takes as he wanted.

'She'll be out in twenty minutes,' he told the crew.

While the crew set up for the party scene, he sat down in his director's chair to wait. And fret.

Who leaked the story on Twitter? If he found out, they'd be off the set and out of the whole business if he had anything to do with it. *Could it have been Pierre?* He'd caught the cinematographer's disapproving expression in an unguarded moment.

94

'Has Pierre ever said anything to you about my work with Roxanne?' he asked Phoebe.

'No?'

'Have you overheard him saying anything about me?'

'No?'

Could it have been the Sound guys? *Bunch of snickering schoolboys.* Always whispering to each other. *Like now.*

'Are they talking about me over there?' he asked Phoebe.

'Sorry?' she said. 'They're probably discussing the setup for the next scene?'

And as for Josh, the lead actor, any time he wasn't in front of the cameras, he was on his phone, on social media. *Could he have sold me out?*

'Do you think you could 'borrow' Josh's phone while we're shooting the next scene?' he asked Phoebe. He could check whether the actor had messaged anyone about private on-set business.

'I'm not comfortable doing that,' Phoebe said. 'Are you okay, Griffin? You're sounding a bit…'

'…paranoid? Is that what you were going to say?'

'No.'

The sound of a chuckle drew his gaze. He caught Shane and Nick glancing his way. *Two jackasses who laugh at everything. Are they laughing at me?*

'Got something on your mind, boys?' Griffin called.

'Just that we'll need the diamond necklace for the next scene,' Shane said.

'Of course,' Griffin said. 'Let's get it while Roxanne's dressing.' They'd already lost enough time with his late arrival.

'Sure,' said Shane. 'The producer wants us to take a security guard along.'

#

'Nice place,' said Nick, checking out the Avoca house.

95

The security guard said nothing. His eyes, like searchlights, swept back and forth looking for danger—probably hoping something would happen to break the monotony of the day. A security guard's job must be a bit like a pilot's, Griffin thought—hours of tedium, punctuated by moments of sheer terror.

'The safe's in the bedroom,' the director said. 'This way.'

He led them up the stairs and along the hall, but before he'd even entered the room, he knew something was wrong. A new framed poster leaned against the wall by the door, as if someone was preparing to hang it. For Hitchcock's *To Catch a Thief*.

'Oh, no! No! No!' Griffin plunged through the doorway to find the safe door wide open and the contents gone. He fell to his knees and patted each of the metal walls to be sure.

'It can't be!' Griffin turned to the guard. 'The necklace has been stolen.'

'What?' said Shane.

'Stand back!' The security guard squatted down to examine the safe and the area around it. 'When did you last see the necklace in there?'

'This morning!' Griffin said. He'd slept in the living room but got dressed in here. 'That's to say I didn't check inside but the safe door was still closed then. Someone must have broken into the house after I left today,' he said. And they'd brought the *To Catch a Thief* poster with them. To play mind games with him. He didn't mention that.

But how did the burglar open the safe when only Griffin knew the combination?

'It could have been someone with safe cracking skills?' the guard said.

'No, wait.' Griffin had noticed a small piece of exposed plaster on the wall opposite. 'That paint chip wasn't there before.' He examined the chip, then turned back to look at the safe from there. 'I think something was here—a small camera,

96

maybe. From this angle, you'd get a pretty good view of the combination I pressed to open it.'

'So you're saying someone planned to steal the necklace?' Shane said. 'They put a concealed camera here to learn the combination, and then took it?'

Griffin nodded.

'Diabolical,' said Nick.

'Do you mind if I take a few photos for my report to the studio?' the guard asked.

'Knock yourself out. And here's a card with the number of some police detectives who were in the area last night chasing a burglar. You might want to talk to them.'

The guard waited at the house for police to arrive and dust for fingerprints while Nick drove Shane and Griffin back to the set.

'What do we do about the necklace?' Nick asked. It was a key part of the next scene.

'We could borrow one from a local jeweller?' Shane suggested. 'Offer them a credit on the film or pay rental for the piece?'

'Yeah, good idea,' said Griffin. 'Do it.'

Griffin was grateful Shane had a cool head to think things through when his own mind felt like the inside of a firework—all it needed was a spark to blow into a million pieces.

Not long later, Shane returned with good news and bad.

'The good news is we've got a substitute necklace—top quality—being couriered over. Should be here in fifteen minutes.'

'Excellent!' Griffin said. 'And the bad?'

Shane bit his lip. 'The set insurance won't cover the theft of that necklace from the Avoca house. Because it wasn't officially on set at the time. It was in a private home.'

'What? What do you mean?'

'Sorry, mate,' he said. 'Because the jewels weren't with the props department, the insurers won't pay up.'

'But, but I'm the film director. If it's in my care, surely it's still part of the set?' Griffin said.

Shane shrugged helplessly.

If the insurers wouldn't pay, would Griffin have to? Somewhere around US$50,000 for the necklace, he believed. That would absorb most of his writer's fee for the project.

'But what about the guy who stole it?' Griffin said. 'Shouldn't we find him and make him give it back? Or pay up? Not me, I was just trying to help.'

He could hardly focus on the morning's shot list. His mind kept boomeranging back to one question. *Who took the necklace?* It had to be someone who knew he had it, and had the opportunity to steal it?

He looked around at the people on set. *It had to be one of them.*

But who could have got their hands on a micro surveillance camera? All the camera guys, presumably. And their buddies. And, while Griffin was busy directing, anyone could have nicked his keys and headed to the house to empty the safe?

Perhaps Nick? An unpaid props assistant? No-one would notice his absence. And he was mates with the camera guys.

Or Roxanne could be behind this? As revenge for his treatment of her.

Or Phoebe? Who'd just this moment emerged from Roxanne's trailer and was ducking booms and dodging cameras and leads to get back to him. After all, what did he know about the girl? She arrived on set one day, as if she'd fallen out of the clear blue sky. Like an angel. *But what if she's a golden-haired devil instead?*

'Okay,' said Phoebe. 'The courier's brought the replacement necklace, which is gorgeous. But there's a problem. The jewels are sapphires, not emeralds. And Roxanne's party dress is green to match the emeralds.'

'Oh, for God's sake!' Griffin said. 'Get the costume people to find her a blue dress to match.'

'But, err…?' Phoebe said.

'What?'

'Roxanne doesn't like blue.'

'You're kidding me!' Griffin clutched his head and paced. Did he have to sort out every teeny detail on this film? 'Aaaargh!' He kicked the nearest gum tree, a scribblybark—named for the distinctive scrawls on the trunk.

Looking up, he found a dozen pairs of eyes on him. *Haven't they seen a director losing it before?* 'What are you all looking at?'

Two people strode through the set towards him. Not crew members. Detectives Feeley and Sedgmore.

'I'm so glad to see you two,' Griffin moved to greet them. 'Any news?'

'As a matter of fact, we do have some news,' said Sedgmore.

'Fantastic. You've caught the criminal?'

'Not yet, but we are about to do so,' Sedgmore replied, then nodded to Feeley, who stepped forward, and addressed Griffin.

'On behalf of Interpol, we're arresting you, Griffin Chance, for the murder of Sophia Renly, Chloe Barclay, and Alicia Marlowe,' she said, as Sedgmore cuffed his hands behind his back.

Pierre hoisted the camera on his shoulder to record the moment. A dozen cast and crew got out their phones to video it.

'Murder! What?' Griffin shrieked. 'Is this a joke? I didn't murder anyone. I don't even recognise those names.'

Roxanne, dazzling in a blue cocktail dress, bounded out of her trailer, pushing to the front. 'Oh, my goodness!' She covered her mouth in surprise.

'This script of yours reads like a confession to a trio of murders, disguised as suicides, that have been baffling police for some time,' said Sedgmore. 'The first victim supposedly leapt off a cliff after a disappointment at work. But investigations revealed the presence of a second person on the cliff that night. You, Mr. Chance.'

99

'It wasn't me,' Griffin said. 'I don't even know the woman.'

'The second victim supposedly took poison to end her life, but evidence suggests an unseen hand slipped it into her drink. Yours.'

'This is insane!'

'And the third woman didn't throw herself under a train. Someone pushed her. Three guesses who.'

'I want a lawyer. It wasn't me!'

Feeley moved real close to Griffin's face. 'Then how did you detail the end of these three women's lives so accurately?'

'The script provides all the answers we've been looking for to questions about these three deaths,' Sedgmore said. 'You'll get fifty years for this, Chance.'

'Oh my god!' Roxanne shouted. 'You made me play someone you murdered?'

'I didn't do this!' Griffin shouted. 'Please, someone help me.'

The police began leading the director away. Pierre ran along beside them, filming it all. And the crew followed, stumbling into each other as they kept their phone video on the director.

'You got away with the murders.' Sedgmore turned towards the cameras. 'But like most arrogant killers, that wasn't enough. You needed the world to see how clever you were. So you wrote this script.'

'Not so clever now, though, are you, Mr. Chance?' Feeley said gleefully.

'It wasn't me! I'm telling you. I don't even know those women. And I didn't even write that script—Juliette McKenzie did!'

'Say what?'

Everyone stopped dead. Pierre moved the camera closer to capture the director's heavy breathing.

'The words are not mine,' Griffin said. 'Someone named Juliette McKenzie sent me that script. I changed a few things and put my name on it. Juliette McKenzie is the one you need

100

to arrest.'

'Wait a minute,' Phoebe came forward. 'Didn't you say you'd proved it was your script because you registered your drafts with the Guild before her?'

Griffin sighed. 'A friend at the Guild altered the date of origin of the script as a favour to me.'

'So you're not a murderer?' Feeley seemed so disappointed.

'No. I'm not!'

'But you *are* a plagiarist,' said Sedgmore.

'Technically, yes, I suppose I am,' he said.' But there are precedents for directors improving on a writer's script and sharing the credit.'

'Really?' Sedgmore said, then turned to Pierre. 'You get all that?'

The cameraman gave a thumbs up.

'And it's on Twitter now,' said Nick. 'I reckon you're about to go viral, mate.'

So Nick was the Twitter traitor? *I knew it!*

'Where is this Juliette McKenzie, the alleged author of the script?' Feeley asked.

'I'm afraid she died in a road accident.'

'That's rather convenient, isn't it?' Sedgmore raised his eyebrows. 'We can pin all the murders on a dead woman, who can't defend herself.'

'Not so fast,' an extra called from the back of the group— the woman who'd played dead in the ice box came forward. 'Rumours of my death have been greatly exaggerated.'

'What the—?' Griffin said. *I knew she looked familiar.*

'I'm Juliette.'

'But I saw you on the road,' Griffin said.

'And you didn't come to my aid,' Juliette said. 'No surprises there. But I'm sorry to tell you it wasn't actually me.'

'He fell for the old dummy-under-the-car trick,' Nick said, looking around at Shane.

Griffin glared at him. 'You were in on this?'

101

'Juliette and I went to film school together,' Nick said.

'So you're Juliette McKenzie?' Griffin said.

'No, I'm Juliette Longhurst.'

Phoebe stepped forward. 'And I'm McKenzie Tyndall. Juliette and I wrote the script together.'

Griffin gave her his most hateful glare yet. 'What did you do with my old assistant? You didn't harm her, I hope?'

'She's having the time of her life at a film conference in Hollywood,' McKenzie said.

Roxanne's famous laugh peppered the air. 'Oh, this is too good.'

'You can arrest these two now,' Griffin said to the two police officers. Feeley unlocked the handcuffs and Griffin shook his arms free. 'They're your murderers, not me.'

'You're free to go, Mr. Chance,' Feeley said. 'Here,' Feeley handed the cuffs to Nick. 'You'll be wanting these back in props, where they belong.'

'And the fake police ID too?' Sedgmore said. They passed the IDs to Shane.

They waited as Griffin gawped at them, figuring it all out.

'You're not real cops?' he said to Feeley and Sedgmore.

'Correct.'

'And there was no crime? That was all just made up to—'

'Make you admit the truth,' McKenzie finished his sentence.

The red-head bowed. 'Joanna Feeley, actor, at your service.'

'And Ralph Sedgmore,' said her partner. 'I reckon that was a pretty good audition for a cop role. Are any coming up, do you know?'

'Not for you two,' Griffin said. 'If I have anything to do with it, you'll never work again. Nor will any of you.' His accusing finger swept across the entire cast. 'You're all finished.'

'And there's the power flex.' McKenzie shook her head. 'Just like Harvey and his pals, you used your position of power to get something you didn't deserve. Our script.'

102

'We couldn't do much about it before,' Juliette said. 'You were right, no-one would take our word over yours. But now…they'll have to.' She smiled at Pierre, who was still filming.

Griffin scowled but couldn't deny it. Then a spark of hope flared. 'You stole the necklace!' he said. 'You had the access, and the means. You're thieves and everyone will know that! You won't be laughing when real police come knocking on your door.'

'Sorry, don't know anything about a necklace.' McKenzie turned to Juliette. 'Do you?'

'No.' Juliette turned to Nick. 'Do you?'

'No.' Nick turned to Griffin. 'Do you?'

Griffin saw their smug smiles and wanted to scream. But the camera was still rolling so he kept it together. He'd have to pay for the lost jewels, he knew. After that, they'd probably hand the necklace in, for a reward. Or sell it on—*like the crooks they are!*

'By the way,' Roxanne said, 'you might want to check your phone. I believe the producer's just sent you a message. He saw the Tweet and terminated your services immediately. And I'm to let the cast know another director will replace Mr. Chase the day after tomorrow. So we have a day off!'

Griffin's jaw clenched and his fists twitched with his desire to hit someone. But all he could do was send death stares at them all before picking up his things to leave the set, the film—the business.

'Oh, and Griffin,' McKenzie called after him, 'just because you're paranoid, doesn't mean people aren't out to get you.'[1]

---

1 Quote from *Catch-22* by Joseph Heller

The Suitcase

Jason Fischer

'Why would you do it, Jim?'

'I didn't do anything.' As he lied, he remembered her seamed nylons beneath the tight skirt.

'If that is the case, then why did she take him?'

'We don't know she did. We don't know that at all.' The young doctor stared at his wife, feeling a deep shame.

'What will we do?'

'For now—wait, as the text said.'

She wiped mascara-stained tears from her eyes. 'Let me see it again.' Scrolling through, she read, 'We have your boy. I assure you he is safe. Wait for further instruction and tell no one.' Not hiding the disgust in her voice, 'If you did nothing then why does that, woman,' the word was over pronounced in a venomous way, 'have your number?'

'Look, I understand you are upset, I am to, but we must keep our cool.' Jim wished his nerves matched his voice, his stomach flipped, and his heart raced as he thought about what they could be doing to his only child.

'We need to call the police, or better yet, the British embassy.'

'I don't think that would be wise.'

'Presently, I don't really care what you think.'

Wanting to lash back and ask how she could think of leaving Carson alone in the hotel room, he thought better of it. 'Please, hear me out. I couldn't sleep. You know how I am after a long flight, so I went down to the bar for a nightcap. The woman you saw sitting next to me w…' He was interrupted by his ring tone. They both stared at the unknown number.

He clicked the answer button. His wife, in a flash, was at his side whispering, 'Speaker.'

The voice matched the voice of the woman he met downstairs. 'Dr. Muir, have you told anyone?'

'Where is my boy?'

'This is not how this is going to work. I will forgive you that outburst. Now, answer my question. Have you spoken to anyone?'

Feeling more paranoid than he had ever in his life, he glanced out the window of the high-rise hotel looking to see if it was his imagination or if he was actually being watched. Feeling foolish from his lapse of memory, they had specifically chosen a room with a view of the lake. All he saw were white caps over the expanse of water. He wanted to scream and let out all that was building up inside this last desperate hour, ignoring the heat in his face and pain in his chest he said in a disgusted tone, 'I have not contacted the authorities if that is what you are asking.'

'I knew you wouldn't. You are just not the type.'

There was a pause, thinking of a movie he'd once seen where a marshal used the background noise to track someone down. Jim closed his eyes, concentrating on some audio clue. All he heard was the forced heat blowing through the vent and a muffled conversation from the room next door.

'This can be very easy if you simply follow my instructions. Do you have something to write on, doctor?'

'Yes.' He grabbed the notepad with the ultra-modern hotel logo from the tiny desk. 'As soon as we are done, go to room 2042. The door will not be locked, so all you need to do is push it open. Inside, you will find a suitcase. It is black with rollers and a retractable handle. Take that suitcase and go to the bar two blocks north of you called the Jilted Olive. Once you are there, text me at this number and I will call you with further instructions.'

'What's in the bag?'

'Now, now, doctor, I thought we understood one another. You do as I ask and this will all be over very soon.'

Margret, to his right, opened her mouth to reply. In a flash, the surgeon clamped her mouth shut with his free hand. Shaking his head with wide eyes, he slowly mouthed, 'Quiet.' Returning to his tormentor, 'Fine, I don't need to know, frankly I don't give a damn what is in it as long as my boy is returned. What assurance do I have that he will be?'

'You only have two options here; cooperate and trust you will get your son back or don't and never see him again. Please, for your own sake, just do as you are told.'

There was silence, then the call disappeared from the screen. Feeling like someone just placed a weight around his neck, he stared at his wife. Neither made any effort to hide their terror. Jet-lagged and with his nerves pushed well beyond endurance, Jim put the phone back into his pocket.

'Can't you trace the call some way?'

'I tried searching the number on Google when I first got the text. It didn't come up under anyone.'

'Isn't there some other way to track where it came from?'

He quietly whispered, 'If there is, I am not aware of it.'

'Then we must call the police.'

The truth was, he desperately wanted to, but felt somewhere deep inside where intuition was stored that it would lead to a very bad result. 'We can't.'

The look of recognition came over her face. 'What's happening, Jim?'

He stepped forwarded and cradled her under his chin, his beard stubble made a scratching noise against her tussled hair. 'I don't know, but I need to go.'

She jerked her head back violently, 'But where, you can't possibly be thinking about handling this alone!'

'We have no other choice. I am going to go get the suitcase.

Maybe it will give me some clue. If it doesn't, I will have to take it to that pub.'

'I'm going with you then.'

'No.' He put both hands on her shoulders, stopping her interruption. 'Honey, please, you need to stay here. I will call you as soon as I can.'

'Please, James, what happened downstairs? Why is this woman doing this to us?'

'Penny, I swear to you I don't know any more than you do. That woman sat next to me and started talking. Honestly, I did my best to ignore her.' He could still smell her perfume, the guilt rushed over him again. 'We don't have time for this.' He pushed away and headed out the door, ignoring her protest, knowing if he hesitated for even an instant, he would give in to the fear and not be able to leave.

The door to room 2042 opened with a light push. It was a near duplicate to his own, two bedrooms, two baths, a room with a couch and a minibar. Next to the table in front of the couch was a black suitcase. It was hard plastic and had a sturdy lock fastened to it. Jim considered trying to pry it open but quickly he dismissed the idea. Not only didn't he have an adequate tool to open it but he also didn't want to have to explain his actions to his tormentor if it came to that. He rifled through every drawer in the room and searched closets, looking for some clue. The only sign that anyone had ever entered the room was the abandoned suitcase. Knowing it wouldn't do any good, there were no distinguishing qualities, he took a picture of the suitcase from every possible angle. It gave him some sense of control. Thinking of his son, he took his unasked for burden and left.

Exiting the elevator, he entered the lobby. Bright lights, and what seemed like hundreds of voices, assaulted his already overworked senses. Cringing from the anxiety and feeling like everyone in the large room was staring at him, he made his way along the marble floor, the wheels of the case bouncing along beside him. The room smelled of some sort of smoked beef; the scent permeating from the attached restaurant that housed the bar that started his tortuous chore. At this time of night, he expected much less activity, yet everywhere he looked, there seemed to be groups of young couples laughing, talking, and barely disguising their lust. Jim looked with a pathetic interest at each face, somehow hoping against hope that he would see the woman from the bar and could immediately end whatever kind of charade he was swept in. Wishing he'd thought to take his overcoat, he walked through the revolving door. His claustrophobic feeling was soon replaced by the need for warmth as a bitter cold attacked his thin suit coat. Pulling the lapel of his jacket as high as he could, he walked down Huron toward the bar. Even in his distressed state his thoughts viciously lashed out at his wife for insisting the trip be taken during the winter, her instance on visiting Chicago during the holiday season was not driven by her desire to see the great city with all of its decorations but to accommodate the convention she was to attend next week. Even at the late hour, the street was alive with cabs, buses, and cars moving at a pace that seemed much too fast. Off in the distance, he could hear the metallic roar of the L rush over the elevated tracks. The unfamiliar surroundings reminded him somewhat of London, yet everything seemed to move much quicker and had an odd sense that danger was hidden in the many strange faces and dark buildings.

The suitcase with its tiny wheels could not navigate the uneven sidewalk. Every few steps, it threatened to topple over. Finally, Jim collapsed the handle and attempted to carry the plastic shell. It took a great effort; the plastic encased suitcase was extremely heavy and whatever it contained had space to move. As he rattled the handle, he could feel something with indefinite mass shift slightly from side to side. For no real reason, he assumed it was money. Like many foreign to the city, he thought of mobster payouts and dirty politicians. As he

108

saw the sign of the bar for the first time, he considered the situation and the wisdom of his actions—maybe Margaret was right. There were authorities who were trained to handle such things, even if the thought petrified him. Once again, the panic came over him in a wave; he looked up and down the street, for what he didn't really know. If someone was cunning enough to abduct an eight-year-old, they would certainly be smart enough to observe him without being detected.

With freezing fingers, he unlocked his phone, no calls or new messages. Crossing the street to the bar, he shut down the questions of doubt that were pulling at his sanity. As soon as he entered through the glass door, he saw her in her short skirt at the corner of the bar. With a full head of steam, he weaved through the half-drunk patrons. He saw her pick up her phone and a second later felt the vibration in his pocket. Struggling to hear through the heavy bass laden music in the background, he pressed the phone hard enough against his ear for it to cause the skin to tingle. He thought he heard, 'Stop!'

'What!' His exclamation turned the head of a very peculiar looking Russian man who stood next to a barely-clothed girl who was half his age.

'You were followed. Don't come any closer. Shake your head if you understand.'

Jim glanced into the enormous mirror at the back of the bar. Behind the many bottles of exotic liquor, he saw the reflection of two men at the entrance. The shorter of the two had a very noticeable bulge under his left arm. Jim complied and nodded his head.

'You need to get out of here now!'

'What about the suitcase?'

'Take it. Go now!'

Jim pushed through the crowd and was jostled by zoned-out revelers. Looking frantically for an exit, he located a hallway off to the right. Fighting to pull the suitcase along with him, he ducked into the darkness. There were bathrooms flanking him.

A few steps beyond was an unmarked door. Thankfully, the handle turned easily. Hoping it wasn't a dead end, he slammed the wafer-thin door shut behind him. His heart was pounding. Even this far removed from the bar, the music was extremely loud. He looked around the room, increasingly frantic. There was a collection of boxes labeled "fragile", and a small desk off to his right. A few feet above it was a window letting in moonlight. In one sweeping motion, he jumped onto the desk. The window was locked. Wondering if he could even make it through, using two hands, he swung the suitcase. The plastic shell was too heavy to gain any velocity. It bounced off the glass, shooting a vibration down his arm. Quickly, he looked back at the door. It was still closed. Feeling like any minute someone was going to come rushing in, he grabbed a lamp from the desk and went at the glass once more. With a crash, his target gave way. Not noticing the hundreds of shards sticking out of the frame, he tossed the suitcase through and then hoisted himself out into the alley. He landed awkwardly on his side, out of breath from the effort and bleeding from his fingers. He grabbed the suitcase, pulling it along behind him through the alley, heading toward the light and street noise, wondering what to do next.

#

Investigation, hour one.

The phone rang. On the second ring, a very lively voice for two in the morning said, 'What's up, Chuck?'

'I'm assuming I didn't wake you?'

'Wake me? It's still evening.'

'Rex, it's a little after two in the morning.'

'Geez! I'm re-plumbing the bath. Guess I got caught up in it!'

'What are you doing to my bath? No, no, forget that. We can talk about that some other time.' There was a loud, deep

110

sigh. 'I need you to get into the city right now.'

Rex sensed the irritation in his voice. They had agreed no more remodeling work would be done in his ex-partner's second house without discussing it. Knowing he could be up against it, he jumped into the conversation. 'What's going on?'

'I just got a call from an English colleague of mine. His daughter is in town on vacation and from what he said, his grandson was abducted, and his son-in-law is missing.'

'Where?'

'The Loop near Water Tower.'

'Did they call the precinct?'

'No, they were against it.'

'Ransom demand?'

'Oddly, no. Do you want me to send a car for you or are you okay to drive?'

Rex knew the question was a veiled attempt to check in on his sobriety. It was understandable, considering it was only two weeks since he'd stopped. Asking such personal questions came with the territory, considering he lived rent free. 'Charles, I promise I am good. Going to throw on a clean shirt and will call you on the drive. How long ago was he taken?'

'Don't have that pinpointed. Sounds like less than two hours, though.'

'That's good. Talk in a few.'

#

Jim didn't dare go back to the hotel. He ran for what felt like a mile away from the bar, his lungs burned from the effort, the exhaustion temporarily made him forget the harsh weather this close to the lake. Looking back, he was confident he'd lost them. To him, there was no doubt they were police. With damp hands—the cuts were not severe but abundant enough to make slick smears on his aching palms—he grabbed his phone and contemplated calling back the girl who'd introduced herself as

111

Claire. There were two missed calls from his father-in-law, and a few from an unknown local number. Just as he was about to hit send, the phone rang.

'Did you make it?'

'Yes, I got away. Who were they?'

'Where are you, doctor?'

'I can't see a street sign. I can see the lake and a sculpture that looks like a silver bean in the distance. I did as you asked. Please give me back my son!'

'Not until we can trade.'

'Tell me where!'

'Are you sure you're clear?'

'They're nowhere in sight.'

'Take the L train north, get off on the Belmont exit. Go down the stairs heading north, and you will find a club called The Anvil. I will meet you there.'

Just as before, the line went dead. Jim panicked as he rifled through his pockets, remembering he'd left his wallet back at the hotel. Fortunately, he found a few loose bills in his front pants pocket. Pulling the suitcase behind him, he headed back to State Street. Feeling exposed on the street, he ducked down an alley, using the rattling sound of the L as a compass. The alley was littered with boxes and other less recognizable debris. Steam poured out from the grated sewer cover. Jim stood directly above it. The smell was horrendous, but it was worth it for the heat. Taking in deep breaths that were just beginning to trigger a gag reflex, he heard a loud clattering just off to his right. His heart felt like it was going to jump out of his chest as the shadows enveloped him.

#

Investigation, hour and a half.

Rex sat in the sedan, watching the entrance to the Tower Hotel. Through Charles, he'd arranged to meet Margret. Not

112

knowing what he was walking into, he watched her walk east toward the lake. Knowing there might be surveillance from one of the many high-rise windows, he had arranged for her to walk four blocks over. When he was confident she had no tail, he dodged traffic and caught up to her. If this was an abduction and the ransom hasn't come yet, he knew he was taking a calculated risk, but with no army of investigators, he had to take it. He pulled up to her. She was pretty but looked haggard through the open window. 'I work with Charles on behalf of your father.'

She almost leaped into the car. 'You are Rex Haining?'

She sounded like a character from masterpiece theater with her perfect English diction. He pulled from the curb, checking his mirrors. 'Yes.'

'It's horrible. It's all so horrible.'

'Yes, it is. Please excuse me but we haven't much time. I need exact times or as close as exact as possible. When did they take your boy?'

'It had to be very close to midnight.'

'Are you sure?'

'Yes, I looked at the clock when I left the room, and it was a quarter to. Oh, why did I go? Why didn't I just stay there with him? If I had, none of this would have happened!'

'You don't know that. Hold on.' He spun the car around in a swift U-turn and headed in the opposite direction, looking back. No cars followed. 'You just got in today?' Gripping the handle of the door with very wide eyes, she replied, 'Yes, we touched down just before noon.'

'Did you go straight to the hotel?'

'Yes.'

'Did you take a cab there?'

'No, we rented a car.'

'Where did you eat dinner?'

'Please, Mr. Haining, what does this have to do with that woman taking my boy?'

113

'I need to know who you've seen since you arrived here so I can determine when and why they chose your husband to move their product. There is a chance this all went down in the bar with that woman, but I need to know everything. Where did you eat?'

'What product are you talking about? Is this about drugs?'

'It sounds like they need your husband to be an involuntary mule. Frankly, it's preferable than a ransom demand. Now please, no more questions. Where did you eat?'

'We ordered room service. Jim and Carson wanted to go out, but I was so tired. I always suffer from the worst jet-lag.'

'When you went down to the bar, did you get a good look at the woman?'

'Yes.'

'What did she look like?'

'A whore!'

'Can you please be more specific?'

'She had red dyed hair; it was just past her shoulders. She was quite robust in her,' she made a rounded motion near her chest, 'Well, you know. She was sitting so I can only guess but would say she was around my height, so maybe five four?'

'Her face?'

'All I saw was way too much makeup.' The jealously flashed over her, flushing her cheeks. 'You can find my son, can't you?'

He didn't answer. He just pulled into the parking garage. Glancing at her Dior jacket and Burberry purse, he worked to trigger her memory. 'What exactly was she wearing? Was it expensive?'

She wrinkled her face as if she'd just got a whiff of an offensive odor. 'A tight pencil skirt that looks like she bought it off the rack and an almost see-through plunging blouse. It may have been a Lauren, but I couldn't say for sure. Her stilettos were Manolos. They were the only item of quality she wore.'

Knowing he had her concentrating, he pounced, 'At the

114

neckline, was she wearing any jewelry?'

'Yes, a garish gold chain with an elephant that sat right into her cleavage, the tips of her hair curled down around her neck accentuating her oval face.'

'What color were her eyes?'

'Blue, she had on what had to be false eyelashes and her lips were so large they were almost cartoonish. I do believe they were natural. I couldn't see any liner.' Margret's face looked like it just came out of a trance she now looked surprised at her own response.

'Thank you. I know this is difficult.' Seeing the car, he came there to meet he spun into the empty parking place. 'I am going to have you go back to my colleague's office with a girl who works for him. Her name is Penelope. Stay with her and I will contact you if I have more questions.'

'But why can't I stay with you?'

'I have work to do. Stay here a minute.'

Rex got out of the car and leaned against the driver's side of Penelope's Subaru. With her hair in a bun and wearing a very unflattering pajama top, the second-year lawyer who did most of his friend's research and assisted on his pro bona work looked like a high-school student. With her bright smile, she rolled down the window. 'Oh, I feel like we are in a spy movie!'

'Are you sure you are alright with this? I don't know how long she will be with you and heads up; she is a few seconds away from hysterics.'

'With what she is going through, I don't blame her. Don't worry about me. I'm always jealous when you and Charles talk about your cases from the old days. Finally, I can be a part of one.'

'I just wanted to make sure you didn't feel like you had to go along.' He gave her his wide grin. The one she once playfully said made him look like Harrison Ford. 'You are a huge help.' He dug into his pocket and pulled out Margret's

115

phone. He grabbed his own and waved it over using the app that he got from a seedy connection. With a flash, the technology paid off. Margret's home screen opened, bypassing the code. Not looking up, he said, 'Is she staring at me?'

'Yup, and she's really pretty.'

'Didn't notice.' He pulled up recent calls, found her husband's number and dialed. It went directly to voicemail, twice. Quickly he went through texts and emails, nothing of any significant interest caught his attention, 'Here's her phone. Give it back to her when you're at the office. When she asks, say it must have slipped from her purse and you grabbed it. Under no circumstances are you to let her use it away from you. We need to know everything she says and who she talks to.'

'Why lie, didn't she hand it to you?'

'No, I swiped it from her purse.' He equally liked and hated the look of admiration she gave him when hearing of his improper act. 'If a call or text comes through, I don't care if she is in the bathroom, be there and call me immediately.'

'This really is like working on a case then?' Her smile instantly disappeared. 'Their boy's life depends on us.'

With more of a smirk than a smile, he said, 'Don't think like that. Just do as I ask, and all will be fine.' He escorted Margret to the car and called Charles to get a report, hoping he was able to pull a favor and get the security footage from outside the hotel. Knowing they should call in help for a job like this, he got into his car and headed back to the hotel.

#

The L swayed, feeling like it might tip over as it took the curve. Inside the empty compartment, the light was dim and there was the faint smell of body odor and burned plastic. Thankful for the warmth, Jim was pondering the same question his wife was asking clear across town—how could all of this be happening? He was a collection of bruises and scratches. He'd barely made it out of the alley. Two bums had pinned him, taking his suit coat and the suitcase. Warmth was a necessary concession, and since the men had taken off in different directions, he'd had little choice but to go after the suitcase.

He looked at his bruised knuckles and felt ashamed, but he'd been forced to give the would-be thief a pummeling. He'd had to get the suitcase back.

With his jacket gone, so was his phone, leaving a visit to the bar he was headed to the only way to communicate with the vixen who was putting his family through hell. Wishing it was only that easy to blame her for his momentary lapse in judgement, Jim leaned his head against the glass and tried to let go of some of the tension. He wanted to blame his near indiscretion on tiredness or drink, but the truth was when she'd showed an interest in him at the bar, an unyielding passion he thought was a remnant of the past had been unleashed. That passion, intermingled with a sense of invincibility, made him forget he was a dedicated surgeon whose every moment was spent caring for others. From the moment he saw her earlier in the day and she slipped him a note to meet her in the bar, he could think of nothing else. That hour in the bar talking with such a beautiful girl had brought back his youth and sense of wonder. Knowing now how wrong he was, he stared at his haggard reflection in the dirty plexiglass and wondering what he would actually have done if Margret hadn't come down. He wished he could simply rewind time—just this once—go back a few hours and undo all that had been done.

But all that was useless, wishful thinking now as he looked down at the city traffic. At this time of night, there was a somber quality to the streets—thoroughfares that would be buzzing in a few hours. He gripped the suitcase tightly in both hands as he heard the mechanical voice come through the speaker, announcing the Belmont stop. He moved to the sliding door, waiting to make the short walk to the bar where he'd face his penance.

The door opened with a squeak and the wind once again chilled him. All he knew was it was no longer time for pity or self-reflection. His path was clear. He had to rescue his son.

#

Investigation, hour two.

Rex entered the hotel and saw a small man standing behind the concierge desk. As he headed that way, he took stock of every face he saw committing the images to memory. When he got to the desk, he flashed the badge quickly, mindful to cover the name at the bottom. He had been out of the force for well over two years now on partial pension at the grace of his former captain. The badge belonged to Charles; he retired as soon as he finished law school and was happy to lend his expired credentials to his ex-partner who paid back his debt by taking on free-lance work. Rex never resented the indentured nature of their relationship. The few jobs he took on were not favors but essential to his only friend. The tradeoff of free room and board for detective work also kept them together, if only in brief periods, which suited both men's egos quite well. 'I'm Detective Sergeant Hill. Can we talk?'

'What's this about?' The man stood on his toes and squinted at the badge.

'It would be better for us both if we talked in private.' He hooked his thumb at two drunk men holding hands on a couch a few feet away. 'I don't think you want your guests overhearing.'

The little man grabbed a walkie-talkie off his desk and said, 'Joshua, this is Robert, I have to...take care of something. Please come to the front desk immediately.'

There was static and then, 'Just rounding the back elevator, be there in a minute.'

'Detective, if you would please come round we can step into my office.'

118

Rex went around the long faux marble counter and entered the room labeled "manager". The two men sat in chairs that looked out of place in the modern décor of the room. 'I saw two cameras in the lobby. Do you have one in the lounge?'

'Yes, but I cannot give you access to them.'

The over-officious man who paraded as manager had just made the easy route impossible, but Rex easily hid his disappointment—after years of long, hard training, he could hold extensive conversations and have no changes in his facial expression other than blinking. 'I am aware. I wanted to know, as it may be necessary to secure them. What time did you begin your shift?'

'I started at eleven.'

'You have been at the front desk the entire time?'

'Yes, sir. Do you mind telling me what this is about?'

'We will get there. From your post you could see inside the bar. Did you see a redhead wearing a short skirt and a low-cut blouse?' The flash came across the concierge's eyes and forehead. As quick as it came, it disappeared. He fidgeted, first shifting in his seat, then drawing his arms nearer to himself.

'No, I can't say I did.'

'Robert, if you knew she was a working girl and looked the other way for a couple of bucks, it's alright. It happens all the time up and down the mile. In fact, I have been known to patronize such bars now and again.' He gave a knowing smirk, selling the fabricated point. 'I promise you, that is not why I am here. Look, can I trust you?'

'Of course you can.'

Rex looked around the empty room, pretending they were conspirators. 'Her pimp got himself into a jam and we are trying to track him down. I'm following a tip to his girl, thinking she might be able to give a legitimate address. I just need to ask her a couple of questions, then—scout's honor—' he raised his two fingers and touched his heart, 'I will be out of here and hopefully back home by the time the sun comes up.

You know how it is—I'm on a double shift and freaking exhausted man.'

'She left about an hour ago.'

'What's her name?'

'Sarah. I don't know her last name.'

'When she left, was she with a…customer?'

'No.'

'Did she go upstairs?'

'No, she left the hotel alone.'

'Has she ever used one of the rooms here?'

'You promise this is off the record?'

Rex almost felt sorry for the guy. If he was actually CPD, he would have him. This wasn't a television show where things like off-the-record conversations held any merit. 'Of course.'

'Yes, she gets to use empty rooms for a small fee.'

'Cash or barter?' He flashed the knowing smile once again.

'I don't usually like to speak for others, but if it is important, I guess I should. I've never taken part in it, but there's a rumor some of the other guys here have been known to barter.'

'Are any of them working tonight?'

'If I tell you, will they be safe too?'

'All I need here is to talk to her. If she gives me a lead, I am outta here.'

'Steve Carver. He's a floater and has had such relations.'

'What's a floater?'

'Oh sorry, he doesn't have a defined role. He floats by need as a bartender, concierge, or bell hop. Between you and me, he spends most of his time sleeping and dodging work. I honestly don't know why they keep him on.'

Because he is giving a kickback to whatever other scams he is running to the manger, Rex immediately thought. 'Could you radio him and get him down here?'

Like an obedient puppy, he grabbed the transmitter. 'Steve, you there?'

As they listened to the static, Rex asked, 'I know you don't have to, but is there any way you could either tell me who rented room 2042 or possibly look the other way when I look at your computer? I can get the official paperwork if it is absolutely necessary, but it's a ton of paperwork and will waste an hour.'

'No problem.' He spun in his chair and clicked away at the keyboard. 'The room shows as vacant.'

Rex knew everything just got more complex as Steve's voice came over the transmitter, 'What's up, Robert?' As Robert was asking the unknown man to come to the office, Rex's phone buzzed.

He walked back to the lobby, flashing the concierge, his index finger motioning back in a second. 'What you got Charles?'

'I am in your old office at the precinct going over the surveillance of the hotel.'

'I don't even want to know what favor you traded for that. And?'

'I did a quick scan on fast forward of all entrances. Not surprisingly, at this hour didn't see a single child.'

'When you go over it again, you don't have to look before eleven forty-five. The boy was with someone until about midnight.'

'Sounds like you're making some progress.'

'So far, nothing worthy of remark. Is there a parking garage attached to this place?'

'No, only front entrance, back service door, and alley entrance. These use a valet to the garage down the street for their guests. From what I saw, the only camera that had any movement was the front entrance.'

'Nothing in the service entrance—not even trash bags?'

'No, and you know you don't have to tell me to look for anything he might have been hidden in. I haven't been out of the game that long.'

'I wasn't trying to be rude buddy. I just like to think out

loud sometimes. I have to get back to something. Talk to you later.'

He walked back to the office. The man who'd taken over for Robert gave a look as if he was about to say something. Rex gave him the side eye, daring the comment, and walked back into the room.

As he sat down, he texted Penny. *Any news?*

Her father-in-law called not much was said other than him trying to calm her down and trust the 'competent' man he hired. English people talk weird.

Keep trying the doctor every couple of minutes, please.

Have been and will keep it up.

Thanks. Got to go.

Putting his phone away, Rex looked to his interviewee, 'Any response?'

'No, and there might not be. He isn't exactly an exemplary employee.'

Rex nodded. 'Do me a favour and try him again.'

The walkie-talkie clicked. 'Hey Steve, where you at?'

Robert's voice echoed from somewhere just behind them.

'Is there a service corridor through that door?' Rex pointed at the door directly behind the little man.

'Well, yes, but I don't see why he wouldn't come through the front?'

Rex didn't bother saying out loud, because he is listening to our conversation. With the swiftness of an athlete, he moved from his chair and was around the desk in a flash. Very carefully he twisted the knob and violently pulled the door open. A few feet to his right was a large man with a goatee holding a walkie-talkie. He quickly turned and bolted down the hall. Rex was at him full speed in a half step. The hallway was narrow and dark. The man disappeared as he made a right turn. Rex was seconds behind. He braced himself as he turned, half expecting an attack, but there wasn't one. Straight ahead, there was an exit door closing. Rex burst through the door, the frigid

122

air assaulting his lungs. In a few strong strides, he grabbed the man by the collar and threw him up against the brick wall, pinning him.

'Where you going in such a hurry!' The man reeked of sweat and marijuana.

'I didn't do nothing.'

'Then why did you run?'

'Because I know how these things go. I heard your talk. Now you're going to take me in because I was helping that whore and that foreign dude she was with.'

'Slow down and answer my questions.' Rex was leaning close, using his left arm to pin Steve against the brick. 'What foreign guy are you talking about?'

'There was some weird guy. I don't know his name.'

'What did he ask you to do?'

'I ain't saying shit. Haul me in and get me a lawyer.'

Rex saw two ways to handle this. Thinking of the small child who was hanging in the balance, he quickly said, 'We can do that, but you realize you are going to be brought up on kidnapping charges, right?'

A surprised look came to his face. 'I had nothing to do with that!' The fear in those words made the former detective tense. He pushed harder on Steve and kept his hand in a fist just beneath the neck, gripping the collar of his uniform. 'What do you know then? If you lie, the next time I touch you, you won't recover from it.'

'Look, I promise you I didn't know what he was up to.'

With a firm push, Jim spat, 'You have two seconds to explain all this or I'll grant you your wish and you can explain kidnapping charges to the DA. If what you're telling me is true, I might be able to help talk this down.'

'Look man, this foreign dude offered me and Sarah ten grand. She was supposed to keep the doctor in the bar, and I was supposed to get him into the doctor's room.'

'What's the guy's name?'

'I swear I don't know.'

'How did he contact you?'

'He approached me in the bar last night.'

'What did he look like.'

'About six foot, thinning black hair and a real crazy mustache. He had an accent that might have been French, but I really ain't good at that.'

'What did he want in the room?'

'Think he told me?'

'What happened next?'

'The whole thing got jacked up. I got him into the room, and I stood by the door. Half a minute later, he comes out of the bedroom talking really fast to himself in a weird-ass language. Then all of a sudden, he grabbed me, and bum-rushed me out of there. Now I know you are going to have a hard time believing this, but I felt a kinda responsibility cause I let him in. So, I hid out in the room next door. After a few minutes, he comes walking out with something under a blanket. Now at first, I think he took something—what, I don't know. Who knows what foreigners think? Maybe a crazy expensive rug or something like that. But then just, before they get on the elevator, I'm pretty sure I saw a hand hanging out from beneath the blanket.'

Filled with rage, Rex grabbed the man with both hands, lifting him into the building.

'Wait, wait, wait, man—don't hit me! There wasn't nothin' I could do. For all I know, it was his kid and him and his wife were fighting or who knows what.'

'Where's the boy now?'

'I don't know. He took him away.'

Rex could see in his eyes he was telling the truth. 'What's in the suitcase he had Dr. Muir get?'

'I don't know man, I swear.'

'You sure about that?'

'Really, man. No clue.'

'Have you had any contact with him since then?'

'Yeah, he called me from the lobby phone and told me to call Sarah and keep the doctor away for at least a half hour longer.'

'Explain that part?'

'The original plan was to have her get him out for fifteen minutes to a bar down the street. Then all of a sudden, he said he needed more time, so I called her. She wasn't too happy when I told her to make something up.'

'What was the plan to exchange the suitcase for your payment?'

'He was going to call Sarah at the top of the hour and give her instructions.'

'So you had no way of contacting him? You were simply waiting on him?'

'Yeah.'

'And you were going to trust a hooker to give you your share?'

'Fuck yeah. She has a good thing going here because of me. It's not like the score was enough to get her out of this racket. Then I would have been following the doctor.'

'Yeah, and you didn't know what heat the exchange was going to bring, so you figured you would just hang back here.' Rex didn't give him a chance to respond to the insult. 'Call her right now!'

Reluctantly, he pulled the phone from his pocket, making a big production out of it. The call rang and went to voicemail twice.

'Text her to call you.' He watched his fingers move with amazing dexterity. Rex considered calling Charles and demanding they call in the police. A trace on the phone was their best bet to intercept any kind of exchange. He checked the thought, believing he knew how the suggestion would be received. 'You got your keys on you?'

'Yeah, why?'

125

'We're going upstairs to check out that room.'

#

Dr. Muir approached the nightclub. He was shaking and felt as if he was going to pass out from a mixture of adrenaline and fear. Glancing at the sign at the door, it was less than a half hour to last call. There was a tall man that looked like a linebacker flirting with two young women with multicolored hair who were smoking in the corner. They were all underdressed in youthful defiance of the harsh wind whipping down the street. The smoke hovered above them, partially obscuring the neon logo of The Anvil. The doctor was expecting the man who had to be the bouncer to stop him, but apparently, he was either off duty or more interested in his prey than noticing a bloody man with a suitcase. The bar was playing some kind of German speed metal at a surprisingly low volume. The room was less than half full, and the patrons who were left were all glossy-eyed with their heads bobbing collectively to the music. Jim saw the prostitute in a corner booth. Bright-eyed, she leered at him. Hair that only an hour ago had been perfectly arranged hung over her face as if she'd just came in from a windstorm. She got up, pulling her skirt down, flashing whoever was looking in that direction a glimpse of her garters. She gestured with her head to the back hallway. Jim pulled his albatross along, no longer seeing or hearing anything else in the room but the woman who was going to lead him to his son. She entered the ladies room. Seconds later, he caught up and pushed open the door that had the word "women" scratched out and replaced in childish lettering with BITCHES. There was a girl who looked like she could still be in high school standing at the mirror. The second she saw Jim, she frantically pulled down her sleeve and turned her back. Through the dirty mirror, he saw her shoving something into her purse. In short quick strides, looking at the floor, she left

126

the room.

Jim glanced at the other stalls. They were all empty. The room smelled almost as bad as the steam in the alley. The thought made his knuckles ache. As if it were a discus, he tossed the bag in Sarah's direction in a sweeping motion; it landed far short of her well-heeled feet, spinning as it slid. 'Where is my boy?'

'I don't know.' Hyperventilating, the words came out all choppy. Her face scrunched up, crinkling her makeup.

'I don't know what type of game you're playing here, but you're going to give me answers.'

Jim moved swiftly towards her. Before he had his hands on her, he saw her lacquered nails move in a flash and then felt a wetness on the right half of his face. At first, he thought she'd spat on him, then the stinging came to his nostrils and eye. It was pepper spray. Somewhere deep in his memory, he recalled a rotation in the E.R. when he smelled the exact same odor when treating a man the police brought in. With his right hand, he swiped at his eyelid, desperately trying to stop the burning. With his left, he made contact with the tops of her exposed breasts and shoved her with all his strength and pent-up rage. She exploded into the stall and stumbled onto the toilet.

Squinting through tear-stained eyes, he kept his focus, his fear now guiding his limbs as he grabbed her around her throat. Knowing exactly where to press and how long it would take before she blacked out, he hissed, 'Where's my son?'

He released his grip slightly, letting just enough air in for a response.

She was flailing, her legs kicking the graffiti-covered walls of the stall and her fingers grasping the surgeon's hands.

'Please let go, please!'

Knowing any more pressure would knock her out, he shook her. 'Answer my question!'

'I was paid to get you out of the hotel. I don't know why he took your child or where.'

127

Her spit was warm on his freezing hands. Involuntarily, he released his grip as his mind tried to process what she'd said. The words came out of his mouth. He hadn't known they were there until he heard them. 'Who would do that, and why?'

'I have no idea. He was handsome, with a large mustache, and he spoke with a thick accent.' She gripped Jim's wrists with all of her strength. 'Please loosen up. I can't breathe.'

Ignoring the request. 'How do I find him?'

'I don't know. He calls me from a different number every time. They're all from the hotel.'

'Do you understand he has my son? I need to find him!'

'There's nothing I can do about that!'

'What's in the suitcase? Is it drugs you're bringing back to him?'

'I have no idea. All I know is that he told me what to say to you.'

With his face burning and his right eye nearly swelling shut, he increased his grip. 'Cut the bullshit. Why did you lure me up here?'

'I swear I don't know the plan. He told me to get you out of the hotel, that's it.'

'How are you supposed to get the suitcase back to him?'

'I have a number I'm supposed to call.'

He released his left hand and fished through her purse. Handing it to her, he practically hissed, 'Then do it.'

Tears were smearing her mascara in streams that ran over her highly blushed cheeks. She pulled up the notes on her phone and hit send. Through the speaker the recorded voice said, 'You have reached the Chicago Transit Authority, our office hours are—'

Jim shook her and said, 'Call again!'

The same voice repeated the message. All apologetic, she looked up at him. 'I don't know what this is. I know the number is right. I read it back twice when he gave it to me.'

Jim lifted his hand and cocked it back into a fist. In the

corner of his good eye, he saw his own bloody knuckle. An instant before he moved to punch her, he saw a well-remembered image of his hand holding a scalpel before surgery. Thinking of all those he saved and what he was close to doing stopped him in his tracks. Seconds away from losing his humanity, he let her go. She fell off the toilet and pulled herself into a ball in the corner between the porcelain and the wall of the stall. 'Do you see what you've done? He took my child.' His voice cracked on the last few words, making it sound like a pathetic whine.

'I swear I'm sorry. If I knew he was demented, I never would have done it. I thought this was just going to be a simple exchange and nobody would get hurt.'

'Demented? What do you mean?'

'Doesn't he have to be? What kind of person goes through all this unless they're crazy?'

Jim hadn't considered the possibility he wasn't dealing with a thief or a drug dealer, someone who could be reasoned with by the lure of money. He never once considered he might be dealing with a psycho whose motives evaded logic.

He stared at the suitcase with his good eye. For the first time, he thought about the weight inside in correlation to the size of his child. His stomach turned and his heart nearly stopped. 'It can't be…it just can't be.' The words were spoken to slow his frantic thoughts. He grabbed the stiletto heel from the mosaic floor and crawled to the suitcase. He began prying the small lock with the pointed tip of the shoe. As he worked, he imagined the smell of decaying flesh. Not making any progress, he mindlessly pulled the hooker's purse to him by the strap. Digging through assorted makeup, he found a Swiss Army knife. At the very end, it had a small, serrated blade. Forgetting about the lock, he began sawing frantically at the plastic loop it was secured to.

#

Investigation, hour two and a half.

Steve was getting jittery, his muscles quickly spasming, Rex noticed the movement in the corner of his eye. He had given the room a quick once over, to investigate it the way he wanted to would take an hour. '.When you came in you said the mystery man went right into the doctor's bedroom, right?'

'Yeah, right through there.' He pointed with a hand that was laden with cheap jewelry clashing with the tattoos that went to his knuckles.

Rex went to the wall safe inside the main bedroom. From behind him he heard, 'I don't know the combo, man.'

'It's alright I can get it open.'

'How you going to do that?'

'Like this.' He pressed the keys, and the door clicked open.

'The fuck—you some kinda super cop or something?'

'Yeah, something like that.' He smirked as he shoved the handwritten note into his pocket, thinking for a doctor it wasn't too bright leaving the combination sitting out in the open. Inside he found cash, passports, a manilla envelope with a stack of papers nearly a quarter inch thick, and an expensive-looking necklace. He grabbed the folder and sat at the workstation. There was a laptop sitting on the desktop. He picked it up to lay out the papers and noticed it was still warm. Something familiar went off deep inside his mind. Quickly, he stood up and grabbed Steve by the arm.

'What are you doing, man?'

'I got to make a call and need privacy.' He pushed him toward the balcony.

'It's freezing out there. You crazy?'

Rex grabbed a towel that was hanging over the couch. 'This will keep you warm.' He shut and locked the glass door.

Pulling out his phone, he took a few steps into the room. 'Penny, I don't have a lot of time. Can you ask Mrs. Muir if she used her computer before she left?'

'Sure, one second.' After a murmur in the background,

130

'No.'

'Did her husband?'

'No.'

In the background, he heard near shouting, 'Have you found him?' Ignoring her, Rex said, 'Ask her if she's sure.'

He didn't have to wait for Penny to repeat the question he heard. 'No, neither of us used it since before dinner.'

'Keep trying her husband.'

'I will. I have literally called every two minutes.'

'Good job, don't stop. Got to go.'

He looked over his shoulder. Steve was staring daggers at him with the towel over his shoulders. Rex dialed Charles. Without salutation he heard, 'Rex, please tell me you are making more progress than I am.'

'Some. Not enough. Hey, what did you say the father-in-law did for a living?'

'I didn't, but the short answer is he heads a pharmaceutical research firm. They work on experimental drugs.'

'And Margret works for him?'

'Yes, I am not entirely sure in what capacity, but she does. What are you thinking?'

'That we might be following the wrong assumption here. I need some more time to think this over.'

'Hunch or facts?'

'A little of both. Did you find anything?'

'Going out the door, there was one suitcase large enough to hold a small child. I don't think that's it though. It was held in one hand by a petite woman.'

'How big was the suitcase the doctor took out?'

The question they both knew the answer to was met with silence.

#

The doctor had the suitcase open. His knees ached from

131

kneeling and his fingers were bleeding. He couldn't stop himself from sobbing.

Sarah got up and put her shoes on, the heels clacking on the tile floor. She grabbed her purse, and Jim's attention.

'You're not leaving!'

'Look, I'm very sorry, but like I told you, I don't know anything else.' She tried to look around him and see what was in the suitcase.

'You are the only link. I have to find out what happened to my son.'

'What's in there?' She pointed with a long-painted nail behind him.

He stood, lifting the handle, 'Nothing!' There were some old clothes and small bags of what appeared to be sand.

She stood still for a few seconds. Almost to herself, she said, 'Why would someone want you to smuggle that stuff out of the hotel?'

'I don't know.'

'Well, there has to be something in there.' She walked past him and started to inspect the contents. 'That fucker still has to pay me. What the hell is he going to pay for this junk?'

The lights in the room flashed on and off, signaling last call. Jim gripped the knife in his right hand and grabbed Sarah's hair in his other. He pulled her to him and put the knife beneath her bra on the left side. 'With two pounds of pressure, the blade will go right through your ribcage and enter your right ventricle. There will be a very sharp pain followed by gushing blood, and in less than a minute, the best surgeon in the world will not be able to save you. Nod if you understand.'

Her head quickly went up and down, the motion causing her almost unsupported breasts to jiggle.

'How did you get here?'

'I drove.'

'Well, finally something is going right. We're going to bend down, slowly, and you're going to refill that suitcase. Then we

132

are going to walk out of here like a couple of lovebirds with my arm around you. If you make any move to ask for help, remember,' he gently dug the knife into her skin, drawing blood, 'with just a slight twitch you will no longer be upright.'

She silently did as she was told. With everything secure, she pulled the suitcase behind her. Jim was having a hard time keeping his hand from shaking as they walked through the almost empty space. Twice, the bartender looked for more than a second. Jim didn't meet his stare. Once they were out the door, he asked, 'Where's your car?'

'The Lexus over there.'

He pulled her along, wondering how someone like her had a car like that. She didn't fight, but she kept herself stiff, trying to create even a tiny separation between them. When they got to the driver's side, she grabbed the handle. The electronic lock sprung open.

'You've made it this far. I would advise you against doing anything foolish now.'

She obeyed and inelegantly climbed over the center console and slid into the seat, allowing him to get in after her.

'Get out your phone and unlock it.'

She handed it over. He dialed his wife's number.

#

Investigation, hour three.

Rex had let Steve in from the cold and brought him to the bathroom. He ran the fan. With the faint buzzing noise in the background, Penny patched him into the call after she briefed him with the details. Jim immediately asked, 'Do you know where my son is?'

His desperate voice was hard to hear. 'Dr. Muir, the quick answer is no. We haven't much time. Please, just answer my questions. You are sure there was nothing of any value in the suitcase?'

'Yes, I went through it twice.'

'Sarah, where were you to meet the man to give him the suitcase?'

'He didn't tell me. I was to call him once I had it and he was going to give me instructions.'

'No instruction on what to tell the doctor?'

'No.'

Jim's voice came over the speaker. 'But why go through all of that for that garbage?'

Rex was quiet. It was all coming, in a near whisper, 'What is the password to your computer?'

'Why does that matter?'

'Because I need to check something.'

Mrs. Muir spoke. '*Puppy Love*—capital *PUP*, lower-case *py*, love with an extra *e*.'

Rex tried it twice. It wouldn't take. 'Are you sure?'

'Yes, I just changed it before we left.'

Rex's cadence picked up. 'Was anything missing in the room?'

'No, I mean I don't think so. Honestly, I never thought to check.'

There was a long silence. Rex leaned back. He bent his arms with his fists pressed tight together, knuckle to knuckle, almost touching his chest. Like it had so many times before, he was completing the mental puzzle that had been evading him since taking the call from Charles.

Penny said, 'Rex, you still there?'

No response, nothing short of a gunshot would pull him out of the trance before he'd completed his thought.

'Rex?'

Steepling his fingers, he breathed out. 'Yes, I'm here. Sit tight. I have to check something out.'

He went to the bathroom and looked at Steve, who was sitting on the edge of the tub. 'Get Robert on that thing.' He pointed to the walkie-talkie on his belt.

134

Steve stood and straightened his wrinkled clothes. 'Hey, man—I'm getting tired of playing your bullshit games. Are you even a cop? You sure don't act like one!'

Rex swiftly entered the room, and with a quick jab, he doubled the man over. He pulled the walkie-talkie out of his belt and said, 'I guess I don't.' Turning the knob at the top of the transmitter, he contacted Robert and got the information that would end the search.

#

Rex was battling his greatest weakness other than drink. His feet and hands were slick with sweat as he gripped the railing and carefully stepped onto the balcony of room 2844. His fear of heights had been with him for as long as he could remember. Doing his best to not look at the street so far below him, he clung with all his strength to the railing, thinking of the young boy who needed him to be strong. His vertigo was making him dizzy. The distance between the two balconies was less than two feet, and his weight was balanced perfectly in the center. Cantilevering over twenty-eight stories up, he could vividly imagine his body flaying in the wind, bouncing off lower balconies on its way down. Only once, back when he was on the force, had he seen a jumper. Right now, in graphic detail, he saw the flattened face grinning at him, looking like when the cartoon coyote got hit in the face by a frying pan. The thought of moving in either direction brought his pulse into his palms, and he felt warm bile crawl up the back of his throat.

In a single, graceless gesture, he let go with his right hand and pulled himself onto the other balcony. He hugged the railing with both arms and for the first time felt the bitter cold and wind accentuated by the high altitude. He carefully lifted his leg over the painted steel, and when he felt the concrete beneath his shoe, the fear subsided.

Back to his old self, his senses came alive. He knelt and

pressed himself against the glass.

Through a one-inch gap in the heavy drapery, he saw a well-built man sitting at the desk over a black laptop. The familiar tingling that only came when a hunch paid off ran over him. He dug into his pocket and got his pick out. In less than a minute, he had the latch open. Knowing the second he slid the glass door open, even a touch, the cold wind would alert the man of his presence. Rex sized up the distance. It was at least eight feet. If the man had a gun and kept his nerve, it would all be over in a less than two seconds. He pulled out his phone and texted Charles. *I'm in position.*

What's the play?

I don't have a clear line. Knock on the door. As soon as he opens, I'll charge him.

Now?

Wait.

Rex stood up and down repeatedly, bending the knees, trying to get his circulation going. He gripped the door handle with his hand.

Now.

The wind was too loud for Rex to hear the knock, but he saw the man's head jerk in the direction of the door. He opened the top drawer of the tiny desk and pulled out what looked like a taser. Standing, he closed the laptop and carefully walked to the door. He leaned his head against the door, peering through the glass peephole. Rex felt the adrenaline coursing through his veins. Seconds felt like minutes as he focused on the man's hand. Twice it went up, but neither time did it make it to the doorknob. Finally, it slowly unlocked the top lock.

Rex pulled the door open and the heavy drape, sucked out by the wind, wrapped across his legs. The foreign man spun at the noise, and Rex, fighting to free himself of his fabric captor, kept moving forward. With a crash, Charles kicked the door in, sending the man tumbling toward Rex. He was thrown across the couch but held onto the taser. Charles was on him as Rex called, 'Right hand!' But it was too late. There was a flash of blue electricity and he stabbed towards Charles's abundant mid-section. Just as it made contact, Rex was over the coffee table and with a chopping motion knocked the taser from his hand. Rolling forward, Rex continued his tackle and pinned the man against the floor. He quickly spun his head around and looked at Charles. He was gripping his midsection and rolling his tongue inside his mouth, looking like an animal chewing straw. 'He get ya?'

'Yeah, not too bad though. Besides my fillings, all is fine.'

#

Investigation, hour six.

The group was assembled back in Charles' office. Carson sat between his parents. He could barely keep his eyes open, even after the shot the EMT's had administered. Rex sat at the edge of the desk with Charles behind him, wearing a suit jacket over a pajama top. The booming voice of the father-in-law came through the speaker. 'Could someone please explain all of this?'

Rex, in his even tone, addressed the room. 'Mr. Holland, the name of the man who kidnapped your grandson is Albert Hutchinson.'

'I'm aware. The police called me and told me that. But why would my former employee kidnap my grandson, and why didn't he ask for a ransom?'

'Because he intended to let him go after he got information from your daughter's computer. He was attempting to gain access to a formula he said you stole from him.'

'That is complete bull. It's true he started the project, but he couldn't complete it, so we took over. When we suspected he was trying to sell the formula, I let him go.'

'Be that as it may, his goal was to create a diversion so no one would notice he'd swiped the computer.'

137

Jim asked, 'So the suitcase and everything else was just a diversion?'

'Yes, and a brilliant one if you think about it.'

'But what if we'd called the police?'

'My guess is he was counting on it.'

'But why?'

'Their first move would have been to wait for a ransom demand and in the meantime conduct a thorough search of the room, which obviously would have meant no one could touch anything, further concealing the decoy computer.'

'But what if they'd opened the suitcase?'

'They would have sent the sand to the lab for analysis buying time. Remember, his only goal was to create a diversion that could not lead back to him. Sending you out on a wild goose chase was the perfect way to do that. If I hadn't happened to touch the computer and notice it was warm, he very well may have gotten away with it.'

'But if it was only a decoy, how was it on?'

'Best guess he was going to copy files to it and when he couldn't get past the password quickly, he took it back to his room. From there, he would get the information he'd come there for, remove the disguise only one person had seen, and leave the hotel. Eventually, the drug he'd used on Carson would wear off, and by then he would be well on his way.'

Penny interjected, 'But how did you figure all this out?'

'When it became evident the goal was not to exchange the suitcase or fulfill a ransom demand, it came down to motive, which is difficult to determine when you have no idea who you are dealing with—so I simply followed the clues.'

Penny mouthed 'wow' and shook her head. 'How did you know what room he would be in?'

'I called the hotel manager and asked who was signed into Wi-Fi in an unrented room. Like I said, once it was obvious there was a wild goose chase, the plan become easier to detect.'

The next half hour was spent with enthusiastic thank-yous

and unending irrelevant questions. Rex, with his natural impatience, sat back and let Charles take over. The politics of dealing with people was always what he was best at. For the first time in almost half a month, the craving for a drink felt uncontrollable, as it always did after the adrenaline of a case had worn off. Knowing he needed a distraction to prevent the inevitable backslide, he thought about what he was going to work on in Charles's house on the golf course. Learning how to remodel was a poor substitute for drinking, but so far, it had been effective. Hoping he would be back in his sanctuary before the traffic picked up, Rex got up and carefully left the room. The only one who glanced in his direction was Penny. With her warm smile, she gave him a playful finger wave.

#

Jim had just put Carson to bed, and Margret, with the aid of one of her pills, slept quietly next to their son. It was nearly eight am, although exhausted, he was still too nervous to sleep. Sitting on an uncomfortable couch, he watched the lake in the distance. The water rolled slowly with the wind, a few sporadic white caps the only interruption to its trance-inducing motion. Jim thought of what he'd done this evening and wondered if it was possible to bottle up what he'd uncovered. The pacifist who'd devoted his life to saving others couldn't fool himself into believing he wouldn't have killed the prostitute if she'd resisted, and that the instinct wasn't driven by fear or protectiveness, but by sheer hatred and a need for retribution. Although relieved to have his son back, Jim couldn't share in the joy to the extent the others did, knowing he'd uncovered an evil lurking in his heart. Despite this, for the first time in hours, he finally managed to relax, and soon drifted off to sleep.

139

Rebecca Redux

Elizabeth Elwood

Last night, the dream came again. I had returned to Manderley. I drifted weightlessly along the twisted drive that wound its way east, then west, meandering between black stunted oaks and pale white beeches, their branches entwined into a vault above my head. The trees closed in on me, their spindly boughs creeping out to clutch me as I passed. What was this strange black and white world? Was it our *Manderley, or was it the Manderley of fiction? I felt confused. I was desperate to be free of these tortured, menacing woods, yet afraid of what lay at the end.*

Then, suddenly, with the supernatural powers bestowed on those who inhabit the land of dreams, I was transported out of the forest. Now, I was in the bedroom, standing beside the carved bedstead with its quilted coverlet; staring at the familiar curtain hangings, the flowers on the mantelpiece, the brushes and combs on the dressing table, and the candlesticks and the clock on the wall. Even the satin dressing gown was there, delicately laid out beside the monogrammed nightdress case. And she was there, too, ghost pale, her dark eyes black shadows against her pallid face.

'Why don't you go?' she said. 'I'm the real Mrs. De Winter, not you.'

Her figure looked hazy and insubstantial, for a grey mist was swirling in from the mullioned window that overlooked the sea. I moved towards her but the fog settled around me, its grey threads clouding my vision, and the terrible words echoed eerily in the dim light of the room.

'It's you that's the shadow and the ghost. It's you that's forgotten and not wanted. Why don't you leave Manderley to me? Why don't you go? There's not much for you to live for, is there? Why don't you jump? Go on. Don't be afraid.'

And then...and then...

#

And then she woke up. It was a horrible dream, and I was sad to hear my wife recount it. Poor Beryl, the pretty little film fan, so enamoured of Laurence Olivier and so enraptured by Hitchcock's cinematic rendition of Daphne du Maurier's *Rebecca*. How hard it was for her to follow in my first wife's footsteps, yet the moment she realized that my wife's name had been Rebecca, she began to see herself in the Joan Fontaine role. Beryl did, in fact, look a lot like Fontaine, a fortuitous resemblance as it happened, if hardly appropriate in terms of film casting. After all, Maxim's second wife was supposed to be a plain little thing, and one could hardly call Joan Fontaine plain. Still, plainness is more than a matter of skin and bone structure. Ironically, my first wife had resembled the actress too, but Rebecca had had glamour and intensity, whereas Beryl radiated nothing more than amiability from that delicate countenance. Amazing what different personalities can come from similar features.

Of course, the fine details of appearance are of professional interest to me, being an actor by trade. Sadly, not in the Olivier bracket: I could emulate his matinee-idol performances, but never did I attempt the challenge of Shakespeare. Success in film eluded me too, though I did once have a tiny part in *The Lady Vanishes* and was an extra on *The Thirty-Nine Steps*. The war put a temporary spoke in my career plans, but I emerged intact, and still had enough contacts to get lead roles with reputable repertory companies, which was how I met my first wife.

Rebecca was an actress, too, and we met in Manchester while starring in a production of du Maurier's play of that name. It was my first engagement up north, and I have to say I was not thrilled with the rain-drenched city or the decrepit converted-vaudevillian theatre that was our venue. However, I did not regret taking a break from my home company in Brighton, for Maxim was such a plum role. Rebecca played my shy second wife, cast because of her resemblance to the star who had taken that role in the film, and we made the arrangement permanent after the show closed. She was happy to move south with me and concentrate our efforts there. Rebecca had disliked the draughty old Mancunian theatre too, with its rumbling plumbing and squeaking floorboards, and looked forward to the lively audiences of Brighton. Our subsequent success as a team playing drawing-room comedies or classic whodunits earned us enough to buy a lovely old house in Cornwall that had survived the coastal bombing raids, and, mischievously, we named it Manderley, after the estate in the play that had brought us together.

Life with Rebecca was, well, what can I say, exciting at best, enraging at worst, for her beauty and vitality brought her many admirers and there were multiple occasions when jealousy consumed me. She was extravagant, too, tearing down the blackout curtains and replacing them with lush velour and rich brocades. The heavy walnut furniture was replaced with teak or rosewood, and every pay cheque disappeared into some new, up-market acquisition for the house. Our fights were monumental; our reunions passionate, if not tender. Then, as the years wore on and the parts grew less frequent, the cost of maintaining our country home became more difficult. Manderley began to deteriorate. Damp caused the wood to swell—one had to get up on the window seat and shove from the top to open the bedroom window—pipes rusted and leaked, lath and plaster cracked, and the roof developed an ominous

142

sag in the west wing. It was just a little here, and a little there, but it all added up, and it gradually depleted what finances we had left. Naturally, being short of money did not improve our relationship.

Then, as fate would have it, around this time, I returned for another engagement in Manchester and came across Beryl, a bedraggled waif, valiantly ignoring the downpour that rattled the gutters and bounced off the pavement as she stood by the stage door, hopefully waving her autograph book. She was a sweet child, sadly alone in the world, and offered unconditional adoration, as opposed to the turbulent and erratic passion of my wife. Beryl had seen me play Maxim in that fateful production of *Rebecca* when she had been thirteen years old and, she shyly informed me, had kept the picture of me that had accompanied the review of our production in her scrapbook, alongside her photographs of Olivier in the film. Such devotion was irresistible, and I realized that an opportunity had arisen that could not be ignored. The prospect of a peaceful, prosperous retirement opened up before me.

Unlike Maxim in the film, I did not accidentally kill Rebecca in a fury, provoked by her taunting me about a pregnancy that did not exist. I coldly decided that she had to die. Moreover, I ensured that her life was well insured. I intended to be a wealthy widower who could retire from the stage, rather than suffer the humiliation of being reduced to playing doddery old household retainers.

The problem that faced me was the fact that I would be the first person suspected if anything happened to Rebecca. Her death had to be arranged far away from Brighton and the theatrical colleagues, who knew how volatile our relationship had been. Fortunately, we had treated our country estate as a retreat, and had not socialized with our neighbours or the people from the village, so in Cornwall, there were no witnesses to our quarrels. As a result, I was able to select an amiable couple as acquaintances for our final summer there. I needed to put on a show of marital bliss and harmony that would ensure their support when Rebecca, like her namesake in the film, went sailing one night, never to return. Sure enough, when the time came, their testimony to our happy relationship was sufficient to convince the local constabulary to deal quietly and efficiently with my tragic loss. I was free to quietly court Beryl and resume my life as planned.

Manderley, now maintained by an efficient housekeeper, beckoned. Beryl and I were married in a private ceremony. She was enchanted at the prospect of moving to Cornwall and becoming mistress of my country home. Unlike Maxim, I had talked to her about Rebecca, so she was aware of my first wife's faults and was confident in her own ability to make me happy. She was not worried about a quiet country existence, which was a good thing because we were totally isolated. Most of the landowners were in town for the winter, and the one couple I had befriended had left for a protracted stay in France.

Therefore, Beryl set off for Manderley in a blaze of enthusiasm and anticipation. It was only when she saw the photographs in my scrapbooks and the portrait of Rebecca as Caroline de Winter—I had acquired the picture that had been painted for our stage production—that she became uneasy. After all, she had only seen Rebecca on stage, dulled down as Maxim's shy second wife. There had been no pictures in the program to show how truly glamorous she was. Poor Beryl felt suddenly insecure. I would see her glancing at the portrait, and then frowning at her own appearance in the mirror. I tried to reassure her, but I fear that her discomposure was not helped by Mrs. Davenport, the housekeeper, who was familiar with Rebecca's performances and, I suspect, slipped in many asides as to how spectacular my first wife had been on stage. Beryl became nervous, agitated and clumsy. She became hysterical when she broke an ornament that had belonged to my deceased mother, crying piteously that she knew just how Joan Fontaine had felt when she hid the ornament away, rather than let

144

anyone know that she had broken it. I suppose I should have been more sympathetic, but I sometimes thought she was playing it to the hilt and enjoying living the part that had so fascinated her. But perhaps not. Maybe I was only ascribing my actor's analytical nature to her, whereas in fact, she felt life as it happened, real and immediate. Either way, the accident, when it happened less than a month into our marriage, was sadly predictable.

I was away in Manchester at the time, that fateful, draughty venue having tempted me back with the opportunity to audition for the lead in *Sleuth*. The call came to the theatre just as I was to go on stage and deliver my piece. I felt a chill of apprehension when the old boy who manned the stage door announced that there was an important call for me. When I followed him to his office and picked up the phone, I recognized the speaker right away. That deep baritone voice with the Cornish brogue was unmistakable. It was the detective who had investigated Rebecca's disappearance the previous year. Inspector Mallory sadly informed me that I needed to return right away. There had been a very unusual development. He would explain when I arrived, but the upshot was that my wife was dead. I could hear a distraught Mrs. Davenport in the background, insisting that she had to speak with me, and a moment later, she came on the phone.

'Oh, sir, I feel so responsible,' she cried. 'She was exhausted and in a terrible state. She'd been having dizzy spells, nasty bouts of vertigo, and I thought some fresh air would help. I went to open the window, but she pushed me back and started carrying on about how we all thought she was so helpless. She insisted that she could manage, and before I could stop her, she climbed up and forced that bedroom window open. It shot out so suddenly, and she lost her balance. I tried to catch her, but I was too late.'

Mrs. Davenport's voice dissolved into sobs but the essence of her message was plain. My wife had fallen to her death. It appeared that our beloved Manderley had done for her in the end.

The following week, after the inquest was over and I was able to plan the funeral, I sat with Mallory in my study, a cozy room with a tall window that overlooked what was left of the rose garden. It was the one room I had not allowed Rebecca to alter, and it was as close to the Manderley of fiction as one could get, with its comfortable, solid chairs, great open fireplace and book-lined walls. A decanter of scotch sat on the small occasional table between our chairs, the crystal glasses beside it twinkling in the firelight. Mallory shook his head in sorrow as he reviewed the train of events that had ended so tragically.

'It's beyond belief,' he said sadly. 'To have Rebecca return like that, literally from the dead, only to die again the moment she arrived home.'

I nodded.

'Mrs. Davenport was astounded when Rebecca appeared at the house that night. She said she could hardly believe her eyes.'

'Your poor housekeeper was beside herself when we arrived,' said Mallory. 'She couldn't enlighten us at all. She'd done her best to look after your wife, giving her something to eat, and getting her ready for bed, but she hadn't been able get any sense out of her. No explanation as to why she'd gone away. No apology for all the distress she'd caused.' He frowned disapprovingly. 'Your wife must have realized that the abandoned sailboat would have made everyone assume that she'd died in an accident, yet I gather she acted as if she'd only been away on holiday.'

'But she wasn't behaving rationally. Mrs. Davenport made that clear. Rebecca was flushed and agitated. She obviously wasn't well.'

'Yes, we heard that, too, from the porter at the station and the driver who brought her to the house. They thought she might have been drunk, because she was weaving all over the place. But it's still a very frustrating mystery. Do you have any idea why she would have staged her own death?'

'I suppose, if she'd simply walked out, she knew that I'd have followed her—I would have, too—and in hindsight, I think she was probably desperate to get away. I myself was having difficulty coping, and I guess I never realized how the house had drained her, how tired she was of our financial struggles, how she longed to escape.'

'But to let you think she'd drowned. That was cruel.'

I sighed.

'Rebecca could be cruel, but I would have forgiven her.'

Mallory drained the last dregs of his glass and set it down with a frown.

'Then you're a better man than I am, Gunga Din. I'd have had difficulty accepting her back after pulling a stunt like that. The post-war years have been difficult for a lot of people. We've all had to put up with rationing. Many came back to find they'd lost their jobs. Your wife should have realized how lucky she was, just to have a home and a husband who genuinely loved her.'

'Well, Rebecca was always erratic and unpredictable. That was part of her charm.'

Mallory made a harrumphing noise. 'I suppose. Well, she's certainly been punished for her sins, now, whatever they were. She should never have climbed up to open that window if she'd been having bouts of vertigo. It makes you wonder what would have brought those on, doesn't it? Whatever she was up to this last year obviously took its toll on her. Still, I'm sorry, old chap. This has been hard for you. You've really been put through the mill, losing her twice.'

He waved a refusal to my offer of a refill and got to his feet. 'I must get home,' he said. 'Take care, old fellow. I'm truly sorry for your loss.'

I saw him out and watched as his old Daimler disappeared

into the night. Then I turned back into the hall, reflecting how surprised he would have been if he had known the truth of the matter. For it had not been Rebecca who had fallen to her death; it had been poor Beryl, who thought her life was emulating *Rebecca*, but it was a completely different plot. I wasn't playing Olivier as Maxim; I was merely playing a husband who used the resemblance between two women to enrich himself. Come to think of it, that would make another good film plot for Hitchcock. Perhaps he'll make it one day. Look-alikes, dizzy spells, a fall from a great height. He could call it *Vertigo*. That would make a very good title.

Well, it was sad that young Beryl had to die, but that secret second marriage was necessary because I simply had to have a body. The life insurance company had refused to pay out on a presumed death by drowning, and I really did not want to wait seven years for Rebecca to be declared dead. Neither did she want to spend that time, drabbed down with grey hair and pale makeup, continuing in the role of Mrs. Davenport. No, Rebecca needed to be dead in order for us to make the claim, and so Beryl had to die in her place. We had contemplated having Rebecca come back to life as Beryl and having them simply trade places, but she rather balked at assuming that persona, too, so we shall simply have to meet again elsewhere, preferably abroad, and enjoy another torrid romance before settling down once more as a married couple.

Of course, we cannot remain at Manderley, but neither of us mind leaving the old house now. Somehow, it has lost its appeal, for I can't help seeing Beryl's anxious little face peering at me from every corner. I gather Rebecca, having shed her ghastly Davenport guise once I dropped her at the station, returned and reduced the poor girl to such a state that it's a miracle that she didn't simply jump out that window. However, if the truth be told, she had to be given a shove, and I'm rather glad I only had to plan her demise, and did not have to carry it out.

148

As for Rebecca, who engineered her end, the nightmares recur more and more frequently. I wonder if they'll ever go away.

#

Last night, the dream came again. I had returned to Manderley. I drifted weightlessly along the twisted drive that wound its way east, then west, meandering between black stunted oaks and pale white beeches, their branches entwined into a vault above my head. The trees closed in on me, their spindly boughs creeping out to clutch me as I passed. What was this strange black and white world? Was it our *Manderley, or was it the Manderley of fiction? I felt confused. I was desperate to be free of these tortured, menacing woods, yet afraid of what lay at the end.*

Then, suddenly, with the supernatural powers bestowed on those who inhabit the land of dreams, I was transported out of the forest. Now, I was in the bedroom, standing beside the carved bedstead with its quilted coverlet; staring at the familiar curtain hangings, the flowers on the mantelpiece, the brushes and combs on the dressing table, and the candlesticks and the clock on the wall. Even the satin dressing gown was there, delicately laid out beside the monogrammed nightdress case. And Beryl was there, too, ghost pale, her dark eyes black shadows against her pallid face. My appearance had stunned her. Trembling, she had climbed onto the window seat. It was as if she was desperate for air. Her figure looked hazy and insubstantial, for a grey mist was swirling in from the mullioned window that overlooked the sea.

'Why don't you go?' she said valiantly. 'You left him, and now he's married to me. I'm his real wife, not you.'

I could see she was afraid, for all her pretended boldness. I moved towards her but the fog settled around me, its grey threads clouding my vision, and my terrible words echoed

149

eerily in the dim light of the room.

'It's you that's the shadow and the ghost,' I hissed. 'It's you that's forgotten and not wanted. Why don't you leave Manderley to me? Why don't you go? There's not much for you to live for, is there? Go on. Don't be afraid.'

I knew it would only take a slight push.

'Why don't you jump?' I cried.

And so she did.

Highwayman's Hitch

Cameron Trost

I stepped down from the carriage and dropped my duffle bag at my feet. I was near the end of platform three of Lincoln Station, and fellow commuters eager to get home, or wherever it was they were headed, were already hurrying towards the station house—an elegant edifice of yellow brick and slate roofs built in the Tudor revival style. One of the more modern touches was the coffee shop it accommodated, but I was in need of something stronger.

A woman in a long dress started waving from halfway along the platform and I recognised my cousin even from so far away. I grabbed by duffle bag and walked briskly over to her.

'It's so good to see you again, James, despite the circumstances.' She shook her head.

'It's been too long.'

She looked me up and down. 'It has been,' she agreed, meeting my gaze. 'You look tired.'

'A little, but I'm fine. As for you, well, you're looking fabulous as usual, Willow.'

My father had been a no-nonsense sort, taking after grandpa, but Aunt Penelope had always been the eccentric sibling. I can imagine the look on grandpa's face when he discovered his first granddaughter had been named after a tree.

'Still a terrible liar,' she admonished me, wagging her finger. But she really did look great. She was wearing a moss-coloured dress and brown leather boots, and her dark hair speckled with grey caressed her shoulders. She had a natural beauty about her—"a lass of the land" was the sort of thing grandpa used to say.

'Still so modest,' I replied. 'But how are you?'

Instead of replying, she nodded uncertainly, and after a moment's hesitation, she hugged me.

'Without weddings and funerals, we'd never see much of each other nowadays,' she said, taking a step back but keeping her hands on my shoulders.

'Weddings?' I asked.

She shrugged and smiled wistfully. 'Yeah, just funerals then.'

I looked up, noting the dreary autumn sky that loomed over the station's footbridge, chimney stacks, and crenellated clock tower.

Willow followed my gaze. 'And the weather's set to worsen tomorrow—rain forecast.'

'Fitting,' I found myself saying.

'No doubt.'

'Is everyone else already settled in at Havercroft Manor?'

She giggled the way she always did when I referred to the old family home that way. It was a big country house with two floors and five bedrooms. Not quite a manor, but for someone who'd spent much of his life in a Barking bedsit, it wasn't far off the mark.

'Mum's here, of course, and Ryder got in this morning. Apart from us, it'll mostly be grandpa's few remaining friends tomorrow.'

'Well, it gives us a chance to catch up, I guess. I can't remember the last time I saw your brother.'

'He can't wait to see you, James. You can't imagine how much he misses you. The special memories you lads have with grandpa—' She fell silent. 'It's only natural after all, isn't it?'

'I suppose it is,' I replied. 'He had to teach us how to be men. That's what grandfathers do.'

'They probably have to make up for the mistakes they made

152

with their sons.'

'With my dad?' I asked, even though her meaning clear enough.

She shrugged.

'I can't say you're wrong, but dad didn't turn out all that bad.'

'No, he didn't,' she admitted. 'Our parents pulled through all right.'

'They did,' I said, 'all things considered. But it's hard to know for sure, isn't it? I mean, there's not much to compare with. Our parents are the only ones we've ever know.'

'Do you think grandpa ended up making men out of you and Ryder?' she asked, and the cheeky tone in her voice told me she wanted to lighten the mood. I wanted to answer from my heart, but instead, I played along.

'If you have to ask, the answer is clear,' I said with a wink.

She laughed.

'What's your mother going to do?'

'I don't think she should stay here all alone now that he's gone. The house is too big, and it's not healthy, is it?'

I knew exactly what she meant.

'We'll talk about all that after the funeral,' she said. 'I guess it would be a shame to sell.'

I nodded. 'It would be. On the other hand, does anyone want to live here?'

The look she gave me said it all. 'You're happy in London, aren't you?'

'I don't know that "happy" is the word, but I'm by no means planning on moving out here and becoming a farmer. That and—well, you know.'

'The memories,' she said sullenly. They were as much a part of the house and grounds as the red bricks and pantiles, the ancient oaks and laurel hedgerows—and the lakeside pergola. 'The bittersweet memories.'

I nodded. 'I'm not sure we could find tenants, let alone

buyers.'

'We could turn it into a youth hostel,' she said, and it took me a second to realise she was pulling my leg.

'Or an orphanage while we're at it. I'm glad to see you've finally mastered the fine art of the straight-faced joke,' I congratulated her.

'I've been working on it.' She winked. 'We'll work it all out. Anyway, let's get going.'

We headed for the station car park and I immediately recognised her weary khaki Land Rover.

'The old beast still going strong?'

'Not dead yet.' She paused, and a furrow formed on her brow. 'Oh, poor choice of words.'

'No point tiptoeing around it. He was an old man and he passed away. That's all there is to it. I know that doesn't make it any easier but that's how it is. No one gets out of life alive.'

'No,' she said lowly as she climbed behind the wheel, but she let the vowel linger a tad too long.

There was something on her mind, but I waited until I'd put my bag in the back and got into the passenger seat.

'What is it?' I asked as she turned the key in the ignition and the old beast woke with a shudder.

'He died of natural causes, of course,' she pointed out.

I was lost for words for a moment. 'Right—of course.'

She was staring through the windscreen, making no move to put the Land Rover into gear.

'What exactly are you saying, Willow?'

She turned to me. 'It's just that he had a shock to the system shortly before he died.'

'A shock? Spit it out then. What happened?'

She was frowning.

I stared at her, hoping she'd crack like the star break in the bottom left corner of the windscreen.

Before long, she did.

'Ernie Carter came back to town.'

154

An uneasy silence fell between us. Ernest Carter was an old family friend who'd grown up with our parents. He'd always been "a bit of an odd one" and sometimes he'd found himself in "a spot of bother". From what I'd heard, it was with such terms that his behaviour had been downplayed whenever his name had popped up over a cup of tea or a game of cards. But that was before the tragedy. It was Aunt Penelope who'd first spoken out against him in the wake. Her little sister, Caroline, the youngest of the three Havercroft children, had confessed to no one but her, and Penelope had never forgiven herself for keeping her sister's secret—for not exposing Carter for the monster he really was until it was too late.

'Are you serious?'

'I'd never joke about that,' she replied gravely.

She put the Land Rover into gear and started driving.

'Is he still here?' I asked bitterly.

'You haven't been following the local news, have you?'

'I don't make a habit of it. Why?'

'He was murdered,' she said, and it was as simply as if she were giving the time of day.

'Well, that's good news,' I heard myself saying.

'Yes,' she whispered, then found her voice and added, 'but it's terrible to feel that way, isn't it? Doesn't that make us monsters?'

'No, Willow. It really doesn't. Not one little bit. When did it happen?'

'A rambler came cross his body near Bracken's Wood yesterday evening. Four days after he came back to town. Not even two days after grandfather's death.'

'He killed him,' I told her.

'The shock killed grandfather. There's no doubt about it, is there? That's the conclusion we've come to.'

'No doubt at all. To be frank, his spirit died with Aunt Caro all those years ago, but Ernie's return must have been the deathblow.'

Willow sighed.

'That pathetic excuse for a man ruined our childhood,' I said. 'He stole our innocence.'

She didn't reply. There was no need.

'Do the police have any leads?' I asked, staring at the gloomy clouds.

'They're tight-lipped about it. All we know is that he had a rope around his neck.'

'Hanged?'

'They haven't released the details.'

'He must have had a long list of enemies. I hope whoever did it gets away with it.'

Willow hesitated before nodding.

'We have a right to feel that way, Willow.'

'You're right. He ruined so many lives.'

'Including ours.'

'In a way, we didn't do so poorly, did we? Then again—'

'Go on,' I encouraged her.

'I've been getting—no, forget it. It's nothing.' She fell silent and made a show of concentrating on the road.

'Don't shut me out, Willow,' I said. 'I know you, and you know me.'

She placed a hand on my knee for a second before removing it to change gears.

'You've been getting therapy?' I asked softly.

She was holding back tears now.

'So have I. You're not alone. There's no shame in it. We do what we can to cope with our ghosts.'

She turned to me and offered a wan smile.

'Are you still seeing what's-his-face?'

'Old news, dear cousin. I'm single these days and fine with that particular aspect of my life.'

'Good for you.'

'You seen anyone since Lana?'

I shook my head. She knew the tune. We led different lives

156

in many ways—Willow shared a flat with a couple of friends a stone's throw from the Manor and together they scraped a living selling honey and handiworks at county markets, whereas I lived alone in a bedsit overlooking a bustling street and somehow still hadn't escaped the mind-numbing stability of my job as a photocopier service technician—and yet we bore similar scars. We were wounded in ways we'd probably never fully understand.

Our conversation soon turned to grandfather and our fondest memories of him. We remembered all those tall tales by the fire at Christmas and I relived him trying to teach me to sail and fish. I recalled how patient a man he'd been, and how he'd always hidden the darkness gnawing away at him behind winks, grins, and laughter. The man had been a rocky isle in treacherous marshland, and all of a sudden—just like that—he was gone, as though swallowed into the bowels of the earth.

'We wouldn't have made it without him,' Willow mused.

I questioned whether we'd made it at all and dreaded to think what would have happened without him. We'd lost grandma so long ago I couldn't even remember the sound of her voice, but none of us would ever forget the slightest thing about grandpa.

#

We found Penelope and Ryder in the living room. They were sitting on the timeworn leather sofa, flicking through a photo album. On the wall behind them hung the same three bucolic paintings that had been there for all long as I could remember; the green meadow speckled with daisies, the golden harvest scene with haystacks and scythes, and the hunter emerging from the woods with the hound at his heels and the rifle and pheasant in his hands. Penelope was sipping a gin and tonic and Ryder was nursing a dram of whisky. Mother and son took so clearly after grandpa. They were both tall and slim with

157

hunched shoulders. Penelope's posture in particular reminded me of how he'd stood and moved. But whereas grandpa's face had been rugged and his hands strong and rough—the result of long days spent outdoors all year round—Penelope and Ryder's features were soft, and Penelope moved with a kind of offhand elegance no one else in the family had ever possessed, almost as though she really were the lady of a manor.

'Good to see you again, despite the circumstances.' Aunt Penelope smiled sympathetically.

Ryder raised the bottle of Bruichladdich and I nodded. He poured a glass and passed it to me.

'I told him,' Willow announced, pouring herself a glass of champagne.

'About Ernie?' Ryder asked.

Willow nodded.

'I can't say I'll shed a tear for him,' I said with a shrug.

'Silver lining and all that,' Ryder declared. 'Quite right. Let's save our tears for grandpa.' He raised his glass.

'To the old man's memory,' I replied. 'We'll not see his like again.'

'Farewell, grandpa,' Willow whispered breezily before smiling at her mother and taking a sip of champagne.

'I'd shake his hand if I could,' I said adamantly, knowing my meaning would be clear.

'Will Burnside's.' Ryder narrowed his eyes and fixed me with their icy blue. 'No doubt about it.'

'You think so?' I asked. 'Because of Julie?'

'Because of business. Word is Ernie had run up too many debts with the wrong people and never tried too hard to make good on them.'

'People like Will?' I asked.

Ryder nodded.

'I still don't know why he came back to town in the first place,' Penelope said, closing the photo album.

'He had no shame,' I found myself saying.

158

'After all these years,' Penelope said, shaking her head.

'He probably figured enough water had flown under the bridge,' Ryder muttered.

'If so, he was wrong,' Willow said. 'Some waters stay forever stagnant.'

'I heard the police took Will in for questioning but didn't hold him,' Ryder said.

'They haven't come to see us.' Penelope tutted. 'It's almost offensive when you think about it.'

Ryder stared into his whisky. 'You think so, mum?'

'What do you mean?' I asked. 'What happened is—' I paused, trying to find the right words, '—well, what happened is common knowledge.'

Ryder closed his eyes and stayed silent. When he opened them, he said, 'Ernie wasn't a young man, but he must have been as tough as ever. He was found in the woods with a rope around his neck.'

'And?' Willow asked.

'It's unlikely the police consider either of you capable of it.'

Penelope opened her mouth to retort but closed it promptly and strode the length of the room.

'You could have done it though,' Willow pointed out. 'Or you,' she added, turning to me.

'But we weren't here,' Ryder replied immediately.

'They don't know that, do they?' Willow said.

Ryder shrugged. 'I have no idea what they know, but I have an alibi for yesterday.'

'You do?' Penelope asked.

'I'll only divulge if absolutely necessary,' he replied with a cheeky wink.

'Will we meet her one day?' Willow asked.

'We'll see, dear sister. When and if the time is right. It's not a decision to take lightly.' He gave her an apologetic look. 'Nothing personal.'

'I know, Ryder,' she said quietly. 'We all know how it is.

159

Play it by ear.'

'I wasn't here either,' I added.

'You have an alibi?' Penelope asked.

'I arrived at Lincoln Station less than an hour ago and I don't have a car,' I said with a shrug.

Ryder nodded. 'Station security footage can confirm that if it comes to the crunch.'

Penelope raised her empty hand with the palm facing the ceiling as if to say "all settled then" and sipped her gin and tonic.

'Enough of this—let's dance, mum!' Willow said chirpily, and they scurried over to the record player together.

'No dancing for us?' Ryder asked me. 'Your legs are probably sore.'

'A little stiff,' I said, stretching them out.

'I can tell. Now, what were we talking about?'

'Alibis,' I reminded him.

'Oh, yes—security footage.'

'I was saying it will show me getting off the train and being greeted by Willow on the platform.'

Ryder drew a deep breath. 'You got on the train at King's Cross?'

I nodded.

'It'll be much harder for them to check that with so many passengers milling about.'

'Not easy at all, and I was wearing my flat cap this morning because the air was quite chill in London.'

Ryder glanced at his mother and sister. Penelope was putting one of grandpa's favourite vinyl records on. The atmosphere brightened as they started dancing and singing *Delilah* together, their silhouettes outlined by the twilight entering the room through the bay window that overlooked the garden—the distant lake. I hadn't seen her body, but I saw her in my mind's eye at that moment, just as I had over and over again throughout my life—Aunt Caro sprawling on the floor of

160

the pergola, an empty bottle of sleeping pills and an empty glass beside her. Gin and tonic, I'd always assumed.

'You didn't tell her about the message I sent you saying he was back in town?' Ryder asked quietly. There was an enquiring glint in his eye.

'It must have slipped my mind, I guess.'

He frowned and sipped his whisky. When he lowered the glass, he was wearing a faint grin.

'Do you remember that day together with grandpa?' Ryder asked. 'The three of us together in his garden shed.'

'The day he taught us about knots?'

Ryder nodded.

'I remember,' I said. 'I haven't confused a splice for a hitch ever since.'

'Me neither,' Ryder laughed. He drained his glass and bowed his head to hide the tears welling in his eyes.

I looked at my cousin and aunt. They were fluttering about like drunken butterflies, wild yet delicate. They were oblivious to us.

'It was one of the best days of my life,' I managed to say, controlling the swell of emotion inside me.

'Pure gold,' Ryder whispered. 'We'll never have that again.'

'Nothing even close,' I agreed.

'I'll never forget that day,' Ryder said. 'Do you remember that one he told us was used by bandits to make a quick getaway?'

'The Highwayman's Hitch,' I told him. 'The quickest way to release a horse tied to a post. I could do one with my eyes closed even now.'

'I've never forgotten the rope he used to teach us.'

I didn't know what to say.

'I went into his shed this morning to have a look around, mostly to reminisce, but also to start working out what the pair of us would do with all his tools.'

I nodded slowly.

'It's a funny thing, but I couldn't find that rope.' He shrugged. 'He'd always kept it coiled and hanging from the same hook—but it wasn't there.'

I looked him in the eye but didn't utter a single word.

'I think grandpa's old bicycle is missing too,' he went on. 'I didn't even know it still worked.'

The women were lost in their moment of happiness, spinning and singing. They couldn't hear a word we were saying.

'It's in fine condition—chained to a street lamp not far from Newark Northgate Station.'

'The last stop before Lincoln,' he mused. 'Quite a ride from Bracken's Wood.'

'Especially at night. It was he who taught me to ride.'

'I remember,' Ryder told me. He closed his eyes for a moment. When he opened them again, he looked at my hands.

There was no point holding back now.

'Grandpa's gardening gloves are missing too,' I admitted. 'They won't be found.'

He raised his eyebrows and nodded. 'Mum never goes into the shed. We're the only ones left who know what should or shouldn't be there.' He tapped his nose.

'Thank you, Ryder.'

'No, James.' He took the whisky bottle to pour us another round. 'Thank *you*.'

Relish

David Carroll

I

I was walking down the road again, alone.

Easy to ignore the pair somewhere behind me, out of sight. Just as easy to ignore the group of figures and bulky equipment at the bottom of the hill, almost half a mile away. When my eyes met those figures they slid off again without acknowledgment, and as I walked toward them, they seemed to wait patiently, unhurried.

I concentrated on being alone. I would be used to these walks. I would breathe easier out here, but not have time to admire the expanses of green or the gently unplanned rise and fall of the terrain. This spot had been chosen well: the wire fences along the road were intact, the foliage luxuriant, not yet unkempt.

Perhaps the only reason I would think that things were not as they should be—that any house I approached with my neat suit and display case could offer no more than swinging doors and shambling death—was the silence. No motors, no long-distance cries, no nothing, and if it was the animals that normally filled this oppressive quiet, then our intrusion had scared them away.

Alone. Just me, under a cloudless sky.

I kept my eyes up, a confident gaze on whatever town might lie ahead. I stumbled, my foot hitting some unevenness in the road. My case twisted strangely in my hand, the loose bricks inside tumbling somehow, and I had to drop it just to keep my own balance.

And then I was just tired and pissed off, and I muttered 'Christ' under my breath to hide my nervousness at the silence. I looked up and the distant figures waited just as before. If there was any discussion I couldn't see it, and eventually one held up a large makeshift sign that read, quite clearly, DO IT AGAIN.

I waved, grabbed the case, and climbed back up the hill. Kim had stood up, offering me consoling murmurs, her machete hanging too casually in her grip. Phil remained in position, scanning the rougher terrain on the far side for any movement at all.

I stretched, preparing. A confident gaze, a steady pace. A belief in a land full of people, where fences are mended and cows are milked, and not the most desolate and fucked-up locale you ever have seen.

Except for the cities, I thought. Except for hometown Los Angeles, and just about every other city there ever was.

One of the figures below was holding up the big green piece of cardboard now. I waved again in acknowledgment, and moved backward until the crest was between us three and those thirteen. Kim looked over my face carefully, looking for flaws. But the make-up was simple and had survived even my sweat. She nodded. I took a tighter grip on the fake leather handles of my display case.

I walked up, over and down the hill again, alone.

#

The real trouble started later, though. The real *immediate* trouble that is, and I reckon it was the flashes that did it. STEEGERS HOUSE, EXT. had turned out to be a small and comfortable-looking cottage not too far outside the limits of a town called Delano, north of L.A., in the thin strip of farmland protected by the Sierra Nevada range. The area had been reported clear, the tallest structures within a hundred feet were the all-important group of spindly trees in the front garden and a medium-sized fence. Even the paint looked fresh. The original inhabitants had been some kind of religious nuts, judging by the debris our crew had tossed into one of the back rooms, clearing the entrance and lounge for the attention of our illustrious set designer. To get it out of the way, I'll mention now that this scrawny individual was the most stuck-up arsehole on the shoot, but he had nonetheless been part of the crew who'd set everything up a couple of days ago, so I suppose that's deserving of something. Now he was wandering around shifting props—that would only be seen for the briefest of moments—by increments of quarter of an inch, much to the annoyance of Peggy, who was trying to photograph anything and everything for continuity before the big camera moved inside. I, not needed for a while and wanting to keep out of the sun, moved further into the house.

After the false starts and occasional mishap of this morning, everything seemed to be going smoothly. We had arrived not long after noon and the recheck of the area had gone without incident. We started with a minimum of establishing shots of the house and trees, first empty, and then with Ted Tensing (who was playing Steeger himself) in varying positions, including accepting a letter off a suitably dressed Phil. We did a single take of myself walking along the road, pausing and moving to the front door—not too fast, not too slow—and our illustrious director had nodded briefly. Joanne had to do pretty much the same thing, except she had to do it three times before the nod was given, and we moved on to the close-ups.

It had taken maybe half-an-hour to set up the camera and circular track again, but this was almost as rehearsed as the lines themselves and there were no arguments—just quiet consultations about lighting adjustments and battery

165

consumption and sound levels. Joanne and Ted did a scene—her character was answering the ad for a room to rent—and then she and I did one. Confined to the track, the camera would swing quickly and with reasonable precision to one side or the other for the different angles, and if nothing else, we weren't worried about planes overhead.

'Numnumo Relish, madam,' I said at my answered knock, not quite meeting her eye. 'Finest relish for meats and savouries there is. World-famous, I should say, loved in Europe, loved in America, available to you.' I looked up to see the response to my introduction, judge whether or not to continue. I was speaking as softly as I could, of course, because nothing draws them to you like the sound of the human voice, but Jake on Sound would break in if we faded away. A spark of recognition flared between us.

'Ah...' I said, losing the course of my spiel.

'Smith, isn't it?' Joanne said delightedly. 'You were at the party last week...came with...' she paused, uncertain.

'Smethers,' I corrected. 'Yes, I was...uh, there.'

'Well, come in, come in. I'm Nancy if you don't remember. What were you selling again? It wasn't perfume was it, because you wouldn't believe how many...'

'Numnumo,' I called out after her, trying to catch up. 'Relish, it's quite good you know...no deleterious acids in it, doesn't affect the heart...'

But by this time, we had both disappeared inside, and after waiting a couple of seconds, we came out to see what the verdict was.

And so on.

All well planned, well practiced, and nobody wanted to stuff up.

Now I was in the back rooms, Peggy was taking her photographs and the rest of the crew were outside shooting Ted Tensing roughly cutting down the trees (described as larch in the original script but looking more like malnourished maple,

166

even to my uneducated eye) with an old rusty axe. Even that was done all but silently. The wonders of movie magic.

There were two bedrooms back there; the master one, sunny and sparse, and one belonging to a boy of, I guessed, fourteen or so. The blinds were down in that one. Clothes were discarded on the floor or pushed under the bed, books lined a study desk, a pad of paper and a pen were ready to be picked up and used. The pad had writing on it, and all of a sudden, I didn't want to move forward, to see if the work had been abandoned mid-sentence. I didn't want my vague feelings of loss to collapse into specifics.

The house was still in good shape—nobody had died there, it seemed—and only the kitchen smelt pretty bad. In the bedroom, there was only a stale smell, very faint, of mildew and sweat like my own, and of a young boy's dreams.

I considered the room for a while—the picture of Jesus smiling secretly at me, the bed tidy, and the cupboard doors neatly closed—and I didn't want to open them, to see what had been grabbed or not, to see if this boy had torn anything before pushing the door shut. I knelt on the bed and felt behind the cupboard—yes, two magazines, cheap pulp against my fingertips. Monster mags, or girlie mags, or the boy's own mags that had never really seemed to exist outside a few suburbs back in L.A.? The badly reproduced photos and tales of bloody conflict in the war magazines my own children had once upon a time stashed away?

I restraightened the bed, the indent of my weight slowly settling, and turned away, the flashes of Peggy's work playing strange shadows on the walls.

That called them to us, I know, I am sure, because the only other beacon was my melancholy, and the dead do not feel such things.

Someone ran in and said Hitch was looking for me, and I went out for some group shots with Stuart (playing Constable Slugger with a nice detached air) and Erich (Rex Linley) in the

167

newly renovated garden. That was when the attack came, as my thoughts were ebbing back into some sort of rationality, and Phillip Franks shouted a panicked yell just about as loud as he could.

Too many zombies—four going for the main group in the front garden, another two round the other side of the house, and another two on the fucking *road*. How in hell's name had they gotten there without being spotted?

As I stood there in logistical outrage, Jake Stanton was already wrestling with one, which had fallen to its knees, snapping teeth grasping for flesh. Kim had her machete out and swinging, scoring undead meat but not stopping anything, and one of the two closest was coming for me.

My machete, I thought, my…

He grabbed me with obscenely soft hands and pulled me towards him and I screamed, throwing my weight backwards out of his reach. He kept coming, his ripped mechanic's uniform flapping strangely, and *they're fucking slow*, I know they're slow, but it was on me going for my cheek.

I swung my arms against it, pushing it away momentarily, enough to build up the momentum to scramble backwards into STEEGERS HOUSE INT. It grunted as something hit it in the leg, steel peeling away flyblown muscle. But its attacker moved on and it didn't take its blank stare off me.

I heard shots then, and more shouts—any pretence of silence abandoned. Somebody was sobbing, babbling, and I had my own gun, of course I did, yes.

The one-time mechanic just kept on coming, grabbing my leg now and worrying at it, its tongue lolling, forgotten, getting caught on and off the dirty teeth. It still hadn't got through the heavy canvas guards under my trousers and I kept trying to scramble backwards and grab my pistol out from my shoulder holster all at once. I was still screaming; I don't think I ever stopped.

It smelled like the kitchen, but worse. It had simply gone off.

168

Safety catch off, yes. Fire, fire. Anywhere. One through its shoulder, throwing its arm back loosely, one nowhere, out the door maybe. Then it was going for my gun hand, the nearest available living matter, and its lungs were still trying to remember what to do because I felt the damp halting breath of it on me as a shadow came over us and a flash of steel sent its head bouncing away, expression unchanged.

Still hungry as the machete swung again, splitting the skull over the left eye and letting the hunger out.

I don't know who did it, I really don't, because I threw the twitching, seeping body off me and crawled into a corner until somebody came and checked to see that nothing had broken my skin.

I was better after that, and went back out in the sunlight to see what was happening.

We had done well, I suppose. Most injuries were shallow scratches from a variety of causes, but none were bites, so the chances of infection were minor. A stray bullet through the flesh of Stuart Daniels' arm was the most serious wound (and not my bullet either—I checked), not to mention some severely shaken individuals. That was about it. After all, we had been armed and outnumbered them two to one. No problem, I thought unsteadily, no problem at all.

Except there was a problem, and the two designated guards and a few others stood round softly arguing about it—or rather arguing with the director (who was sweating in the late afternoon sun, but looking unruffled nonetheless) and losing.

I looked in disbelief as they started moving lights and the camera for another shift. The body in the hall seemed to have human proportions again with its head removed—*John Wi* it said on the torn mechanic's name patch—and was shoved out of the way.

Didn't they know that every eldritch fucking zombie within several miles radius was converging on this spot?

And of course they did. Phil and Kim were already starting

169

to fire with careful precision into the heads of the forerunners to what would soon be a major invasion.

Cleared area, my arse.

The camera and lights were positioned, the cables were hastily yanked out of the way, and the sound quietly and curtly told it would not be needed. All this without discussion but under precise orders from the big man himself. Without the track it was done in less than five minutes, which I would have found hard to believe had I not had ample demonstration of his abilities back at base.

I knew which shot they were setting up—the last shot of the schedule, the one the interior had been prepared for.

The sharp retorts of the rifles became more rapid, and I was given one of the weapons and told to stop gawking and go outside and use it. And of course, we couldn't stand behind the door or we'd get into frame—any zombie crossing that line would be in real trouble.

I aimed and fired and clumsily reloaded, as I had recently been taught to do. I shot down men and women and children and only head shots counted so those staggering to their feet with shattered ribcages were just wasted lead.

It wasn't easy, but the house had partly been chosen for its isolation and Kim was working my side with her pistol, presumably Phil on the other, shooting anything that was still moving within fifty feet.

But more of them were coming, many more, just shambling through the fields, taking their time.

And then it was finished, the tape safely stowed, and we simply filed onto the truck, Doug Enright at the wheel.

I've seen the footage since then, but I knew exactly what it looked like, regardless. The opening doorway, the vital glimpse of vegetation and distant horizon (and even indistinct moving figures) that said this shot wasn't done on any soundstage. And the large, immediately recognisable figure of Alfred Hitchcock, silhouetted by the sudden glare of real sunlight and then

170

turning away. Shutting the door.

We braced ourselves for the bump as Doug drove forcibly through the zombie pack and then we were clear.

Silent and exhausted we sat there. Stuart clasped the quick bandage around the chunk taken out of his arm and looked very ill. The rest of us ached and didn't look much better. Somebody laughed and asked Hitch if he had had this much trouble shooting *The Birds*, and the big man shook his head ruefully, and said you just wouldn't believe.

II

It works out like this. Studio One, as we called it, was actually a huge ex-lecture hall underneath the second largest football stadium in the city of Los Angeles, California, the US of A. And that wasn't the only thing down here—somebody had plans for this place, really big plans, and a viable population of over seven hundred bodies should give you an idea of the scale of things.

Not all in the lecture hall, of course, but spread over four levels of internally powered, lushly furnished, and rent-free accommodation. Deep enough to survive a war or two—including any of the Soviet's little surprises—and big enough for room to move. The televisions produce multi-coloured static and I've found Jack Snow's name scribbled on a toilet wall. All the comforts of home. If nothing else, it certainly kept out the problem of several million of the walking dead. Nobody was quite sure if *that* was one of the Soviet's little surprises or not, but the most popular theory at the time held it was one of Nixon's efforts to increase Democrat support.

The studio itself was a mess, the results of five weeks carpentry and wiring and plastering and welding and people tripping over each other. There were six main sets, built in a single block, stacked two across and three up. Each was twenty feet deep, twenty feet wide and nine feet high. Two of the middle dividing walls were removable, and access to the top four "rooms" was by way of a perilous series of ladders and platforms, plus a narrow flight of stairs belonging to the set of my character's flat. This montage was fronted by a vast tangle of cables, lights, microphones, panels, screens, speakers, a number of cameras—one mounted on the platform of a medium-sized cherry picker that had been mostly removed from its truck body and allowed to move horizontally along a rail—and half-filled shells of junked and cannibalised miscellanea. The dressing rooms were just a series of impromptu screens along the right-hand wall, with make-up near the bottom. The costume designer, less fastidious than the set designer, usually had her wares scattered over three rows of seating, also on the right. For the entire duration of the shoot, she sat in the centre of those rows, in a space where the seats had been forcibly removed to make room for her material, equipment and sketches, a nesting bird on a well-decorated branch. Most of the actual needlework was handled elsewhere, as was painting, minor construction, the modification of scavenged props and the like. Completed props were sorted by scene, location, or—there was general suspicion—by some more esoteric system, and spread out on the rows above the costumes. Short term repair-work was behind that. Apart from the on-going electrical maintenance work down the front, the left side of the room was the repository for the junk created by all of this activity, and there was a makeshift but well-stocked food stall near the back of the hall. In sum total, it was a...strange sight.

I helped build it and *I* don't really believe we did it. But we did it all right, and the strangest sight of all was always that of Alfred Hitchcock, who during construction would move from one person to another and always know what they were doing, and could usually suggest a way of doing it better.

Here he was master of the domain, and so when he became

172

involved in a long and loud argument, everything and everyone stopped, and listened.

I came in at just the wrong time, hurrying down the shallow steps of the auditorium to see what was going on.

Mr. Wurman of the committee looked ready to explode— into quivering masses of subcommittee, I guess. 'I don't care, Mr. Hitchcock, about your schedule or your achievements. I know the number of men you are purporting to keep busy. But the simple matter is that the terms of the agreement have been breached and this…' he waved generally at the fifty by thirty-foot tableau, 'cannot be allowed to continue.'

Joanne was looking worriedly down from the second storey of my "flat", and she shrugged at me, shaking her head, before concentrating again on the two standing in a little space of their own.

'I have explained,' said Hitch with what sounded like infinite and tired patience, 'the achievements thus far of the shoot, not to impress you with our technical ability, but to demonstrate that there is no point in repealing your…kind sanction of this project. Our sets are constructed, the drain on resources has been completed. All that needs be spent now is the time of my actors and crew, and I do not believe the committee has the work to keep even a quarter of that august company occupied. The engineering and mechanical skills you are so concerned with have been dispensed with.'

Yeah, I thought with a silent grin, and the cherry picker doesn't freeze up every half an hour either.

Wurman looked round in frustration and discovered my presence. I lost the grin. His eyes narrowed, briefly, and then he was calm again, assuming a politician's intimacy. 'That simply isn't good enough, Alfred. It's not the point. That man over there…' And everyone was looking at me now. 'I've heard all about the trip yesterday. You let that man—'

'Julian Sadlier,' Hitch prompted, at least proving he knew my name.

173

'—Mr. Sadlier walk through the countryside unprotected for the sake of this…melodrama. The guards were backing him up, I know, I know, but they were simply too far away, from him and from the rest of the group. It was simply unacceptably dangerous. If the latter incidents had happened at that time you would have lost somebody. Simple as that, yes, Alfred?'

I stepped forward. 'I'd like to say something here,' I said firmly.

'Alfred?' he said again.

'You seem to enjoy the word "simple", Mr. Wurman. I trust you have a special affinity for it.' And the director just turned away.

It wasn't the best insult in the world, and it seemed to take Wurman a second or two to recognise it as one. 'This is through, Hitchcock,' he finally said, with both anger and conviction. He brushed by me and stomped up the central steps. 'Not this scene, not any, and if you are thinking of going outside again, don't expect to get back in.' On that note he dismissed us, head down and striding fast up and out of the room.

'Real concerned citizen, isn't he? Caring and sharing.' I walked over to Hitch, who had an expression like he'd been rolling in dog shit.

'Mr. Sadlier,' he said without a glance. 'Glad you could make it, but I don't recall a rifle being called for in the next scene.'

The weapon was dangling forgotten in my hands. I'd popped in to see how things were going on the way back to return the weapon after sentry duty up top.

'Yeah,' I said. 'Yeah.' But his attention was elsewhere.

'Miss Brown, I believe you were walking down to address Mr. Wernicke. Yes?' He spoke softly, as he always did, so that if you were making too much noise you'd drown him out and nothing would happen.

Miss Brown, who was plain old Joanne to me, nodded, and I

174

winked encouragingly. The crew moved back to their positions and it all started happening again.

I returned the rifle and came back for some scenes of my own.

#

That night I walked through the wide corridors of our underground haven and marvelled anew at the silence. It was a different silence to that above, where the buildings of the city or the hills of the country provided at least the hint of an echo. Sound went nowhere down there, somehow absorbed into the walls and the unimaginable weight above our heads—even, I suppose, in the vaster weight beneath our feet. It was a property shared everywhere in the complex, even in the ungainly shape of our studio—a good thing for the film, and even for the actors themselves. But at that point, I was less sure of my intended words and my concentration was free to slip.

I found the right door, knocked and waited.

It was certainly well-lit, though, and the designers had made up for their dampening of the aural sense with an excess of visual stimulation. For the majority of murals in those corridors, the word gaudy was inadequate.

I knocked again and heard an impatient shuffle in answer. The door opened and Hitchcock stared out, blinking bleary eyes at the light. In the dusk behind him, it looked like only one lamp was servicing his rooms. His eyes focused on me; I couldn't say if there was recognition in them, but he was clearly waiting.

'Hitch,' I said. 'Uh, I thought I'd come and say, about this morning…Can I come in?'

'If you feel you must, Mr. Sadlier.' He retreated, leaving me to open the door fully myself. I did so, closing it behind me, and found somewhere to sit. I had to pick my way carefully across the floor to get there.

175

In the half-light, he looked old and slow, both fat and gaunt all at once, with full cheeks and only the hint of a chin, but with lines etched deeply. On the set each day, he was certainly active if not energetic, but now he manoeuvred himself into his comfortable chair with some difficulty, looking round as if he'd lost something. What remained of his hair was mussed, and his legs tried to tuck under the chair to hide his bare feet. He was still wearing the suit, it just looked more uncomfortable on him than it usually did. The smell of brandy was potent, as if a bottle had been spilt and left, but it didn't quite cover that of stale cigars.

There were books and papers everywhere, and I knew immediately that he had employed some willing souls to fill this room for him—he had not brought all this down by himself. Perhaps it had been the same souls who had arranged the minutiae of a stunt with Ted Tensing, a stalled and pitch-black elevator and a nest of kittens above the hatch. That wasn't the only incident either, and though Hitch had all but openly acknowledged setting these humorous little interludes up, no-one had worked out how or when. About the clutter here, I guessed that whether all this was from his own collection or elsewhere, his instructions had been specific. But any ordering was lost on me and I saw only stacks of mismatched volumes, with reams of scribbled paper on most available horizontal surfaces.

Hitch emptied his glass and looked at me suspiciously.

'You're not going to break into some tiresome commiserations about family are you?' he said, before I could speak. 'Do you have a daughter, Mr. Sadlier?'

'I…one of each,' I said, cautiously, not wanting this subject at all.

He moved his bulk in his chair, looking satisfied, but only waited for me to continue.

'I just wanted to say, about this morning, that I don't want to be used by Wurman against the shoot. I mean, that scene

176

didn't bother me, you know, and if they try anything against you, I want to be there to back you up.' It all came out in a bit of a rush, but I think it sounded reasonable enough.

And Hitch laughed, just a little. 'Let me tell you about Wurman,' he said, leaning forward, in a sudden conspiratorial good mood. 'There's a man who pisses more than he drinks. He may be on the committee but he has not got a popular opinion on any subject under discussion. Maybe, he thinks, if I can stir up some trouble, I will start being noticed.'

'Well, tell people that, some of us are worried about it.'

'You tell them, if you feel so inclined. Have you noticed that out of the four chefs they have found for this place only one of them is any good?'

'They do seem a bit disorganised at times...'

He had sunk back into his chair again, and we studied each other. I suspect he was just waiting for me to go away, so I didn't.

'How did you get your name on the role list, Mr. Sadlier? Or did you manage to slip in unannounced like half the people down here.'

'I was on the list alright. I stayed at home like a good little citizen and thirty-six hours after the phone went dead it started to ring.' That was lying by omission, but it was good enough for then and there. 'They told me the password and where to meet, and to bring some identification. You were in England, I believe?'

His eyes flicked up at me, annoyed. 'Yes,' he said, 'Shooting a film. I flew back when I could.' He shrugged.

'So, anyway, it turns out I'm a carpenter because I spent a couple of months in a workshop. The guy who ran the place was a friend of mine, put my name down instead when he was offered the position.' That was Art, and he was a good friend. 'He was claustrophobic, reckoned if the Russkies ever did drop anything serious on us then, well, at least they wouldn't have to put him in a coffin.'

177

He actually smiled a bit at that one. 'So you enjoy it down here?'

I shrugged. 'It's alright. I think Joanne even prefers it. Her hay fever, you know.'

Hitchcock picked up the bottle by the side of his chair and carefully poured out a measure of brandy, not offering me any.

'I am just wondering why you are so keen to risk your position down here by standing against the committee. If the situation were as bad as you originally thought.'

I didn't get it. I'd heard various stories about this man from time to time, everybody had. 'His own best publicity machine,' someone had said to me once, and I think it was even Art. I'd met Hitch once before, just glancingly at an audition, and on the set of *Relish* of course, but I didn't know what to expect in this encounter. This certainly wasn't it.

But then, they'd said he was neat, and the room around me showed no sign of that either.

'Is the situation that bad?' I countered.

'Not yet, Mr. Sadlier.'

He mused on this for a while, and said nothing more. After his third sip of the drink, I got up and left.

When I got back to our room, Joanne told me Jake Stanton had tried to swallow a bullet earlier in the evening. She didn't say much else and after half an hour, we went to bed and slept fitfully.

#

Breakfast wasn't any different from normal. The incident wasn't exactly noteworthy to the community at large these days, but as the cast and crew gathered in our makeshift studio, the talk grew more worried. Jake was unhurt and being tended to by Kim, and when Hitchcock turned up, looking sombre and sober and with a mostly wrinkle-free suit, he seemed in no hurry, applied no pressure. Eventually we started work on some simple shots of Ted as Steeger, talking himself quietly out of the latest police set-up. Lucy Campbell, who had played the 'Farm Girl' in a few scenes and generally helped out otherwise, took up the vacant position on sound.

But among the commiserations, I wondered if everyone knew what wasn't being said. That Jake had lots of problems anyway, but "they" are going to blame the film, and perhaps use it against us.

And relief that he had had the presence of mind to plan it the way he did. Because these days, anything else is just too, too messy.

III

Steeger eats Nancy, if you don't mind me giving the end of the story away.

I think everybody down here had either read the script or had the nuances explained in sordid detail sometime before shooting began, so it was never going to be much of a surprise. But it is, of course. It is always a surprise being on the set and discovering the characters you could only vaguely sketch, even from rehearsals sometimes. Joanne as Nancy manages a buoyancy, half expression, half body language, that gives the character an almost aching naïveté that isn't on the page. And I am Smethers. Just Smethers, mild-mannered traveling salesman, currently peddling Numnumo Relish, finest relish for meats and savouries there is, and so on. No particular hidden strengths are uncovered during my tenure in the movie, and apart from a wry observation or two, most of the good lines are reserved for Erich's Linley. And Steeger, of course—Ted's usual expressive voice reduced to an eerie, barely amused monotone.

It's called *Relish*, as I hope I've already said, and it's based on some old story which *nobody* seems to have read. Script by Hitchcock, directed by same, and he was to be editor, no doubt, and if producing it meant arguing with the committee, then he did that too. And I bet the original story didn't have a domineering mother in it either, but as I'm being effusive about our cast, let me just say Yvonne is doing a great job. And here is the other surprise, because Hitch always explains quietly what he wants to shoot, and where from, and it's just...Hitchcock. Hard to foresee, or explain exactly, but it's the rhythm of the thing, more than the camera angles or whatever. I think the whole point of acting, the mark of a good movie actor, is the ability to maintain that sense of rhythm, take after take. Of course, I know people who reckon that's bullshit, and without the music and the editing and everything else, you've got no idea.

Whatever works, say I, and I've spent enough time in carpentry and taxi-cabs not to defend the position too loudly.

So there I was, trying to look meek and mild and stuck in a corner.

Filming was continuing, of course. Wurman had disappeared somewhere and we all turned up like clockwork. We had spent all day doing a party scene and then there was just me and Joanne and Sue, and the camera more interested in Sue's hand crumpling Joanne's skirt and lifting it higher.

'Detail shot—do it again, please.'

There was a shot earlier that panned across the crowded room, my character's own flat, as graceful as the cherry picker would allow, and then moved over the small table (you know, showing off, and the audience not aware we're all somewhat precariously stuck ten feet up in the air anyway) and in towards a corner. It dived past the crowd and towards the kissing mouths of the two women, who separated at the last minute, revealing my worried expression. Not exactly the best zoom I've ever seen, but I suppose it was as good as the equipment would allow.

180

And so Joanne's hand slides under Sue's blouse and the camera follows the ripple up and over. We were trying to record as much sound live as we could, but for the party scene we were going to add most of it later—letting us use the cherry picker at all, for a start, which made a godawful noise. So there was no sound-man crowding close for these shots. The cameraman was Ian Holt, who had a sure hand with the technology and was about as gay as you can get. But I'm not, so I suppose I was thinking about the shoot to keep my mind off the garish and repetitive show.

And so we have a medium-shot of them moving against each other and Joanne's buttons being undone.

And then another hand under a skirt and stockings falling loose.

Which was about as far as Joanne was going to go. So then we got the nude model in (wonder what profession got her down here, I thought, somewhat petulantly), who seemed nice enough and managed to chat between takes, and we kept going from there.

Finally we finished, and there was one more shot to do that night, which didn't need me—Erich as Rex Linley (amateur detective, my flat-mate, instigator of the current revels, and slick bastard) with his pants around his knees and fumbling under a table.

I grinned encouragingly at Ian and went out for a drink.

#

'And darkness, and decay. And the Red Death held illimitable dominion over all.'

Alfred Hitchcock took a sip from his champagne glass, and warmed to his subject.

'Dreadful party, really,' he said. 'No colour coordination and the entrées...quite awful. Still. I can't help but be reminded of this gathering tonight.'

His gesture encompassed the hundred and fifty or so people in the hall.

'Blue is the colour of a drowned man's skin, and of men trapped and stifled underground. That is the first hall we dance through.

'Purple is the colour of a bruised man's skin, as we beat against ourselves in fear and panic.'

The hall has hushed, of course, and his eyes roved over it. I tried to work out what the hell he was talking about. 'Masque of the Red Death,' Joanne whispered. I considered, but vaguely remembered images of Vincent Price looking smug didn't help much.

'And we know the colour green, the third hall, as we succumb to our wounds and stagger punch drunk.

'And we pass through the orange hall to cleanse our skin and we are scattered shards of white.'

He paused, and the deep absence of sound drew everyone towards the man, suit pressed, hair neat, still old.

'And I would give thee violet, but they withered all when the world died. And all that is left is the last hall, the ebony hall lit by fires stained red.'

He seemed to have finished. He leaned over and grabbed a large chicken wing marinated in something and sat down. It was the signal for everyone else to go for the food, an opportunity they took without hesitation.

'Good party,' said Erich quietly from my right.

'Uh-huh.'

#

'What the...?' said Joanne, quite distinctly. I groaned and half rolled out of bed.

I wasn't feeling too bad, just lying under the light blanket and vaguely bemoaning, as I did every time I didn't have to get up at an obscene hour, the lack of a radio or something in the

182

room. I never was organised enough to grab a record player from somewhere. So I squinted and staggered behind Joanne as she fully entered what passed for a lounge in what passed for our apartment. There I opened my eyes wide and started believing the insistent twitching of my nose.

The room was full of flowers. Garlands and bushels and arrangements and a vase full of roses and lilies spread across the floor. More flowers than I could name, though I saw iris and snapdragon and tulips and what had to be forget-me-nots. And I seemed to smell all of them, a sickly sweet cacophony of aroma that permeated the air, the individual elements pushing at each other as angrily as the murals out in the hall.

Joanne made her way into the centre of the room, pushing through the new carpet, and looked round, unbelieving. She bent to pick up a note placed on the table, looked at it briefly and passed it wordlessly to me. The handwriting was high and unsteady, simply saying 'Until the End of the World'. I didn't recognise the hand. The opposite side was blank.

'What the...' Joanne finally said again.

'It's for your hay fever,' I suddenly said, working it out, too early in the morning for anything faster.

She looked at me suspiciously. 'I don't get hay fever,' she said.

'No, but a certain noted film director thinks you do.'

'Christ, Julian, what have you been doing?'

'Nothing...I just had a hunch and he was being nosy.' I shrugged, and grinned. 'To somewhat spectacular result, I'd say.'

'Well, thanks a whole lot.' I looked at her; she didn't seem to be getting the joke.

'Hey, hang on, this wasn't my idea. I was just trying to save you some bother. You know what he's like.'

'And so while Hitchcock's trying to be the world's biggest prick, you just thought you'd out-bid him. Stay out of it, Julian, or go screw.'

And she walked out and slammed the door.

'Yeah, well that's just *fucking brilliant!*' I screamed after her, and to punctuate the sentiment, I threw the roses across the room and heard the crash of the glass against a stand of gladioli only distantly.

I looked at the shattered mess, the flowers I'd knocked over and the slow welling of water through it all. I suppose I thought about cleaning it up, but I went back to bed and wished longingly for some music instead.

#

'Please...don't...they'll be back very soon.'

Sue pushes Erich gently, without force.

'They left you here for a bit. To be with me.'

'No, no. Ian's just gone to...You know I respect you so much. We all do.'

'Um-hum.'

'We really do. The arrangements are all made. Don't— please don't do that. They'll be back any time now.'

'There's plenty of time. You're right...All arranged. So soft...do you know how long it's been since I felt anything so soft.'

'Please don't do that...Please stop...I'll yell out...really I will. I don't care...Stop!...Please...don't do that...'

'Stop babbling.'

Hitchcock leaned forward, but only a little.

'Stupid cow. You'll do as I say.'

'Help me...Stop it... Help me...'

'You bitch...you stupid bitch...Shut up. Bitch...bitch... what do you think of that? What? Tell me. What?'

Erich crouched over Sue's limp body. Finally he got up and washed his hands.

Hitchcock sank back into his chair. 'Do it again.'

South-south-west, south, south-east, east; since this seems to be literary city, but fuck that because when they found Wurman he was clawing at anything that moved and his kicking legs sent his body spinning jerkily and without rhythm. He had been just inside the door of a little-used storage room on the lower levels, and the commotion as Clive Rosen ran through the complex screaming for a gun roused just about everybody.

Clive shot Wurman again and again and then somebody had to shoot him. Not just because he'd been bitten, but because he'd gone quite literally insane.

Wurman was cut down, though the rope around his neck had already worked through the flesh and had been sawing at his spine with every jig.

Finally, somebody remembered that Jenny Beauman was supposed to have been with Clive at the time. Her current location was unknown.

#

Twenty-seven casualties that night. Twenty-seven and another twenty wounded clean, and if *anyone* had come into what passed for our apartment as Joanne and I huddled together, mostly just listening, it would have been more.

The morning was too quiet. The afternoon saw a full meeting in the largest hall, over seven hundred people, a quick census and some heated argument. Finally, somebody voiced loudly enough what I'd been wondering myself. Why *had* Dean M. Wurman, formerly of the committee, been hanging from the neck just behind the door of an over-rated cupboard?

I looked round for Alfred J. Hitchcock, just to see the look on his face, but couldn't find him in the crowd.

IV

I guess this is a suicide note, after all. There comes a time when you've just got to stop doing things over and over again.

There is no light down here, though the generators seem to be fine and most of the place is still as brightly lit as it ever was. In this hall there is only my flashlight, and I checked all the corners thoroughly first, though there's no need, really. It's only the rarest of zombies that knows what an ambush is.

The six rooms forming their weird tableau are untouched, props scattered arbitrarily, the cherry picker resting its load on A'MENT 2ND's floor, abandoned. There's some water damage and evidence of a small fire in one of the consoles in front of the stage. All the film is gone; I don't know if that was when we left or not. Hitchcock would have had to pull a few more strings than anybody knew about to have gotten his hands on it, and nobody was setting up an archive. Most likely it was just a collector. Most likely it is still under a bed somewhere not too far away, or a couple of beds at least.

The cameras are still here, though. Everything is except for the lights and the film, and the people.

I climbed up the ladders, then walked down the stairs between floors of the apartment, then climbed up the ladders on the other side. Nancy's mother's place is to the right of my apartment, on the first floor; STEEGERS HOUSE INT. is above that and then the police office and jail cell are perched on top of it all. It doesn't look smaller with only my torch, it looks bigger. More crazy shadows, more possibilities.

The opening credits of *Relish* were to have been endless rushing pipes, on several levels, across and down, moving incredibly fast until finally bursting out over the ocean (without a bloody globe in sight, I can still hear the big man mumble) and up into the sky. Title, then more sky, limitless, cloudless, whatever, and my good self walking down that road. A little later we get the flash of sky behind the cameo and that was it.

186

Even the scenes of activity outside Steeger's place were shot incredibly tightly, crowded against doors and fences. No sky, no room to move. And the remainder of the movie in these six rooms, cramped and uncomfortable. I am not talking about the endless close-up/medium close-up of television here. It was to have been a claustrophobic movie, the sort Art probably would have hated and the critics loved. I guess. I don't know. Maybe it was just going through the motions for a man who was too ill to consider anything different.

I sat on the top floor of Studio One, feet dangling over the edge, leaning against sturdy cell-doors, and thought about it.

And if I am only here because I don't want to go into the old apartment, the real one, don't want to see the mush or mummification of flowers we never had time to remove, there are enough specifics here for anybody's grief.

#

Exile killed Alfred Hitchcock. Of course it did. It was tough on us all and most of us weren't seventy and carrying a weight problem and bad habits. The day before his death, five days from L.A., I found a book about him, lying on a bookshelf in a house that seemed safe for a while. I only flicked through it; it was enthusiastically written but slight and didn't hold my interest. There was one movie though, I remember, one scene they talked about that must have been shot seven years before I was born—a boxer receiving news of his wife's infidelities, a stunned moment of film, and all the bubbles in a champagne glass falling flat. Details like that—such a small, unimportant, superb thing, and the mind that could conceive of them. That is my strongest impression of the man, words in a book, that and the image of the bullet taking out the left side of his skull. We buried him, quickly, the first and last burial I had seen in many months. We had followed him into exile and we did that for him, but we had to move too fast for the removal of our main

187

hindrance to be anything but a relief.

#

There have been shots down here now, so the complex isn't as deserted as it first looked. Maybe the zombies are getting smarter after all, those that haven't fallen to bits with their last strands of meat.

That means Kim or whoever is going to need help, or at least expect us to come running and see what's going on, despite the fact she'll have wiped the floor before we can get halfway. Even I've gotten to be a good shot by now.

Again and again.

#

I had a warm drink with a man last week and we toasted a bright new decade, near as we could reckon. He said he'd been all over Hollywood, shot down everyone from Grace Kelly to Sharon Tate. He said it with a hungry look. Maybe it was even true.

#

The streets above are clear, if not empty. Only because they are in the houses and the malls and the stations. There were more bullets than people, I think, before all the crazy shit started. But it is the bullets that are becoming hard to find.

#

So Alfred Hitchcock got himself thrown out of this cosy little hole in the ground and we followed him. Something like ten of us who weren't officially thrown out elected to leave. Mostly from his cast and crew, of course. I don't know if he expected any such display of loyalty, but he certainly never thanked anyone for it.

Why did we follow? They never proved anything. They never connected Dean Wurman's death and subsequent misadventures with anyone, though they tried hard enough. Tried establishing motive and rationale and then said it was a practical joke gone wrong and even I spoke out against that one. In the end, they just threw him out anyway. Popular opinion, critical disapproval, you might say; democracy in action.

And I just didn't think he committed the supposed crime. I don't think he killed Wurman, nor ordered, arranged, or hinted at any felony in relation to, or had prior knowledge of, the death. So maybe the naïveté is mine, or maybe I just took pity on the man who would not speak for himself, just sat before public assembly, staring straight ahead, terrified out of his mind. And maybe I was even right.

#

Joanne thought so. No, Joanne raised the subject, and had her own theories, and I wouldn't have had the courage to go anywhere without her. But she died too.

#

I closed my eyes. Over and over.

V

After that, Kim came into the hall, looking for me. What with the additions and subtractions, she was the only other one left from the party that had been herded from an innocuous door at the back of the sports stadium. There were three more of us down here as well, searching the remnants for anything useful.

189

They had talked about staying here. Kim and I had shrugged and said maybe.

Kim had her own flashlight and it spotted me before I could even think of turning mine off. I waited and heard her come down the long shallow stairs, picking her way through the mess below. She studied the consoles and walked around the first level, started climbing one of the ladders, but stopped before she reached my level. I could see the shifting beam and hear her moving things around in Steeger's lounge/kitchen.

'Well, look at this,' I heard her say.

Not quite believing I was doing so, I made my own precarious way down. I liked Kim, liked her precise movements and unselfconscious manner. She tended towards silence, but could tell a good joke, which was about as dirty as things ever got. After Joanne, that was fine. I had also never asked her what had happened with Jake and everything else that went on in that last hectic week. That was fine too.

I found her standing in the cramped kitchen, where she had found the infamous bottles of relish. One was washed almost clean, the other a quarter full of the actual stuff, thanks to our enthusiastic props man. She opened the second bottle, and the smell was awful.

'Numnumo Relish, madam,' I said gravely, shining my light up into my face. 'Finest relish for meats and savouries there is. Loved in Europe, loved in America, available to you. Free this month, at no extra charge, enough contagion to ravage civilisation as we know it.'

Kim laughed, took another sniff, and wrinkled her nose. 'Come on, Julian,' she said. 'We're getting out of here. The others are just stocking up.'

I took the bottle from her and she made her way over to the ladder. I studied the label, a good professional job, the artwork looking crisp and mass-produced. I replaced it by its mate behind the sink.

I suppose it's the ghosts more than the zombies I'm worried

about. Ghosts of friends and lovers and events, and even of Alfred Hitchcock, whom I knew so briefly after the world had died.

But let the ghosts haunt this empty place.

I turned and climbed down the ladder, then followed Kim's light up and out the door at the back of the hall.

Karma is a Thief in the Night

Roger Johns

I was in the basement, about to put the finishing touches on a window that had been broken a few days before, when my wife Dolores called to me from the top of the stairs.

'Toby?'

The quaver in her voice made me think she was afraid I'd started daytime drinking again, that the busted window meant I was having accidents again, that we needed to have a talk about it—again.

'Yeah? What's up?'

'Two police officers are here.'

I flinched, then let out a long slow breath, as I opened my tool cabinet next to the deep freezer. At least the vodka squabble was off the table.

'What do they want?'

'They're looking into a missing person report.'

'Gimme a second.'

As I laid out my tools on the lid of the freezer, I smiled at the black and yellow biohazard decal Dee had plastered across it as a joke. The venison and ducks my sister brought me from her hunting trips were kept inside the unit, but as a devout vegan my wife avoided it like the plague.

I trudged up the stairs and over to the front door. Dee slipped her hand into mine. Two female officers—Valerie Alexander and Susan Martel, according to their nameplates— stood just beyond the screen, backlit by the midday sun.

'How can I—'

'Are you Tobias Mitchell?'

'Uh oh, my secret's out.'

Dolores stiffened at the officer's formal tone and the use of my full name. Her hand pulled free and her head turned, so she was looking at me instead of the cops.

'Mr. Mitchell, a woman named Rita Caraway—'

'I go by Toby.'

'—filed a missing person report with us, yesterday,' she continued, as if I hadn't opened my mouth. 'Her older son, Mickey, left home four days ago, and hasn't been seen since. When I talked to her this morning, she said her younger son, Alfred, is gone too, and he's not responding to her calls or texts.'

'What makes you think *we* would know where they are?' Dee asked.

'Ms Caraway gave us permission to go through the garage apartment she lets her sons live in. We found your address on a scrap of paper in their trash. In Mickey's handwriting.'

'The address for *this* house?' Dolores woodpeckered an index finger toward the floor, her eyes going wide. 'Why in the world—'

'Mr. and Ms. Mitchell, would y'all mind if we came inside?'

'I mind,' I said, as if she'd asked for one of my lungs, then I turned to Dee. 'Sorry, but it's the principle of the thing. They show up with badges and uniforms, expecting people to just let them do whatever they want. It's intimidation and it really gets under my skin.' I faced back toward the officers. 'We can hear you fine, through the screen.'

Martel looked over her shoulder. I followed her gaze. My eyes narrowed when I spotted a small group of neighbors staring at us from the sidewalk.

'The guys you're looking for aren't here.' I refocused on the cops. 'They've never been here. To that, I'll add that I have no knowledge of the whereabouts of these individuals. So, why

193

would we let you go rooting around inside our house?'

'No one said anything about rooting around, but if we decide we need to, you can be sure we'll get a search warrant and do just that.'

Dee furrowed her brow, her gaze toggling between me and the officers.

'Gee, Susan, you threatening us, because I won't let you scare us out of our civil rights?'

She didn't bat an eye at my use of her first name.

'No need to get aggressive, Mr. Mitchell. I'm just laying out the possibilities.'

I grabbed the edge of the door, ready to close it. 'This isn't a missing person case. It's a roust. And I'm sure I can guess why.'

'You might want to hear the rest of this.' Alexander raised her hand in a stop motion. 'Because, frankly, the situation doesn't look so good for you.'

I paused, my fingers drumming on the doorknob. A wary look hardened Dee's features.

'We took a peek at yesterday's doorbell and security camera footage from the neighborhood. We can do that, you know—without a warrant—because we have agreements with all the major home security outfits. If we're investigating a crime, and the camera owners don't object, they let us look.' Alexander jabbed a thumb in the direction of the street. 'None of your neighbors objected.'

She looked toward the sidewalk. I did too, unable to stop myself. The crowd had grown. Neighbors who normally sported friendly faces now had that string-'em-up light in their eyes. Alexander's slow, cheerless smile made me think of an anaconda.

'You're awfully quiet, Toby.' Martel's voice had a taunting, mean-girl inflection.

'Have you said something that requires a response?'

Alexander continued her recitation. 'The camera footage

194

isn't continuous, but from the time stamps on what's available, it looks like Alfred's van entered the alley behind your house in the late afternoon, not to be seen again until 6:23 pm, as it was exiting the neighborhood. So, it was stationary, somewhere in back of your house, for close to ninety minutes.'

'A white van?' Dolores asked.

'You saw it?' A glimmer of satisfaction rose in Martel's eyes.

'We both did,' I said. 'And if I'm hearing you right, you're saying the van was there, but not who was in it—that you could ID the vehicle but not the driver.'

'We're hoping you can.' She held up photocopied images of two white, twenty-something men.

'Sorry. I don't know them.' I looked at Dee, and arched one eyebrow, studying her face carefully, as she scrutinized the pictures.

She pushed out her lower lip, then shook her head. 'Me either,' she said, showing no sign she recognized either man. Martel's expression lost a bit of wattage.

I leaned forward and raised my voice, as much to irritate the cops as to put on a show for the rabble on the sidewalk. 'The guy inside, whoever he was, was scoping out our house. Maybe others on the block. I went out to ask him what he was doing, but he hopped in the van and drove off before I could even get a good look at his face. And now, here you are, trying to panic us into letting you crap all over our rights because some creep is casing the neighborhood.'

'We think he had a different motive.' Alexander's reptile smile was back.

'You don't even know for sure who was back there,' I objected. 'So, how can you argue about motive? Maybe he stole that van. Maybe he's to blame for the Caraways' disappearance.'

'Nothing can be ruled out, at this time.' Martel paused for a smug three-count. 'But, as *you* just pointed out, the person in

195

the alley might've been there with criminal intent. When you add to that the fact that calls from Alfred's number bounced off the cell tower that covers this area, and that the Caraway brothers are professional burglars—'

There it was. My instincts had been correct, about why we were being hassled. I didn't like it, but I breathed a sigh of relief. Dolores, however, leaned in, and I could see she was about to breathe fire.

'Doesn't our address on that scrap of paper mean we're the ones in danger?' She gave the cops a withering look. 'Shouldn't y'all be protecting us from them?'

'But why this house?' Alexander asked. 'Of all the homes in the neighborhood, what makes yours so special?'

'I'm not a thief.' Dolores laughed. It was the sound she made when she wanted someone to know she thought they were being stupid. 'I wouldn't know what makes them pick one place over another?'

'But your husband might.' Alexander turned to me. 'Our current theory is that the Caraways aren't taking things *out* of your house but putting stuff *in*.'

'Not this, again.' I closed my eyes, and pinched the bridge of my nose. Dolores crossed her arms over her chest, and her chin jutted forward. I could hear her foot tapping.

'You were right, earlier, when you said this is not a missing person investigation. At least, not entirely. Not anymore. The history of the missing men, together with that note in their trash prompted us to check your and your wife's backgrounds for any connections to them. And while your wife is practically a saint, surprise, surprise, we discovered that, during your college days, you pled no-contest to receiving stolen goods, and ended up doing a little time.'

My hands came up in surrender. 'I got in with the wrong crowd. All ancient history.'

'But, not irrelevant. The detectives who worked your case noted that what you pled to was probably just the tip of a very large iceberg. One they'd never be able to prove. And that you might not have gotten tagged with anything at all, if a disagreement between you and one of your suppliers hadn't turned physical, and put him in the hospital.'

Dolores stepped between me and the screen. 'This really stinks. Toby paid for his sins, so what makes you think it's okay to hold it over his head for the rest of his life?' Her voice brimmed with indignation. I felt like howling and pounding my chest. I'd been rousted like this a few times before, but not in ages. Not since Dee and I were married. So, probably, the cops were getting heavier pressure than usual.

'We believe the Caraways are on the prowl and your husband is liquidating their haul. Pawn shops and hometown jewelry stores get too much police scrutiny, nowadays, so the freelance fence is making a comeback. Toby's past, your address on that piece of paper, Alfred's van nearby—it all points to this house as the place where they're cashing out. And, as for Alfred hanging in the alley, basic logic says he wouldn't be moving the goods through the front door.'

'Bravo.' I clapped, lazily, a few times. 'Congratulations, on a truly first-rate imagination. If you ever get tired of chasing the bad guys, you have a bright future writing crime fiction.'

Martel raised a finger, in a hang-on gesture. 'About a week and a half ago, there was a string of residential burglaries in a very well-off area of town. Most of the items reported stolen were the type you got nicked for handling, way back when. So, given the circumstances, it's only natural to think you might be at it again. Or, who knows, maybe you never stopped.'

For a while, those robberies had been big in the local news, but the story had faded in recent days. What had gotten very little coverage, though, was the rash of organized theft operations battling each other over stolen property. That was because thieves didn't file police reports when bigger dogs took a bite out of their plunder. They either struck back or took it as a cost of doing business, and the press was left to puzzle things out on the basis of rap sheets and body counts.

'And you think these Caraway brothers are the culprits?' Dolores asked.

'We do. And, because they're on parole, their mother worries that, whenever they're out of sight for any length of time, they might be up to their old tricks. Her missing person report is sort of a desperation play. She hopes that if her sons hear we're looking for them, maybe they'll straighten up and fly right before they dig their hole so deep they'll never get out.'

'Well, as we said, her boys are not here. And, again, congratulations on a very inventive tale.' I gave her another round of half-hearted applause. 'Call us when your book is published. We'll come to the launch party.' I put my hand back on the doorknob, signaling I was done with their questions. 'So, if there's nothing more, we'll just get on with our lives, and you can get on with yours. Bye, now.'

Martel shot me the menacing sneer of a bully forced to retreat. 'We'll be back, Mr. Mitchell. With a warrant and an evidence crew that'll turn the inside of your house into rubble.'

After a brief, four-way staring match, both officers stepped off the porch.

'Instead of convincing some judge to wipe her ass with my basic freedoms,' I hollered after them, 'why don't y'all try doing your job and leave us honest folk alone?' I stepped onto the porch, about to say something else, when I felt Dolores's hand on my arm. She shook her head and pulled me back inside, pushing the door shut behind her.

'Okay, Toby, what the hell is going on?'

She dragged me into the living room, then perched on the edge of the ottoman. The defiant, stand-by-your-man attitude from a minute ago was gone, and her expression was tending toward hostility.

'Why would our address be on a scrap of paper in some thief's apartment? And why would he be spying on us from the alley?'

Even though her face hadn't given it away when the police showed us those pictures, her questions all but confirmed that she had, in fact, recognized Alfred. And, as grateful as I was that she had lied to the police about it, now didn't seem like the right moment to thank her, or to challenge her assumption that I had recognized him, too. So, I just looked at her, wondering how much to tell her. She deserved to know, but she didn't deserve to be an accessory. Sometimes just knowing something could turn you into one.

I had actually seen the van before she had. As I was finishing a late afternoon jog, I'd noticed it parked in the alley, but hadn't given it a second thought until an hour and a half later. I was in the basement, watching a movie, when Dolores, just back from a pizza run, called down.

'Hey, Toby, some guy's hanging around behind our house.'

I paused the movie. 'He's in the yard?'

'When I drove past the mouth of the alley, on my way into the garage, he was standing on a box or a crate or something, looking over the fence, at the back of the house.'

'Homeless?'

'I don't know. There was a van a little farther down. I'm calling the police.'

'Before you do that,' I'd said, hustling up to our bedroom, 'and make him think he's got a reason to come back later and really cause us grief, let me check it out.'

Calling the police made me uneasy because, by that time, I had developed a gnawing suspicion the guy might *be* the police. Dolores eyed me worriedly, from the bedroom door, as I stuffed a 9mm into the side pocket of my bomber jacket.

'Shouldn't you leave the gunplay to the cops, especially since you're not even supposed to own one of those?'

'It's only in case he decides to do something foolish.' It was actually just camouflage. I'd never pull a gun on a cop, so having it would conceal my suspicions from Dee. I shouldered

199

past her into the hallway, quick-stepped through the living room, then headed out the front door.

At the bottom of the steps, I cut through the yard, trotting quietly along the sidewalk that ran toward the back of our corner lot. Just short of the alley, I stopped and eased my head forward, careful to stay hidden by the nickel ivy shrouding the top of the fence. In the early evening gloom, I could see him at the edge of the pool of light cast by the street lamp. He was leaning against the van, thumbing his phone.

When a noisy car cruised past, behind me, his head swiveled in my direction, then he went back to his phone. After a couple of minutes, he hopped into his vehicle, the engine rumbled to life, and the van dissolved into the shadows deeper in the alley.

It was the same guy I had seen two days before, when I'd been sitting on the couch in the living room, staring out the big front window. Purely by chance, I'd noticed him strolling along the far side of the street—just another pedestrian moving with the afternoon foot traffic. But ten minutes later, I saw him again, headed in the same direction, which meant he had circled the block. Even then, I might not have thought much of it but, while I was watching him, he slowed and turned to look directly at my house. I doubted he could see me, but goose bumps rose on my arms when his gaze stayed on the house far longer than its architectural mediocrity called for.

The next morning, when Dolores came in from her double-shift at the hospital, she asked me if I knew I'd left the trunk of my car open. I'd gone into the garage the night before, looking for a hand tool, so it was possible I'd forgotten to close it—possible, but unlikely. That was what got me thinking the guy might be an undercover cop playing fast and loose with the search-and-seizure rules. And that made me wonder whether I should've been quicker to clear out the freezer. But if he was part of an active surveillance effort, that could've been a disaster.

As the thrum of the van's motor faded, I'd backed away

from the alley and returned to the house, where I found Dolores looking out the kitchen window, munching a piece of pizza.

'Spooked him so bad he took off like a frightened bird.' How easily the lie had assembled itself and crawled out of my mouth. I dropped into a chair at the breakfast table, hoping I looked and sounded more in control than I felt.

'Did he say anything?'

'Not a word. But now he knows the house is occupied by people who aren't afraid to step up, so he'll probably go looking for some other saps to rip off.'

'How can you be sure that's what he was up to? Casing the house, thinking he'd rob us?'

I laughed. 'What else would it be?'

Dolores winced.

I was still jacked up with anxiety over the alley man, so there was a lot of emotion in my voice as I spoke the distressing words.

Two years earlier, during a period of really low self-esteem, I had strayed from the path laid down in my marriage vows. It was only once, it was awful, and I and my also-married partner in crime agreed it was a mistake, and that we would never tell our respective spouses.

But, a few months later, just when I thought I could quit lashing myself over it, every minute of every day, a guy turned up at a restaurant where Dolores and I were celebrating an anniversary. He sat at the bar, dragging his gaze all over Dee, making her visibly uncomfortable.

'Why does that man keep looking at me?'

'Because you're hot,' I told her. 'What else would it be?'

About that time, the guy gave me an I-dare-you stare, then went back to examining my wife. So, I took the dare. But just as I was getting rather loudly in his face—asking him who he thought he was—I knew. He was the cheated husband. Somehow, he had found out and he was baiting me into looking like a jerk, so he could be the martyr as he proclaimed my wickedness to everyone in the restaurant.

I had never been unfaithful again, but broken trust can be like one of the outer planets—often not visible to the naked eye, yet always there, its subtle gravity prone to coaxing even the most innocent bits of life into suspicious orbits. Hence, that innocuous set of words—what else would it be—was forever tainted. And the peeping stranger in the alley was close enough to the look and feel of the leering husband in the restaurant that uttering the question was enough of a reminder of that awful night that it struck a nerve.

My heart thudded. I'd wanted to call the words back, but Dee gave me a wry smile—the one that said, 'It's okay, I trust you. I know it was just a poor choice of words.'

'Actually, I was thinking he could be a stalker,' she said. 'A rapist scouting for a victim, or some sicko looking for a family to hold captive for an afternoon of excruciating fun.'

While I had been thinking in terms of the safety of our possessions, my wife had been focused on our personal welfare. I wondered how often she regretted marrying me.

'Do you want me to start driving you to—'

She waved my offer away, with a sniff and an oh-please eye roll.

'While you were out in the alley, I called Jack Reacher. As we speak, he's extricating himself from some life-or-death situation, so he can be my bodyguard for a while.' She laughed. It sounded almost genuine. I remembered thinking she was far better than I deserved.

'Toby!'

My head snapped up. Dolores was staring at me like I was a child who couldn't pull his thoughts out of a daydream.

'Why would our address be written down by some burglar?'

I hated not coming clean, especially since I'd sworn a blood oath to myself that I'd never so much as shade the truth with her, ever again, but I'd already broken that pledge so many times in the last few days, it hardly seemed worth worrying about, anymore. Besides, things had just turned in an unexpectedly good direction. If I played my cards right, I could have my cake and eat it too. I pursed my lips, and bobbled my head, as if I were giving her question the consideration it deserved.

'Well, they never actually showed us the piece of paper in question, so we don't know if they were telling the truth about that.' I shrugged. 'Let's face it, the police lie all the time, trying to spook people into doing something incriminating.'

'But if that paper doesn't exist, what brought us to their attention to begin with?'

'They're probably under pressure to solve those burglaries they mentioned. The politicians get heat from the donor-class victims, so they push on the police to look at any- and everyone who's ever done anything that remotely connects. I've got a past. They shake my tree.'

'You have to admit, though, that the brother of the missing guy—'

'Allegedly missing.'

'—showing up here in his van—'

'Nothing to say it wasn't a total coincidence.'

Dolores closed her eyes and gave me the slow, lopsided smile of a disappointed mother dealing with a stubborn child who refuses to face an uncomfortable truth. When she opened her eyes, a remoteness was there, in the way she looked at me, that hadn't been there before.

'Do you really think they'll come back with a warrant?'

'If they could've gotten a warrant, they'd have brought it this time. They were here prospecting, and they came away with nothing new to add to the nothing they already had. They're probably harassing the next person on a long list, and have already forgotten we exist.'

Even as I said that, I could think of at least two reasons the cops might not go away. Taking all that lip from me would've pissed them off, so they wouldn't mind finding a way to trigger the habitual offender law and put me under the boot for a nice long time. They had also been way too forthcoming. In my experience, the biggest reason cops showed their cards to a person of interest was to pile on the stress, to force a mistake. For that to work, though, they'd have to keep close tabs on me. But theft is common and surveillance is expensive, so it was hard to imagine I was that high a priority.

As Dee got ready for work, I tried chatting her up, but her one-word answers to my questions and her tepid smile that never reached her eyes told me the visit from the cops had touched off loads of doubt. My last career had been felled by the automation axe, months ago, and finding new work had been a challenge. Now was usually the time she asked how my previous night's search went, and offered me encouragement. Today, though, there was none of that. She spoke only when spoken to. It didn't take a genius to see she was pulling away. It actually felt more like she was plotting an escape, which was painful to think about.

I knew that, even if she did end up moving on, I should be thankful for the time we'd had together, and the fact that she'd found it in her heart to forgive my infidelity, but all I felt was depressed, at the prospect of failure. In all fairness, I'd had it much better than I deserved, for far longer than I deserved. If she had known the full extent of what I'd been up to, all those years ago, she likely never would've married me in the first place.

I hadn't told her everything, and the police had certainly never figured it out. That some of the goods I'd been accused of fencing for others were items I'd lifted directly from their rightful owners. And, in some cases, it was stuff I had strong-armed away from other thieves who hadn't understood how to protect what they had just gone to the trouble of stealing. A few of those take-downs had been close calls, and one of them had even resulted in a death. Coming out on top had been due as much to good fortune as it had been to skill and cunning.

It wasn't until I had a home of my own, and a wife who loved me, that I realized how crazy lucky I'd been to get away with as much as I had. During the years since, I'd also grown enough of a conscience that I was plagued by a creeping regret for all the lives I had messed up.

After Dee left for the hospital, at two pm, I went downstairs to finish fixing the window. She was pulling another double and wouldn't return until after eight tomorrow morning, so I had plenty of time. And, because Martel and Alexander had freed me from my worry that the man in the alley was an undercover cop, I had a plan to take care of things. Perfectly. Assuming the constables weren't keeping their eyes on me, every minute.

Once night fell, I hopped into my car and drove away. I parked on the street, one block over, then hoofed it back to the house and sneaked in through the French doors off the bedroom. From there, I moved through the lightless interior into the basement, then sat in the dark, waiting and listening. Shortly after one o'clock, I stowed my gear in the freezer alcove, and slipped back out to my car. Minutes later, I pulled into the garage, windows down, radio blaring, like I was returning from a night on the town.

Back inside, I checked to see if anyone had entered during my absence. When I was sure I was alone, I turned on a few lamps and moved aimlessly from room to room. Just before two o'clock, I killed the lights and headed down into the dark basement. I retrieved my gear, and stretched out on the old TV-watching couch.

Sleep, when it came, was fitful. During my wakeful periods I felt jumpy, second-guessing my plan, wondering if my routine would be accepted as the new normal. I also wrestled with how to deal with a new point of concern about Dee—a poisonous idea that had slithered into my thoughts during the dark hours.

At seven, my phone chimed, reminding me she would be

home in half an hour, so I packed away my stuff, hurried upstairs, and crawled into our bed, pretending to wake up when she came in. As she got ready to go to sleep, I followed her around, nibbling a bagel, asking how things went in the E.R., blabbing about my latest attempts to entice some company to hire me.

I didn't really need a job. Dee's Covid-driven extra shifts brought in plenty. It was just that being a non-contributor to the household left me feeling inadequate, which, at the moment was vectoring my thoughts back to one of my long-ago escapades. For some of those jobs, the thrill of the steal had been better than sex. My lips spread into a grin at the memory.

'What are you smirking about?' She peeled off her scrub top and tossed it in the basket.

'Oh, you know.' I let my eyes roam over the hollows beneath her collar bones, then drift southward as her pale green scrub pants slid past her hips and puddled around her ankles.

'Down, boy. Mama's tired.' Her languid smile was there, but it looked forced. And the usual playful glint in her eyes, when she was waving me off, was missing. It was odd how the sense of loneliness was at its worst when the person you feared was leaving was standing right in front of you. And how you knew you were about to aggravate the situation, but couldn't stop yourself, because worry destroyed the difference between caution and paranoia, and made you do idiotic things.

'So, I was wondering—'

She looked over her shoulder at me, waiting for me to finish my sentence, but her expression was one of courtesy, not curiosity, as if I were a store clerk instead of her husband.

'Whether our police officer friends decided to pay you a visit at the hospital. They like to split pairs apart, and have a go at—'

'Do you honestly think I wouldn't tell you that, right off?' Her disappointed-mother face was back, with a helping of hurt thrown in.

206

In the early afternoon, when I was alone again, I found myself increasingly nervous that I was being watched. Dee had quit speaking to me, entirely, after I asked her whether the cops had shown up at her work. And while I believed her, that she would have instantly alerted me if Alexander and Martel had to come to the hospital on their own initiative, there was still, technically, an unasked and unanswered question on that subject that left me in limbo.

What if Dee had reached out to the cops, on her own? All she would've had to do, to avoid being roped in with me, was to say that, upon further reflection, the picture of Alfred they had shown us did look a lot like someone she had seen near the house about the time that van was spotted in our alley. I didn't want to believe she'd do something like that, but I couldn't make the thought go away, and I couldn't stop thinking of how things would change, if she had.

As I moved through the house, I peeked between slats in the blinds and through gaps in the curtains, but I didn't see anything worrisome. Although, I did wonder if I could spot someone trained to go unnoticed. I even called the number on the side of a plumber's van parked near the corner, just to see if it was legit—it was—and not some cleverly disguised recon post. I knew I was being paranoid, but paranoid didn't mean nobody was looking.

Once night fell, I grabbed a quick snack and went through the same pattern as the night before, again to no avail. The only difference was Dolores didn't come home with the sunrise. She emailed to say she knew I wasn't being honest, that something dangerous was going on, and it was unfair of me to put her at risk. She said she'd be bunking with one of the other E.R. nurses until she figured things out. She told me to take care of myself, which seemed a lot like good luck, good-bye.

Even with the dull ache of a broken heart pushing my

thoughts in endless circles, I stayed on task. I had no choice. When darkness arrived, I did my bogus drive-away. Then, after sneaking back into the house, I checked the news again, for renewed interest in the burglaries of those wealthy homes. Thankfully, media attention had moved on. So, maybe, absent that pressure, serious surveillance on a nobody like me would be deemed unnecessary. Still, given the contents of my freezer, staying with my plan a bit longer seemed the wisest course.

But, when it looked as if this night would be as uneventful as the last two, my stamina and my commitment began to wane. Still, I couldn't afford to let my nerves make me hasty, so I negotiated with myself for one more night. Then it should be safe to unload the freezer.

As I juggled the pros and cons of the possible places I had in mind for that, the knots of tension between my shoulders began to uncoil. But just as I felt myself really starting to relax, the sound of movement outside the newly-fixed basement window snapped me wide awake.

'Who comes calling at this unholy hour?' I muttered, apprehensive, but thankful I'd stayed patient, and that I'd finally have a chance to get things squared away.

I checked my equipment one last time, then watched, fascinated. The faint glow from the alley was blocked out, bit by bit, as strips of tape were applied to the outside of the window. A crisp kissing noise told me a sharp blow had shattered the taped glass, and the slow repetitive crunch meant my uninvited guest was using shears to cut an opening into the fractured pane.

A shaft of pale light lanced through when the cut-out section of glass flopped inward, hanging from a ribbon of tape. Then darkness again, as a gloved hand reached in to undo the latch, letting the hinged window swing open.

Feet came first. Using the noise of his entry as cover, I stepped close and waited. He squirmed the rest of the way inside, paused, then did a slow one-eighty. Once he was facing away from me, I lowered the loop of coat hanger wire secured to the muzzle of my shotgun, over his head. I pulled back so he could feel the wire across his throat. Then, I racked a shell into the chamber.

'Don't move, Alfred. Not even a millimeter. The loop is attached to the business end of a loaded twelve-gauge, and I'm putting my finger inside the trigger guard right now.' I wasn't, but saying it would guarantee his cooperation. 'Any tension on this rig, and your skull, along with everything in it, will turn into a fine pink mist.'

'Dude. No. Don't do this. Please.'

'I'll let you know if and when it's your turn to speak. In the meantime, eyes forward, hands on your head, fingers laced together.'

Cradling the weapon in my left arm, I reached back and pushed the damaged window shut, then I hit the switch on my head-mounted flashlight and played the beam up and down his body. The grip of a small-caliber handgun peeked above the waistband of his pants. I grabbed the gun and slid it into the waistband of my own pants, then shone my light over his shoulder, illuminating the alcove housing the deep freezer and my tool cabinets.

'Follow the light.'

'Please.' He was shaking. The stink of apocrine sweat grew strong and sickening. 'Come on, man. Take this thing off me. I swear to God I won't do anything stupid.'

'You've already exceeded your quota of stupid, so shut up and do as you're told.'

Our shoes made rasping sounds on the plastic sheeting, as we moved in lockstep across the basement. With my free hand, I slid the kid-sized aluminum bat from the makeshift scabbard slung across my back. Unless he forced me to, I had no intention of blowing this dirtbag's head off and spraying his DNA all over my nice clean basement. We stopped in front of the freezer.

'Open it. This is what you've been hovering around for.' I eased the tension on the loop. 'Keep one hand on your head and use the other one to lift the lid.'

Alfred's breathing had grown ragged, and his head was tilted back, respectful of the wire. Gingerly, he grasped the front the edge of the lid, but his sweat-slick fingers slipped off, causing his body to jerk. He stiffened, and gave up a cringing, nasal whine. After a few seconds, he reached forward, once more. This time, he managed to raise the lid.

'Now, step close and have a look.'

I wanted him positioned just so, to make things easy for me so, again, I lessened the tension on the loop and prodded him forward. By degrees, his head tilted down. His shoulders slumped when he saw the ice-encrusted face of the plastic-wrapped body. Soft noises, drifted through the hole in the window, competing for my attention, but I stayed focused on Alfred.

'I know the iceman is your brother, Mickey, but I don't see much family resemblance.' It had taken a superhuman effort to keep a look of recognition off my face, that day, on the front porch, when Alexander showed me and Dee the pictures of the brothers. And Dee had pulled it off like a pro.

'Different dads,' he murmured, his voice breaking.

'In case you're wondering, your ticket out of this mess is to help me dispose of the body in a way that, if it's ever found, it'll look like *you* did Mickey. Understood?'

He nodded, letting out a shaky sigh of relief. I marveled at how desperate people were willing to believe the impossible.

'You didn't have to kill him.'

I hadn't meant to, either. Only to knock him out, and then call the police. But the bat turned out to be an overachiever, which meant I couldn't call the cops. Not then. I could've sworn, until kingdom come, that I'd been defending myself against a home invader, but I'd've never been able to prove it. And the cops rarely just took the killer's word for how things went down—especially not when he was a former felon.

One look at my past and Mickey's present, and the blue could just as easily have assumed I'd invited Mickey in, that we'd gotten into an argument, and when things went sideways, I'd nailed him. It happened enough, among members of the criminal class, that the odds of me spending time in jail were pretty high.

And, even if the cops had bought my break-in story, because Mickey had been unarmed the proportional-response rule for dealing with burglars would cut against me. And with no witnesses to confirm I hadn't been the one who'd smashed the window, after the fact, to make it look like a break-in, innocent explanations would be tough to come by.

More than likely, I'd've had to post bond, then cough up a fortune in attorney's fees if the re-election-obsessed DA got an indictment. From there, chances were better than even that I'd be convicted of some kind of homicide. That would mean going back inside, for a long time.

But if I never reported the intrusion, and got rid of the body, all those nasty possibilities evaporated. From my own years in the profession, I knew burglars tended to be solo operators, so it never occurred to me that this one had left a note telling his burglar brother where to come looking, in case he never returned home. That's why I'd been so spooked when Alfred first popped up. It made more sense that he was an undercover cop who for some reason had been shadowing Mickey and wondering why the trail ended so abruptly at my house.

But when Alexander and Martel came around, with no warrant, not looking for a body, I'd known the police had no clue. And once they'd shown us pictures of the Caraways, the path to salvation had become clear. All I had to do was lay a trap for little brother. And the surest way to lure a burglar is to signal when the house will be empty—hence, my new nightly routine.

If Alfred never took the bait, and I fell off the police radar over the stolen goods business, so much the better. I could've gotten rid of Mickey's body the proper way, and my problem would've been solved. But, if Alfred's curiosity about the fate of his brother proved irresistible, which turned out to be the case, then I'd simply need to get rid of two bodies. Either way, I'd be in the clear and have a shot at fixing things with Dee.

'Come on, man. Please. Get this thing—'

'You and your brother brought the heat down on me. And you pretty much ruined things between me and my wife.' I yank back on the wire, sending Alfred into a spasm of jibbering terror. 'The police think I'm helping y'all move the goods from those McMansionville jobs.'

'Those weren't us. You were just a weird one-off.'

'What?'

'Mickey had one of those magic eight-ball toys in the car with him, a couple of weeks ago. When he was stopped at the light, in front of your house, he asked it if this would be a good place to knock off, and it said *yes*.'

Surely, Alfred hadn't said what I thought he had said. More noise came through the window, louder this time, but my surging anger pushed it to the edge of awareness.

'On the floor,' I screamed, furious that my world had been turned inside out by some clown and his idiotic impulse about which house to rob.

I booted the back of one of Alfred's knees, collapsing him onto his side, then I rammed the muzzle of the shotgun into the soft tissue beneath his jawbone.

'My life is not your damned play thing.'

As I slipped my finger inside the trigger guard, for real this time, a dot of red laser light winked on in the center of my chest.

'Drop the bat.' Martel's voice had a loud echo, like a bull horn. Alfred squirmed and whined against the plastic sheeting. I inched my head around to see the barrel of a rifle poking through the hole cut into the window.

'Toby. The bat.'

My rage gave way to surprise. Even at my most paranoid, I had never fully believed the cops cared enough about whether the Caraways were using me to move hot merch that they'd be willing to stand vigil on my house this long. They'd get a surprise, too, though, when they saw I had no stolen goods, but that I did have the solution to their missing person case.

'Drop it, Toby.'

I let go, and the bat made hollow drumming noises as the ends bounced off the tile.

'Now, move your finger away from the trigger.'

What she was telling me to do would've made perfect sense in a perfect world. But, in a perfect world, I wouldn't need to explain a dead man in my freezer. Maybe Alfred would testify on my behalf. The thought brought an involuntary bark of laughter, causing Alfred to flinch.

When I considered the felon-in-possession-of-a-firearm charges that would now come into play, plus the fact that Dee had finally seen the light and lit out for saner pastures, the years ahead looked mighty bleak. All because some two-bit thief used a toy to pick my house to rob. It all seemed so unfair.

'Finger away from the trigger, Toby. Real slow. Come on, now. Be smart.'

The shimmering laser dot on my sternum centered my thoughts on the irony of being a long-ago burglar forced into the path of justice by present-day burglars. And, it's not as if I didn't know karma had a sneaky side. That cheated-husband scene in the restaurant was a lasting lesson in how unpunished sins can catch up with you in sly, unimagined ways.

'Last chance, Toby.'

I gauged the heft of the shotgun and focused on the sensation of my finger against the hard smooth curve of the trigger. It felt just shy of the firing pressure. Decisions, decisions.

Scallion's Head

H.K. Stubbs

On Tuesday afternoons, the Seventh Avenue mansion stretched and warped around Abbey as she cleaned the eight bedrooms, sitting room, drawing room, library, and halls. Mrs. Denford had left to pick up Emma from kindergarten some time ago, and the house yawned, cavernous and vacant.

Abbey tucked a lock of brown hair behind her ear, almost done in the second level sitting room. Floors mopped, dried and polished, smelling sweetly of rose and lavender oils. She'd scrubbed the bathrooms until her hands burned and the golden faucets shone. She'd erased Prince Charles's pee stains. Emma had named the puppy Prince Charles because he was a King Charles Cavalier, a very young one, when he'd arrived.

He did his business in quiet corners. Abbey noticed the darker patches where his urine had dried, and the musty scent in the air. Despite the extra work, she adored the long-eared big-eyed dog, and encouraged him to follow her around the house for his company.

Abbey dusted and polished every item in every room, then replaced each one in its correct position. Her cleaning and tidying services restored a home to a state of perfection, so her clients paid a premium for her work. She remembered exactly how she'd left things the previous week, and made their homes look as good as new.

Despite her higher-than-average charge rate, that amount multiplied by the number of hours in the week was never enough to fund Pa's medicines and their rent, food, electricity

214

and gas. Compounding the worries of making ends meet was her anxiety for his well-being when she left him alone for long days, especially if he didn't answer her calls. After his stroke two years ago his weak side made him vulnerable to falls, and several times she'd returned home to find him on the floor, unable to get up without help. If only she could afford a nurse to look after him, or—imagine—if she didn't have to work, so *she* could spend her days with him. After Mother and Father died, Pa was all she had left.

Abbey shook the worries away and bore the loneliness of the room as best she could, focusing on the detail of an antique chair's dark wooden arm. She thrust from her mind her sense of foreboding: that something terrible was about to happen. She searched around for Prince Charles. Gone. Busy charming scraps from Mrs. Cork in the kitchen.

She breathed steadily in a counted rhythm to spare herself the episode of anxiety inching closer, raising the hairs on the backs of her arms. At worst it could steal her breath entirely away. Downstairs, Prince Charles barked.

Hear that—you're not alone, she reassured herself. *Prince Charles is begging Mrs. Cork for snacks. Mr. Geet, the butler, is somewhere. Fleur, the nanny, is on her way. She'll be here soon to take Emma through her evening routine of piano, dinner, bath, and bed.*

Abbey shivered, nevertheless, and glanced back over her shoulder. Just plush green furniture, enough to seat twenty people. Tall windows along the outer wall admitted the afternoon light through maple leaves, and looked out over busy Seventh Avenue. Little Emma loved to hide in the pale blue curtains on either side, on rare days when she was home from school and she and her mother weren't away. She loved nothing better than to spring out and scare Abbey, who would tousle her hair and ask her about school and her drawings. A little sudden fright then torrents of childish laughter and chatter were a thousand times better than this solitude. Prince Charles always gambolled after Emma, and the two of them could make a mess faster than Abbey could tidy. She adored them, nevertheless.

The late Mr. Denford had brought the puppy home six months ago. Emma had loved him immediately, but Mrs. Denford had been angry, and there'd been a big fight, which was nothing new—they were always quarrelling about Mr. Denford's business affairs. Before Mr. Denford's car accident, Mrs. Denford had often yelled at the little dog, but since her husband's death, she was more tolerant. There was a sense of emptiness in the home, but a new atmosphere of peace.

Abbey glanced through the archway leading to the library, dark with the curtains closed, lined with thousands of leather-bound books. The shadows gave an almost haunted aspect to the air.

The shrill ring of the telephone made her jump. Half way through the first ring, it stopped.

'Denford Residence.' Mr. Geet's distant voice was pared down to a monotone drawl, as corners stripped the sound waves bare.

'Very good, ma'am. Yes, I will. Thank you, Mrs. Denford.'

The phone's bell twanged as he hung up. Abbey polished the wooden legs of the chair, eliminating every last trace of dust, as his footsteps approached along the hallway's wooden floor.

'Miss Abbey, are you still here?' He peered over the lounge, one eyebrow raised. 'Oh, there you are, on the floor.'

Abbey looked up at Mr. Geet, bent forward in his black and white butler's uniform, chin thrust out, white eyebrows in need of a trim.

'I'm due to finish at three,' Abbey said.

'Mrs. Denford just called and said she expects to entertain guests in this room this evening. She expressly asked that you polish those artefacts,' he pointed a gloved finger across the room, 'on the mantelpiece above the fireplace. Start with the

216

bust of Mr. Lincoln, if you don't mind. You must take *great care* not to damage him. Mr. Denford brought him back as a souvenir from Mount Rushmore.'

Indignation flushed Abbey's cheeks, and she looked down at her dusting. To think that *she* would damage anything! She ground her teeth, swallowed her retort, and remained pragmatic.

'Of course I'll be careful, Mr. Geet. It would be my pleasure.'

She stood and turned her back on him. The impertinence!

She picked up the Lincoln bust: a stone head carved from cold black stone. He had a pointed chin with a beard like the roots of a spring onion and a deadly serious expression on his face. The bust fit in her hands, but it was very heavy, so she took it to the lounge, intending to rest it on her lap.

But Lincoln fell apart in her hands, his base dropping off.

'Oh Lord, no!' she cried, heart racing. He was broken! She glanced up to see if Mr. Geet had noticed. He was gone, thank goodness.

She looked again at the bust in her hands and saw that he *wasn't* broken. The base was removable, and would slide into place along tiny rails. A small note had tumbled onto the floor, words facing upwards so she couldn't help but read it.

Abbey, you must help. Emma's life depends on your fast, efficient action. Put this statuette in a large black handbag, dress in a blue coat and black beret. Take the bust to Serpent's Fountain at Galleon Square. Further instructions will follow. Do not contact the police! Go NOW!

Abbey gasped. This appeared to be Mrs. Denford's handwriting, like on the lists of instructions she left weekly, but it wasn't signed. She glanced behind her and, in the shadows of the library, thought she saw the butler.

'Mr. Geet?'

She squinted into the shadows, but no one was there. Had it been a trick of the light and her agitated mind?

Go NOW.

Emma's life was in danger. Abbey ran down the hallway to Mrs. Denford's dressing room.

#

Abbey glanced back at the mansion as she strode down Seventh Avenue, adjusting the heavy leather handbag on her shoulder. The mansion's windows reflected sunlight through the trees, and the glare from the tall building across the road. Abbey thought she could discern Mr. Geet's profile, and his white gloved hands, through the window, as he held the brass telephone to his ear. Frowning, she marched towards Galleon Square, feeling ill to her stomach, so distressed by this threat to Emma's life.

Mrs. Denford had seemed anxious when she'd left the house at two pm. Why hadn't she broached her fears about Emma then? Had something happened in the interim that made her call Mr. Geet so that he'd give Abbey those instructions, which would lead her to finding the message and taking the small black bust to Galleon Square?

The blue coat was a snug fit on Abbey's broad shoulders, and the black beret hugged her forehead, tipping toward the left. Her long brown hair flowed down her back, curling naturally once she'd taken out her bun. Mrs. Denford's dark glasses hid her eyes, as she wasn't wearing any make up except for the red lipstick she'd hastily applied to her *little plump lips*, as her father had sometimes called them.

Her coat buttons were fastened from knee to neck, and she'd added a thick black belt to ensure the coat stayed closed. If anyone glimpsed *inside* her coat they'd see what a fraud she was, in her worn blouse and skirt, blotched with bleach stains and holes worn from scrubbing floors on her knees.

A busy three-o'clock crowd bustled down the street. It was a long walk, and Abbey wove her way through the people, avoiding puddles and oncoming pedestrians. Surprisingly, some gentlemen made way for her.

When she'd almost reached Galleon Square, a man wearing a tweed suit, with a bushy moustache above his lip, came marching directly toward her. She stepped to the side to avoid him, but he stepped in the same direction. She stepped the other way, and he did it again. Abbey frowned. He seemed determined to intercept her.

'Ma'am!' He grabbed her arm. 'I must speak with you a moment.'

'I'm sorry, I'm on my way somewhere important—' She shook him off.

'No, don't go! Don't give it to her. Come with me.'

'What? No. I can't!'

His brow furrowed with concern. 'Meet me at Feltham's Bar at five pm.'

'Why?' Abbey tried to analyse his expression. What did he know about her strange instructions? She was no good at reading people, though she'd never forget a face. He glanced over his shoulder and set off briskly.

Abbey shivered. The way he'd looked behind him—was someone following him? She shrugged away her fear and confusion, and continued on her way, clouds darkening the sky above, bringing the night in early. With a break in the traffic, she crossed the road to Galleon Square, and made her way across the cobblestones toward the central fountain, decorated by small cobras around the sides, spraying spiralling ribbons of water from forked tongues.

She felt a tug from behind, heard a growl, and looked back to see a large greyhound pulling on her bag.

'No! Bad dog!'

With a yank, the dog pulled it off her arm, and the bust rolled out.

There was something strange about the way the dog moved. She had a prosthetic leg. An old man snatched the statuette off the ground and lumbered away, pulling on the dog's leash. The dog ran after him, her prosthetic leg clacking along the cobblestones. Abbey tried to chase them but couldn't run in her high heels, and tripped, crashing down, bruising her knee and cursing her clumsiness. The man had gotten away with the bust! What a disaster. On her hands and knees, she crawled back to her bag and picked it up. She staggered to the fountain and slumped down, hands over her face, dreading what might happen now, but daring to hope he was the one the statuette was intended for.

'Do you have it?'

Abbey looked up, half blinded by sun behind the glamorous woman with flowing blonde hair. She couldn't see her face clearly, with the glare of the light, but there was something about her that seemed familiar.

'The statuette? No. A old man just stole it and ran off. Wasn't he the one who was meant to take it from me?'

'What old man? Did you even bring it, or are you lying? You don't care if you never see Emma again?'

'Is she here? Hand her over. She's just a child. Leave her out of this!'

'Then deliver the statuette as required.'

'Didn't you see the old man with his dog? He took it, just now. Look!' Abbey threw her the empty bag.

The woman caught it and looked inside. She shook it and threw it down, crying out in frustration. 'An old man with a dog, you say?' Her eyes narrowed.

Abbey nodded.

'You'd better get it back, and deliver it to me as soon as possible, if you ever want to see that little girl again.'

'Who are you? What's so important about the statuette?' Abbey asked, but the woman darted away and disappeared into the crowd.

#

Distraught, Abbey breathed through her tears, seated on the edge of the fountain. When she'd gathered her wits she retraced her steps towards the big house on Seventh Avenue, toes raw in her uncomfortable high-heels, and calves aching with every step. She tried to think. What could she do to help Emma? Did Mrs. Denford already know that her daughter was missing? What if she blamed Abbey for her disappearance? Maybe none of it was even true, and that crazy woman who'd accosted her was making things up. She had to find out if Emma was home or not.

At a payphone, Abbey dialled the Denford residence. The cook answered the phone.

'It's Abbey, Mrs. Cork. I had to leave early. I just wanted to check that Mrs. Denford was happy with my work.'

'Mrs. Denford's not happy at all. She's very upset.'

'Did I miss something?'

Mrs. Cork's voice quieted to a whisper. 'It's Emma, dear. She wasn't at school when Mrs. Denford went to fetch her. They said her aunt picked her up at lunchtime.'

The chill of dread weighed heavy in Abbey's belly. 'She doesn't have an aunt.'

'No.'

A grave silence followed.

Abbey reflected—the woman she'd met at the fountain might have posed as Emma's aunt.

'Abbey, are you there?'

'Yes. Do you have any idea where Emma could be?'

'No love. But Mrs. Denford is very worried about her.'

Abbey held the phone in both hands for a moment, then hung up and walked along Cotter Street, dazed. The after-work early-mark crowd hot stepped it home, around her, while she drifted between those shooting stars like space junk.

The clock tower across the road clanged out five bells, rousing her from her fugue state. Sausages and cabbage were frying in the apartments above, smelling delicious and making

221

her mouth water. The daylight faded to a thin, drained twilight, as city lights flickered on. Shop windows and street lights glowed in gold and red.

The moustached man had suggested meeting at five pm, and Abbey wasn't too far from Feltham's Bar, so she turned her pointed shoes in that direction. A few minutes later she veered right, into Feltham's Alley, searching her pockets when she came across a blind man with a brown Labrador asleep at his feet. She found some pennies in the coat pocket and dropped one into his cup.

As she pushed open the worn wooden door to the bar, cigarette smoke and cannabis burned her nostrils. A gramophone crackled and played smooth jazz from behind the counter, as the bartender poured two whiskeys and slid them over to his customers. Smoke spiralled upwards, where graceful fingers held cigarettes at the bar and in the booths. The clientele sipped dark spirits and red wine, exchanging plans and plots that merged into a quiet hum. A rare laugh broke the hush.

Abbey slid off her dark sunglasses, searching for the man, then slipped into his booth, on the seat across the table. He slid one of his shots of amber spirit closer to her. She was tempted—it would calm her nerves—but she needed a clear head, so moved it back.

'You came,' he said.

'What choice did I have?' Abbey snapped. 'If I don't get the statuette to that mad woman, I mightn't see Emma again. An old man snatched it and ran off. You're the only one who can help. You seem to know what's going on. Tell me how to get Emma back.'

'An old man with a dog?' He frowned.

'A dog with a prosthetic leg. Who was he?'

'Zeke Dobson.' He grinned. 'And his dog, Roberts. He must have put a phone tap on our phone, or yours, that wily cunt.'

Abbey Blinked. 'He tapped our phones?' She shook her

222

head, struggling to believe what she'd been drawn into. 'So how do I get the bust back from him, and give it to the woman? All I want is for Emma to come home safe. Why do they want it?'

'If you want to find Zeke, he usually sleeps in a warehouse down on pier five, at the quay. You'll have a good chance of finding him there tonight. When it's cold he sleeps at the flophouse on Strip Street, uptown.'

'How do you know these people? Why do they want this bust so badly they're willing to kidnap an innocent little girl?'

'The less you know, the better,' he said. 'You're in way over your head. It's dangerous.'

'You think I didn't figure that much out?'

He stared into his drink, then put it to his mouth and swallowed the strong spirit in a gulp, squeezing his eyes shut.

'What's your name?' Abbey asked.

'Laurent. And I know that you're Abbey Bleakley. I have to go.'

'But you're the only one who knows anything.'

'I've told you more than I should've already,' he said. 'But you've told me things, too.'

'How did you know I had the bust?' she asked.

'I had some idea of her plan, but taking Emma was going too far. I was listening in when she got the call.'

He tossed back the second shot.

'Will you think of me?' he asked, wiping his mouth.

Abbey looked down at her hands, blushing. Why should she think of him? He slipped out of the booth and left as she tried to sort through everything he'd told her. If the woman had received a phone call, that must have been Mr. Geet on the phone, telling them Abbey was on the way to Galleon Square.

She clambered out of the booth and ran after Laurent, but by the time she made it to the alley he was gone, lost in the crowd. Abbey shuffled back towards the big house on Seventh Street, pausing at a pay phone to call Pa. The phone rang on and on.

Every consecutive ring tightened her fear, like a noose around her throat. She dialled again, blood buzzing in her ears. This time, finally, he answered.

'Hello?'

'Oh, Pa. It's good to hear your voice.'

He chuckled. 'Coming home soon, love?'

'Gotta work late.'

'Don't you work too hard, now.'

'Eat the soup in the fridge.'

'Of course I will.'

'And there's bread in the pantry.'

'Don't you worry.'

She hung up the phone.

Not worry? What a joke. Worry was all she ever did. Was that why these criminals had chosen her? Because she seemed vulnerable and anxious? Anger ignited in her chest, that they would try to take advantage of her that way.

Abbey allowed herself to hope that Emma was already home, as she approached the mansion. She looked up at the top windows, from across the road. In the sitting room Mrs. Denford paced the floor, back and forth, with her handkerchief held to her mouth, clearly very upset. Guilt stabbed at Abbey. It must mean Emma was still missing. That was partly Abbey's fault, wasn't it? If she'd delivered the bust as requested, Emma would be home by now.

The dark of night set like hardening shoe polish, smudging out smears of red and purple in the clouds. Abbey marched back down the street, heading for the docks, and onto pier five. Spatters of rain glowed in the light of the lamps along the dock, as her heels clacked along the wooden boards, no longer hurting her feet. Her blisters had gone numb. Water lapped over the rocks below, and lights bobbed up and down on boats anchored in the bay.

The rust-stained metal door to pier five's warehouse hung wide open. Abbey approached and peered into the gaping darkness. The warehouse was empty but for rubbish in the corners, and a lamp down the back, beside which someone was asleep, in an awkward position.

The big greyhound, Roberts, lay next to him, whining and licking the man's hand as Abbey registered what she was really seeing, and moved faster, breaking into a run, her blue coat-hem flapping. Roberts was tied to a pole. She couldn't reach Zeke's face. No matter how much she licked his hand, her master wouldn't wake up. His eyes were wide open but unseeing, revealing the shock or pain in which he'd died. Abbey gasped and covered her mouth.

The stab-wound in his chest had bled over his hand. Roberts couldn't reach the wound, that was why she hadn't licked it clean, but the scent of it was making her whine and pant. Abbey lifted Zeke's wrist to feel his pulse, but his arm was cold in her hand. There was no trace of life left in his body.

If whoever wanted the bust was willing to kill for it, why had they left it on the floor, beside him? Because it was broken now? She reached for it. She could at least *try* to give it to the blonde woman, in exchange for Emma's safe return.

Abbey held the two parts of the bust in her hands. When she put them back together, and pulled them apart again, she noticed a large hole in the middle of the head. The murderer might have taken something that had been hidden inside the statuette. She shook her head, hoping it wasn't so, because then she'd have nothing to exchange for Emma's safe return.

Roberts sniffed Abbey's hand, hoping for a pat.

'Who killed your master, girl, and what did they get for it? If only you could talk.'

Abbey sighed and placed the two pieces of the statuette into her bag. She stood up to leave, checking she'd left nothing behind. Best not to linger at a murder scene. She should call the police, but they'd want to question her, when she didn't have time, or any helpful answers. She really needed to find Emma before the child turned up dead, too. Hope was fading, though.

What leads were left for her to follow? The flophouse on Strip Street, which Laurent suggested, though she wouldn't find Zeke there because he was here, headed nowhere but to the morgue, or a shallow, or watery, grave.

As Abbey walked towards the door, Roberts yelped. Abbey looked back at the dog, pulling against her leash, tongue lolling out, eager. She couldn't leave Roberts here to starve or, worse, eat her master's hand.

'I'll set you free, then,' she said, and unclipped her lead from the pole. Roberts sniffed her late master one last time, and followed Abbey out the door.

'Go on, then,' Abbey said, shooing her away. The dog gave a little *arf*, and followed Abbey along the dock.

#

Abbey dialled the mansion from a payphone. It rang and rang, as Abbey held her breath. It was past nine pm. Cook would have retired for the night.

'Hello?' Mrs. Denford answered the phone, voice tighter than a freshly strung washing line.

'This is Abbey, Mrs. Denford.'

'Abbey! Do you know where Emma is?'

'I was hoping they would have brought her back.'

'They who? Who has her?'

'I still don't know.'

'You know something about it, I can tell. How could you have done this to us?' she cried, hysterical.

'I haven't done anything. I'm trying to help.'

Abbey curled the telephone cord around her fingers so tightly it cut off the circulation to her fingertips. An icy wind bit at her cheeks and bare calves. Roberts shivered, too, and pressed close to Abbey's coat.

'Mr. Geet said you stole my clothes,' Mrs. Denford said.

'Then it wasn't your note, telling me to take the statuette?'

226

'What note?'

'The one inside the bust I was cleaning.'

'I don't understand. Do you know anything that will help us find Emma?'

'All I know is a blonde woman wanted the stone head from your mantelpiece. I tried to take it to her and, when I failed, she said Emma was in danger. An old man stole it before I could give it to her. Then I found him dead, and the bust was cracked open. These people are dangerous. Do you know why they want the bust?'

'I have no idea.'

Mrs. Denford sobbed on the other end of the line.

'Have you called the police?' Abbey asked.

'No. We can't.'

'The note said we mustn't,' Abbey recalled.

'Mr. Geet might tell them you stole the bust and the clothes. We simply can't talk to the police.'

'He might have a part in this. But I'm more worried about Emma than myself,' Abbey said.

'Mr. Geet?' Mrs. Denford whispered. 'I haven't seen him since I got home. Still, I can't call the police. Some of Mr. Denford's affairs weren't exactly legal.'

Abbey had sensed Mr. Denford had played on both sides of the law, but was surprised that Mrs. Denford would not do everything within her power to bring her daughter home safely.

'Do you know who might have taken Emma, then?' Abbey asked.

'No, but I know the kind of people Mr. Denford used to deal with. I would give them the bust and have done with it.'

'I think they had the chance to take it. So they don't need Emma now. That was why I was hoping they'd already brought her home.' Abbey took a deep breath. 'I have one more lead to follow. You keep a look out for Emma. Maybe they'll bring her back tonight. I have to go,' Abbey said. She hung up the phone and led Roberts in the direction of Strip Street, her heels burning in these horrible, impractical shoes.

#

'Ah, 'ullo, Roberts,' said a grandmotherly-looking woman behind the reception desk, arms crossed over her frilly blouse. She peered up at Abbey from beneath her blue eye-shadow, short purplish hair and fascinator.

'Old Zeke ain't in trouble, are he?' she said, looking from Roberts to Abbey.

'A bit,' Abbey said, cheeks burning. She would be in trouble, too, when the cops found his body and started inquiring, because she'd inherited Roberts, apparently. She put it out of her mind, and focused on finding out anything she could to locate Emma.

'Does he have any family?'

'One kid of his ain, but he don't talk to his son. But the niece come by once. I got her details somewheres.' She swivelled on her chair and pulled out a drawer of the filing cabinet behind her, then walked her fingers along the files. 'Ay, Bee, Cee, Dee—'

A cat hopped up onto the counter and arched its back. Roberts sniffed up at it, eager to say hello, but it fluffed up its tail and hissed at him.

'Dobson. Here's you go.' The concierge turned back and opened the file. She took a small piece of paper from a pile of carefully cut squares and wrote down an address. 'Cassandra Lacey.'

'Thank you,' Abbey said, taking the note. 'This means more than you know.'

'Anything to keep Old Dobbie outa trouble.'

Abbey looked away so her expression wouldn't betray the truth, that nothing was going to help Old Zeke Dobson, now. She plastered a smile on her face, turned back and nodded quickly, then set off to find Cassandra Lacey's house, and—

most likely—a frightened little girl.

Abbey considered her options as she marched through the light rain, pausing as a rumbling tram approached, lights blazing, dazzling her eyes. It passed and she crossed the tracks. She reached down and stroked Roberts's head, feeling braver with the dog by her side. She planned out possible scenarios. She could ring the doorbell and confront Ms. Lacey, and ensure she was the woman who'd threatened her this afternoon. Or, if the place was dark, she might sneak into the house and see if she could find Emma, and make an escape undetected.

Under the white street lights, she remembered where she'd seen her before: walking in the door of the servant's quarters, at the back of the mansion. She arrived as Abbey was leaving, back when Mr. Denford was still alive.

Abbey was still ruminating on this when she rounded a corner into a narrow lane, then came upon the small house with a low wooden fence. This was one of the clusters of heritage buildings; a leafy, peaceful suburb, tucked away behind hills and trees, hidden away from the busy city. She kicked off her heels with relief, enjoying the cold footpath against her bare feet.

The house's lights were off and a front window partially raised, so Abbey poked her head into a room and looked around. On the wall was a photograph of the woman she'd met at the fountain: Cassandra Lacey. In the picture, she leaned on a boat's handrail, hair blowing in the breeze, with two men who looked like Zeke—but younger. Abbey guessed they were her uncle and her father. They even looked a little like Laurent.

Abbey carefully climbed through the window and stared around the dark office, which was lit only by a dwindling fire in the hearth. She slid out the top desk drawer and found a letter addressed to Cassandra in Mr. Denford's handwriting.

She recognised the script from ledgers in his office.

Dear Cass, Just a few more weeks, I promise, after Emma has gone to stay with her grandparents for the holidays, I'll tell Sarah it's over. We haven't been happy together in years. She'll be glad to be rid of me. We'll raid the bunker. You won't believe it, when you see it. We'll be set up for life. I mean it. See? Here's the map. We'll take a trip around the world, and set up home wherever you like best. Several homes. Marseilles, Monaco, Sanremo...

Abbey turned the page and found a map drawn on the other side. There was a road, a field, a forest, and a cave. Twenty short lines into the cave, was a spot marked X. But the map had no title, no instructions. Where were you supposed to start? There was no way to orient or locate the map in this great big world. No defining features but a road, a field, a forest, and a cave. This cave could be anywhere. If you didn't know where to start, the map was useless.

A gun clicked, halfway across the room.

'Give me that map.' Cassandra reached forward and grabbed the map out of Abbey's hand. As she snatched it away, the paper flew into the fire.

'No!' she cried, but the hot embers ignited the map instantly, and it burned.

Abbey held out her hands in a gesture of peace.

'I knew you'd come for the map.' Cassandra's eyes were squinted, filled with hate. 'You'd better have brought the key.'

'What key?' Abbey asked.

Cassandra laughed bitterly. 'Oh, don't play dumb with me!'

'I'm not. I swear. I don't know what you're talking about.'

'Mr. Denford said it was for us. Me and him.'

'What is?'

'Don't pretend you don't know. Cleaners are all thieving spies and sluts.'

Abbey gasped. 'Slander! I've never slept around—or stolen anything, in my life. Not until you made me dress in this coat and beret, and bring you the bust.'

'Mr. Denford told you it was for you, didn't he? You were sleeping with him, weren't you? He told you how he and my uncle smuggled it all in during the war. Geet says Denford always had a girl on the side. A string of girls, one after the other. He didn't believe that for me and him it was different.'

'Smuggled *what* in?' Abbey frowned. 'And *no,* Mr. Denford was always decent to me. Look. Here's the statuette.' She took it out of her bag, in two pieces. 'Give me Emma and you can have it. I just want to take her home safe.'

'I don't want the stupid bust. Don't play dumb with me. I need the key that was inside. Where is it?'

'So that's what you were after? I didn't know there was a key. I found it broken and empty. Zeke...your uncle...I'm sorry, but he's dead. Whoever killed him probably took the key. Either that or it fell through the floorboards and into the water. But maybe you already know he's dead. Maybe you killed him. Either way, it's gone. Now, where's Emma?'

'He's dead?' Cassandra's face grew long. 'Uncle Zeke...he's gone?'

Abbey nodded. 'I found him that way.'

'Well it's his own fault. He shouldn't have gotten involved. Thomas had already paid him bringing in the gold, he said. If it wasn't you who killed him, who was it? Who else knew?'

Thomas Denford had paid Zeke Dobson to bring in secret gold from overseas. Now they were both dead. Mr. Geet, whatever he was, wasn't a killer. That left one person who knew anything.

'Laurent,' Abbey said. 'But he said he was helping me.'

Cassandra's eyes widened. 'Laurent. He was here when Geet called. I told Geet I'd make it worth his while. Laurent was in here the other day, too. Maybe he was a snoop, just like you. He only helps himself. Was probably trying to get into your pants. He's got a thing for poor women. Wining and dining them, loving them for a week, gone by the winter,

231

believe me. But it won't do him any good,' she said. 'He doesn't have the map.' Her satisfied grin soured to a grimace. 'No one has the map now. You've ruined everything!'

'You're the one who threw it into the fire.' Abbey frowned. 'What I don't understand is why, or *how*, you got the note into the bust. Why didn't you just steal it if it was what you wanted?'

'Mr. Geet put it in there. He's sweet on me.' She smiled. 'He used to let me into the servant's quarters to wait for Thomas. I said, if he helped me, I'd make it worth his while. He faked the note, made it look like Mrs. Denford's writing. He didn't want the blame for stealing the bust, didn't want to lose his position in the big house. He doesn't know how much gold is in that bunker. I told him the bust was special, Thomas's favourite, and that he'd promised it to me—which he had. I didn't want to have to get rid of Mr. Geet, you see. I'm not a murderer.'

The gun trembled, still aimed at Abbey by Cassandra's shaking hand, almost freezing her with fear.

'If you're not a murderer, let me and Emma go.'

Cassandra slowly brought the gun up and pointed it at Abbey's face.

'You know too much.'

'No,' Abbey said. 'You don't want to commit murder. You'll go to jail.'

'Who's going to know?'

Cassandra cocked the gun and Abbey backed away, but there was nowhere to run. Her heart raced in her chest. If her life ended tonight, what would happen to Pa, with no-one to look after him?

'Please, Cassandra—'

Shoved in the back by an invisible force, Cassandra stumbled across the floor, the gun fumbled, tumbling in her hands. Abbey couldn't see who'd shoved her in the back, until her gaze fell upon the little girl darting back behind the curtain.

Cassandra tripped, plunged toward the floor, and the gun fired underneath her.

'Emma!' Abbey called, and ran to the little girl, crouching before her, checking them both for bullet wounds. They were okay, though her body tingled and burned all over with fright.

'Let's get out of here,' she said. Emma was nimble. They quickly climbed out the window and ran, holding tight to each other's hand. Abbey collected Roberts, who she'd left tied to a tree. The dog wagged her tail and sniffed at Abbey's legs, delighted to see her.

'Did she hurt you?' Abbey asked Emma.

'She kept me locked under the floor, down some dark stairs!' Emma said. 'It was scary, but I broke out when I heard your voice. I'm hungry.'

'You brave kid,' Abbey said, hugging her. 'We'll get you home and give you dinner. Did you hear much of what we said?'

'No,' Emma said. 'What did you say?'

'Nothing much. Your mum is going to be so happy to see you.'

'Who's this?' Emma asked, patting the dog's head.

'This is Roberts,' Abbey said.

'Will Prince Charles like her?' Emma asked.

#

'Mummy!' Emma cried, running in the front door. She ran and leapt into Mrs. Denford's arms.

'You found her!' Mrs. Denford cried. 'Thank you, Abbey. Where was she?'

'Cassandra Lacey had her. I snuck in and we got away. Emma needs some dinner. Cassandra kept her locked up, under the stairs.'

'I helped!' Emma said, proudly. 'I pushed the bad lady over. I think she was going to shoot Abbey.' The little girl's eyes

233

were wide. Her mother turned to Abbey, wide-eyed, also.

'We're both safe now. That's what matters,' Abbey said quietly. 'Is cook in the kitchen?'

'She's in bed, but I'll wake her and ask her to get some food for you both. Emma, come with me.'

'And then we should talk,' Abbey said.

Mrs. Denford registered the gravity of her tone and nodded.

'Yes. I'll just wake Mrs. Cork,' she said, leading Emma away.

Abbey sat on the settee and stroked Roberts's head, resting on her knee.

Mrs. Denford returned and closed the door behind her.

'Thank you for bringing her home safely,' Mrs. Denford said. 'Do you think Cassandra Lacey will come for her again?'

Abbey shook her head. 'When Emma pushed her over, her gun went off, underneath her. Afterwards, she was very still.'

Mrs. Denford gasped and raised a hand to cover her mouth.

'Are you saying—?'

Abbey shook her head. 'I'm not saying anything. I don't really know. But she didn't speak, and she didn't chase us. The less we know about it, the better. Emma saved me. She doesn't need to know the details of what happened.'

'What part did Mr. Geet play in this?' Mrs. Denford asked.

'He set me up.'

'I won't have him in the house again.'

Abbey nodded. 'Do you want to know what it was all about?'

Mrs. Denford held up her hand. 'It was something Thomas was mixed up in, wasn't it?'

Abbey nodded.

'So long as it's over? No.' She shuddered.

'I think it's over,' Abbey said.

'Would you like something to eat?'

'I'd best be getting home to Pa.'

Roberts whined, at Abbey's feet. Abbey's tummy grumbled,

too.

'The dog might like some food, if that's all right. And yes, could I have a bread roll to eat as I walk? And my pay, for today's work.'

'Oh yes, how could I have forgotten that?' Mrs. Denford said.

Abbey forced a smile.

#

It was past midnight as Abbey led Roberts through the park, dead tired but relieved to be wearing her comfortable shoes again. Roberts stopped to sniff the grass and pee several times. Abbey was surprised to see other people out so late walking their dogs, too. When she finally made it up the stairs and into her apartment, Abbey checked on her grandfather, who was snoring in his bed.

The clock struck one as she chopped vegetables and made soup, and found Roberts sitting on the floor chewing at the strap on her prosthetic leg.

'Time to get it off, is it, girl?' Abbey said. She sat down and undid the straps to release it. As she removed the limb, something fell out onto the floor. A silver capsule, about the size of her thumb.

The dog nuzzled her cheek. Abbey patted her then opened the capsule to see what was inside. A silver key fell out onto the floor. This had to be the key Cassandra had wanted so badly. A scrap of paper was rolled up inside the capsule, too. *Take the Ferry from Scallion's Head to Catnest Island.*

Abbey kept her eye on the key, musing that the dock on Catnest Island might be where the map should be oriented from. She closed her eyes and pictured the map in her mind, seeing it so clearly she could sketch it, if she wanted to. She saw no need to draw it, though, when she could hold the image in her mind, entirely secret.

What if she found the cave and even the treasure? Who did it really belong to, now? Cassandra was likely dead. Laurent might be after it. Did Mrs. Denford have any claim to it? She had more wealth than she could ever need. But for Abbey, if there was something of value hidden in the cave, it would change her life, change her grandfather's life, too. But if Laurent had killed his own father, there was the risk he'd come after her, too.

Abbey stroked Roberts's head. The idea of the trip scared her. Going somewhere she'd never been, across the channel and an open field.

'Will you come with me, girl?' she asked the dog.

The dog looked up adoringly at her new human, seeming to say she would go wherever Abbey led.

#

Abbey left early the next morning, when the dawn painted orange streaks along the tips of the wispy clouds. *Red sky at dawn, sailors forlorn.* She hoped the weather would hold until she'd returned from her trip.

Roberts ran alongside as Abbey rode her bicycle slowly to the dock at Scallion's Head. Gulls wheeled in a humid sky as she bought a ticket for the Catnest Island ferry, and waited until 25 past the hour, when it puffed in to dock. She walked her bicycle onto the boat and Roberts followed alongside, ears down and tail between her legs.

'Never been on a boat, before?' Abbey asked. 'It is a bit scary.'

It made her anxious to be going somewhere she'd never been before. And what if Laurent had followed her? She looked all around. There was no one else on the ferry but the skipper and a crew member who'd checked her ticket and pulled in the ropes. At this time of morning, the flow of people would be towards the city, not away from it.

236

An hour later, the ferry pulled up at the dock at Catnest Island. Abbey walked her bike over the gangplank and rode it along the peer, slowly enough that Roberts could keep up. Tall pine trees rose on either side of the road, dampening the light of the bright morning she'd enjoyed near the water.

Abbey followed the route on the map she'd memorised. Up the road and out of the trees, to the wide field on the right. She hid her bike behind a bush and walked through the long grass. The breeze bent the tips of the stalks, rippled through their leaves, and tossed feathery seeds up into the air.

Roberts ran alongside happily, sniffing animal trails and looking away curiously.

'Stay with me, girl,' Abbey said. 'You make me brave.'

The field led to a cliff, on the edge of a forest. Hidden over a small rise was the dark yawning mouth of a cave. Abbey peered into the darkness.

'What do you think, Roberts? Is this it? Do we go inside?'

The dog sniffed a nearby rock and sprayed a mark on the ground, then stepped down into the hole, bending low to drag her prosthetic leg through. Abbey took a deep breath and crawled down into the darkness after her, dreading that she might get lost and never see daylight again.

She drew a torch from her bag and shone it ahead. Just a metre in, the small tunnel opened up into a massive cavern, walls seeping with moisture that formed puddles on the ground.

The map had said nothing about crawling down into the cave, but there had been twenty short lines from the cave entrance to the spot marked X. That could mean twenty paces. Or worse: twenty metres. In the dark, that seemed like a long way.

Taking careful steps over the pebbly ground, and around puddles and mud, Abbey counted each footfall as she moved deeper into the unknown.

Flapping wings came tumbling toward her and she ducked, covering her head, then the bat was gone, out through a small hole above, which let in some light. Roberts barked.

'Just a bat,' Abbey said.

A few more steps and she was twenty steps in, standing on soft dirt.

This would all come to nothing, she realised, with the falling feeling of collapsing hope in her chest. This would be a wasted trip, a day of lost work and an irate employer who might fire her, despite the note she'd dropped in his letterbox.

She'd brought along a small trowel, and figured she might as well dig a little, even though she thought there was little chance of finding *treasure*. What a load of rubbish. How had she been so gullible, to get caught up in these lies? People had died for nothing.

With a sigh, Abbey crouched low and scraped away some dirt. She dug a little deeper, and was surprised by the sweet ping of her spade hitting metal.

'Hmmm?' Hope bloomed again in her heart.

She cleared away a wider section of silt, revealing a metal trapdoor, with a cover that slid aside to reveal a shiny lock. Biting her tongue with anticipation, she drew the key from a little bag tied to her belt, and it fit perfectly into the lock. Abbey bit her lip as the key turned. The door was heavy, and she grunted as she struggled to pull it up and open.

The torch beam shone into the bunker below revealing a well of sparkling gems and gold.

'Oh my,' Abbey said, her heart fluttering with excitement. 'This will buy a lot of dog food,' she whispered, stroking Roberts's ears. The dog wagged her tail.

Abbey reached in and grabbed a handful of gold. It seemed too good to be true. But it *was* true. She could see it with her eyes and hold it in her hand. For the first time in her life, Abbey had fallen into luck, and she would put this treasure to good use.

'You're a very good dog, you know that?'

Roberts panted happily.

Abbey dropped the handful of valuables into her purse, then locked the trapdoor and covered it with dirt, just as she'd found it.

With Roberts by her side, she set off for home with a spring in her step, feeling more positive about the future than ever before.

#

It was late afternoon by the time Abbey and Roberts took the ferry back to the mainland, dark clouds brooding in the sky; the wind whipping up the waves. They sat in the back, sheltered from the wind by the cabin. Someone had left a newspaper on a seat, and Abbey's gaze latched onto the headline.

Man Accused of Double Murder Plot.

There was a photograph of Laurent, with his hand over his face, but Abbey recognised him.

'Police are questioning a man over the murder of his father and cousin. He's been denied bail...'

Abbey took a deep breath, relieved by this turn of events. Had Laurent killed Cassandra, his cousin? Abbey had thought she'd shot herself after Emma's shove, but she might have only been stunned, and he'd come in after she'd left, and they'd quarrelled.

Zeke, though. Laurent likely had stabbed his father, after Zeke had hidden the capsule in Roberts's leg. Terrifying, to think she'd sat across from Laurent at the bar, and been down to the dock just after the murder. Had he still been there, watching her? She shivered, remembering his words, 'Will you think of me?'

At least with him in jail, she could relax. He wouldn't be coming after her any time soon if he was found guilty of two murders. By the time he was released, she, Pa, and Roberts would be far, far away. Beyond his reach.

239

Closed Circuit

Mark Blackham

Camera 15—Morrison Drive: Don was on his way again to visit Mariah. To indulge a weekly dose of orphic candles, crystals, and chants.

In his computer den, Jeff watched Don on ghosting cathode ray tubes.

Smile, you're on candid camera you decrepit fool.

Jeff adjusted his broken leg under the desk.

The monitor picture started rolling. Jeff whacked the yellowed case. The spinning stopped. A line-up of ancient monitors showed scenes from other closed-circuit cameras across the rambling Nancy Wake Retirement Village.

The newest thing in Jeff's computer room was a hospital crutch. Everything else was vintage electronics. Old computer keyboards, floppy disks, hard drives and printers line two walls of shelves and workbench. A third bench held a partly dismantled monitor.

Jeff was proudly old-school. He used old computer equipment to do modern things. He clacked the fawn-coloured function key on a cream keyboard to watch CCTV cameras.

Camera 16—Bowie Lane: Don turned onto Mariah's street. Jeff had found Mariah before Don did—albeit from behind the computer keyboard. He fell in love as soon as she arrived at the village, and stalked her online. The story of her nursing career was on LinkedIn, with lovely testimonials from colleagues. He learned of her retirement hobby from the amateur website, offering occult services to make peace with death and locating

240

dead friends and relatives on the other side.

He was disappointed. She was a bit of a crank. Talking to dead people held no appeal to Jeff. Talking to live people didn't appeal either. He fell out of love with Mariah.

Don turned at number six and took the few steps to Mariah's front porch. Amazon-ordered wind chimes. A silhouette of a lyre on the door-glass. A battery-powered black candle.

Mariah opened the door and flashed a broad smile. She pressed her palms together and bowed slightly. Jeff mouthed *Namaste*. She touched a palm to her right breast. Don mirrored the greeting. The door closed. Don's in again. Simple as that.

Jeff grumbled and banged F8 to cycle to the camera on Aycock Avenue, looking for Don's wife, Lisa.

Lisa couldn't be seen from the street camera, but the front door was wide open.

She's too trusting—especially of her husband.

A shriek of colour sauntered down Aycock Avenue into camera view. It was Gerald in a blue baseball cap branded "Navy", white and blue orthopaedic trainers, slim fit chequered chinos, twill shirt, and flash forward polyester jacket.

Who is your next customer then, wide boy?

Gerald knocked on the door of Lisa's house. She appeared. Radiant in moderate, balanced clothes from up-to-date mail catalogues. Mid-height and mid-weight for her age. Blonde hair curling to her shoulders. Blue eyes wide and still bright. A measured smile and even teeth. Every time Jeff saw her seemed fresh.

Gerald took off his cap and nodded his peppery head. Lisa shook hers side to side.

Don's not there. Mate, you need to be more careful.

Gerald walked to the next house, belonging to the Starcks. He knocked and entered unbidden.

Jeff leant back and rolled his shoulders. He could wait. He picked at a nail.

According to LinkedIN, Gerald had been a pharmacist. He'd

run his own city shop before abruptly closing it. With a commonplace hack, Jeff found the suppressed Pharmacy Guild records. Not for profits use old guys as IT contractors. Old guys are short-cutty and forgetful. They leave coding holes they intend to fill but never get back to.

That's not going to happen to me.

Jeff sipped at blackcurrant cordial. He scribbled out an average-difficulty sudoku puzzle. It took seven minutes, forty-three seconds.

He folded the puzzle into an origami flying squirrel and placed it on the sill alongside the others.

He realised he'd lost his train of thought…

Damn…

He scrolled through his memory: Gerald—the guild records showed disciplinary action late in his career. Self-medication had escalated easily into selling prescription medicines to those without one. He was still a pharmacist, just offering a very specific line of medication.

Gerald stepped from the dark house to the bright porch. There was cash clutched in his hand. He lazily found it a pocket.

He used to be cautious—but now he does house calls.

He stood on the footpath, squinting, trying to remember what he intended to do next.

A man jogged past, upright and springy, in the very newest of athletic kit. His hair, dyed black, shone. His shoes, dyed white, glittered. His white pants and tank top sparkled with his own named embossed in silver: Junada.

As he left the camera picture, other joggers appeared; mainly female. The bastard attracted them like stones in a shoe tread. Here they were—haggard, hassled, and hobbling in cobbled-together aging fitness wear.

Jeff nudged his chair along the battery of screens to the one showing Karen Walker Crescent. Junada jogged on the spot as the collection of oldies shambled past.

Junada's third age was apparently his best ever. It wasn't hard—he'd spent the middle third as a funeral director. His online history was crammed with entry lists for city marathons. Jeff found his medical records, but there was nothing of consequence. The bastard had lived in excellent health.

When not running, Junada sermonised fitness in the day room, where his believers and potential admirers gathered.

The day room depressed Jeff. The villagers were exhausted sheep; saggy ewes and ghosted wethers. Junada was able to raise them from their warm patches of grass, but they were constantly looking for somewhere to lie down.

One had succumbed now, and sat on a close mown lawn, breathing shallow. Jeff giggled at the hapless woman, whose wet oversized shirt had slipped off one shoulder, along with a bra-strap.

Junada bounced over and knelt next to her, arm resting on the damp brown-spotted shoulder. The other runners waited. Junada spoke to her tersely. The woman finally nodded, and she was helped to her feet.

The camera at the village square was the only one that was movable by remote control. Jeff ordered it to scan across the frontages of various offices and facilities—the little grocery store, the administration block, the entrance to the dining and day rooms, the pharmacy, and the medical facilities.

Steele Larsen, the mercurial young counsellor, chatted to Aahana who lived on Ngaio Marsh Passage. Aahana was the centre of what Jeff nicknamed The Coven; women who had hijacked the TV room. They alternated between daytime TV and bitter gossip.

Jeff had never much bothered with the pretty and naïve Steele. He was allergic to people who had spent longer learning for their profession than they had spent doing it. He had a theory that extensive formal training increased blind spots. He had learned not to espouse it, because nowadays everyone had formal training.

Christ, we're living in one humanity-sized blind spot.

His bored stomach signalled it was time for lunch. Jeff did one last check-in:

Don was leaving Mariah's place. The pair bowed at the door and parted.

A scan of cable users showed Lisa online, watching a rerun of *The Love Boat*.

Gerald sat on a bench with a new resident Jeff guessed to be Usinae, a woman who had recently joined the village with Gabrille. They were a modestly famous, being among the first civil marriages—and the longest lasting. It looked like Gerald might be acting as a sitter for Usinae as she experienced his medication.

Junada was taking his fatigued crew through warm downs. The exhausted woman sat to one side in the lotus position, sipping at a water bottle.

Steele was ushering Aahana into her clinic.

Don was on Campion Close—lying face down and motionless on the pavers.

Shit!

Jeff leant in, as if that would reveal whether Don was resting or dead.

Shit!

He picked up his mobile to call the village medics, started dialling, then stopped.

If he called it in, they'd expect him to be there with Don. He can't tell them about the CCTV camera hack.

Jeff moved the mouse to bring up the village chat room and logged in anonymously.

@anonvillager: Emergency. Don Draver has collapsed on Campion Close. Please call the medics immediately.

There were nine other people online.

Come on…

Jeff pulled the keyboard closer.

@anon_wakevillage: Emergency. Don Draver has

collapsed. He's lying right now on Campion Close. Someone please call the medics immediately.

Jeff pursed his lips at the static screen.

Come on you old fools, react!

@marcydavis_wakevillage: Who's this? Is this real?

@anan_wakevillage: Yes. He needs help now. Call medics for godssake.

@LivHumo_wakevillage: No need for rudeness. Call yourself.

@marcydavis_wakevillage: I've called them @LivHumo. On way.

Jeff relaxed a little but he could feel a tremble in his thighs.

A few minutes later, medics arrived in a bright green electric cart. Their bright green one-piece uniforms blocked Don from Jeff's vision. A small gathering of pensioners stood watching. Don was shifted onto a stretcher and lifted onto the rear of the cart. The cart did a five-point turn on the narrow drive and went back the way it had come.

Jeff sucked in air over his dry lips and stood up. He hobbled to his crutch and lent heavily on it to the kitchen for lunch.

He picked out things from the fridge, and stood at the half-open ranch-slider, plate in hand, looking over a patch of grass at the wooden fence. He ate prunes, crackers, and cheese, and drank a glass of orange juice.

When Jeff got back to his computer desk, the village chat room was crowded with posts.

@WaitingRoom: anyone have news about Don?

@FlowerGurl: is he okay?

@Turbopants: a stroke or something. Poor guy.

@Fishingordeath: I heard he fell.

@ForeverMG: Can the person who found him tell us? Are they on here?

@Ashanti: They didn't call—they just posted here. Marcy called the medics

@RobtheNob: what the hell @anon_wakevillage. The chat

room is not for emergency messages. You shoulda called medics.

@AchingEighties: What is wrong with some people

@BowlsKing: The worlds FUBAR.

@PixieTown: My god @anon_wakevillage why?

@SimpleMinds_wakevillage: Fry, both sides, in hell @anon_wakevillage.

Jeff stopped reading.

He sat, not moving, looking at the screen. They all flickered and whined.

Ungrateful bastards.

Jeff opened a browser window, pulled down a bookmark, and opened the private portal to the village medical centre files. He tapped *Don Draver* in the search box. The result window showed the chronical entries. The most recent entry read: Deceased, 11:49 am. 23 January 2029. Sudden Cardiac Death. Autopsy not called. Doctor: Ingrid P. Nightly

Jeff opened the village chat window.

@anon_wakevillage: Don died, heart attack. sorry.

He waited, though he knew what was coming.

@PixieTown: We hope you're next, you awful human being.

Jeff's shoulders slumped.

Ingrates. This is why I hate them.

He turned off the screen.

The blackness snapped in.

He took a pill to get to sleep

#

Jeff was late getting up and felt groggy. He sat in his silent lounge, cupping a mug of instant coffee in both hands.

The phone trilled.

'Yuh, Jeff here.'

'Jeff, it's Tom Doyle, village security.'

'Uh-ha.'

'Terrible shame about Don Draver. Did you know him?'

'Saw him about. Nice guy, but nah.'

'Did you see him about yesterday?'

'I'm not seeing anybody.'

'I understand that about you Jeff.'

'I mean my broken leg. I'm not getting out of the apartment.'

'Oh, sorry, I didn't know.' There was shuffling as Doyle moved about. 'What do you do with yourself?'

'Watch TV, listen to the radio.'

'You online much?'

'Yeah, now and again. Isn't everyone?'

'Didn't it used to be your line of business?'

'Used to be.'

'I hear you were pretty good at it.'

'Why are you asking, Tom?'

Doyle's footsteps echoed as he paced the room he was calling from. 'I don't see you on the village chat.'

'What is this about, Tom?'

'It was an anonymous post on the chat that alerted the medics about Don's...er, event.'

'They shoulda called the medics.'

'That's right. It's strange that they didn't.'

Jeff didn't answer, leaving silence except for the sound of Doyle pouring something.

'Any thoughts from your old work, why someone would post anonymously?' Tom continued.

'I was a techy, not a user-interface guy. That's a psych question.'

'Here's something more your field then. Each chat account is assigned when people join the village. It's not possible for a resident to create a user account. But someone has. How would they do that?'

'Admin access. But you know that's how they did it.'

Now there actually was silence on Jeff's end of the phone.

'Well yeah, it was set up by someone signed in as admin.'

'So your question to me is how they got admin access?'

'Just wondering…'

'Well, ask your genius IT contractors. I'm too old for working that shit out.'

'I did ask them. Apparently, the chat system is isolated from everything else.'

'There you go then. Not possible.'

'But it was. There's some very clever retired IT people with time on their hands.'

'We're just waiting to die, Tom—like everyone else.'

'Yeah, but idle hands and all that…thanks, Jeff.'

'Yuh.' Jeff clicked off.

Jeff pursed his lips. Tom knew about his record. Caught twice, and convicted once, for illegal computer access. He was fishing. Screw him.

Jeff went to clean his teeth. Then he picked up his Kindle. He'd filled it with pirated books. He had once calculated that there were more words in the Kindle than he could read before he died.

His mind wandered. He realised as he thumbed a page forward that he hadn't taken in any of it. He placed the Kindle on an occasional table and went to the computer room.

He waited while everything warmed up. The monitors crackled a little and squealed. Hard drives spun up.

Jeff clacked through the cameras to Lisa and Don's home. The drapes were closed. Either side of the front door were stacked bunches of florist flowers. Jeff checked the cable monitor—the TV was off. He checked Lisa's broadband data. Everything was online and the fridge reported it was full. The phone was in use. The records showed many calls last night and this morning.

Jeff picked at the corner of a fingernail. Don had died. He couldn't have helped.

Poor Lisa.

248

Jeff went through the ritual of his CCTV camera cycle. There was nothing else to do. The cameras found Junada running on his own, in shiny black fitness gear.

The day-room camera showed Aahana's group packed into a dense circle in the TV room. Everyone was wearing forms of black and were visibly torpid. Jeff thought again of a coven.

The pharmacy camera showed pharmacist Debbie Wong packaging prescription medicines. Jeff recognised Gabrille at the counter, though her back was to the camera. She sported a mullet, dyed vibrant red.

Funny how she doesn't hang during the day with Usinae.

The village square was busy. An impromptu men's group sat on park benches. Some wore black armbands. Jeff shuddered at them sharing a flask; *colds kill the old.*

Gerald sauntered toward the group. A paunch-bellied bald man everyone called Cobbles stood up. He met Gerald halfway. Gerald wrapped an arm around Cobbles' shoulders, pulled him close, and slipped a tiny paper square into the sad man's hand. Gerald patted Cobbles between the shoulder blades, and they sat down with the group.

Gerald's always business. But someone always needs his business.

Steele was leaning solitary at her clinic door, sombrely greeting residents with a nod and a reaching hand as they passed. She wore a black armband.

She does try hard.

Jeff clicked through to view Mariah's place. She had set up a shelf of gold LED candles at the door, draped gold cloth in some windows, and mounted an orphic egg on the letterbox. In the lounge, Mariah danced slowly in a small circle—a choreography of repeated slow, gentle, waving movements, all aimed downwards, toward Hades.

Then the camera images went black. The computer was still running, but access to the village system was dead. Jeff then tried to reopen a Wi-Fi connection. Nothing. No signal.

He crutched his way over to the Wi-Fi box mounted high above the kitchen cupboards. Jeff could see red lights. Nothing green or blinking. He pulled over a chair and eased himself up onto it, teetering slightly until he rested against the cupboards. He clicked off the wall power switch, waited thirty seconds, and clicked it back on again. The red lights resumed.

Doyle was trying to freeze him out of the village system—probably while they upgraded security.

Jeff looked around the lounge. It was quiet. He looked out the window. On the edges of the village, there was nothing to see but the brick wall between them and the outside world.

He turned on the radio and made a snack. He thought about Mariah—*how long would she keep the gold sepulchral theme going?*

Later, he turned on the TV and made dinner. He wondered how soon after the funeral the fitness crowd would rejoin Junada. He read the Kindle while wondering what narcotics Gerald was supplying. He drank whiskey while feeling bad for Lisa, until he fell asleep on the couch.

#

The next day was the same. He wondered who was in and out of the Coven. He wondered what Gabrille and Usinae were doing and if it was separately.

He called Steele Larson. 'I'm Jeff Stewart. At number 9 Ian Curtis Close. We've not spoken before.

'Sorry. I do try to get around to all the residents.'

'Can you come over to talk?'

'I'm busy with Don Draver's funeral today.'

'Oh…already? I can't make that. I've got a broken leg.'

'Can I come over after the funeral?'

'Sure. I'm going nowhere. Any time is fine. Thank you.'

'About two o'clock then?'

He thought he could hear the bagpipes of the funeral

procession through the village. That was Wing Lee. She played bagpipes at every village funeral. It was never clear who asked her to.

Steele arrived at 2:09 pm. She declined a drink and sat down before being invited. When Jeff eased himself onto the couch with his coffee, she got straight to the point.

'Why did you call me?'

'Company, I think. My computers have been removed for power testing. My Wi-Fi is dead. I can't move because of this leg. Maybe we could talk.'

'We can talk about anything. How about your computers?'

'You've read my profile.'

'It says you were a white-hat hacker.'

'That was a long time ago. Computers are just a pastime now. Nothing to talk about.'

Larsen shrugged. 'Can you tell me what medicines you're on?'

'No. You're a counsellor, not a doctor.'

Steele's lips thinned. 'You never know what might be affecting your mood.'

'It's nothing I'm on.'

'Side effects can be unexpected.'

'I look carefully at the small print.'

'I can help you better if you tell me.'

'Maybe, but this is my first experience with a counsellor.'

Larsen reached out and tapped the top of Jeff's hand gently.

'That's okay. How would you describe your feelings right now?'

'Not impressed with counsellors.'

Steele frowned and tensed up. 'Why did you call me?'

'I'm missing people.'

'Are you usually sociable?'

'No. People piss me off.'

'You don't say. You miss being annoyed by them?'

'That's a bit obvious. I think I'm missing people for real.'

'How often do you see your friends or family?'

Jeff motioned toward his leg.

'Have they come to visit?'

'No, they're not that sort of friend or family.'

'Have you called them for a chat?'

'They're not that sort either.'

'Would you like to try hypnosis? It could help overcome this...loneliness.'

'I thought talking would be enough.'

'My clients find hypnosis to be excellent for mental health.'

'Can't you just talk me into being sociable?'

There was judgement in Steel's tone. 'Being unsociable seems ingrained with you. Hypnosis is the only tool that will work.'

'Not yet please.'

Steele shook her head sternly. 'Then you've just got to make friends on your own.'

'That's it?'

'You don't appear to want my help. If you change your mind, call me. Start being nice to people.' Steele got up and let herself out without another word between them.

Jeff shrugged. He made another coffee and sat back down. On impulse, he picked up the phone and scrolled through the small-screen menu system. It was an IP system. He found the operator command—locked, of course. But *password* got him in. He pulled up a directory of users and found Lisa's number. He dialled.

'Lisa here.'

'Lisa, my name is Jeff Stewart. I'm on Ian Curtis Close. I knew Don.'

Lisa came over that afternoon. She was as lovely in person as on TV. Her grey hair was dyed blonde. It was styled gently, with a natural wave of age through it. Her hazel eyes were circled by surprisingly unfaded white. She wore blue and gold. Even the dark hallway seemed brighter as she walked down it

252

toward the lounge.

She explained that he had called while she was sitting alone in her house.

'They say that's the worst thing after the funeral...the silence when everyone leaves. You weren't at the funeral.'

Jeff lifted his broken leg. 'It's very difficult to move around.'

'How did you know Don?'

'Round and about. I saw him most days.'

'He never mentioned you.'

'Well, we didn't talk much. You know how guys are.' She nodded, not knowing.

'Did you notice anything different about him recently?' she asked.

His mouth went dry. He hobbled to the sink and brought back glasses of water for both of them. 'Sorry Lisa, in truth I didn't know him well. I just felt I should talk to you.'

'That's okay. I'm glad you did. No one has talked about him since the funeral.'

'So, you'd noticed something wrong with him?'

'He wasn't himself. He became weak.'

'He had a gentle way of walking.'

'Yes, that's him, but it become a shuffle. I tried to get him running with Junada. But he gave it up too quickly—said Junada pushed too hard. He didn't even have energy for...you know—for the first time in our marriage.'

Jeff found an imperfection in his cast and worried it with his fingers.

'Don had a lovely temperament—calm and cheerful. But his moods swung about over the past few months. Sometimes he could even be deeply morose.'

'It can be depressing living here.'

'For many residents, yes, but not Don. He was always chirpy. He stopped seeing his friends. He was out of the house for long periods of time.'

253

'He was on medication?'

'Blood pressure meds, like a lot of men here. It was under control. His pressure wasn't serious enough, for long enough, to cause a heart attack.'

'Are you saying his death wasn't natural?'

'It doesn't feel right.'

'You're bound to feel that way. He died too—'

'—too early. That's right.'

After Lisa had gone, Jeff hand washed the cups and saucers slowly.

Don bought from Gerald. Hard drugs could account for the behaviour changes. Could they have caused his death?

Don was seeing Mariah. But maybe the relationship wasn't what he thought it was. Maybe Mariah's orphic rituals had a more sinister side.

He decided to check the CCTV recordings to see who else Don hung with. It wouldn't take long. Just for Lisa's peace of mind.

But he needed to get back into the village system. The lunchbox computer blinked in standby. His eye caught the rear, where he'd cut holes for the cable connections; USB, video, audio, and LAN.

How long since he'd last used a LAN cable? Twenty years? This village was about thirty years old. Jeff grabbed his crutches and went outside. He scuffed his way around looking at the concrete footing of the house. Near the bins, he found a grey plastic conduit coming out of the ground and into the house. He hobbled inside and found where the pipe would have entered the house in the main bedroom. He found a blank facing plate in the wall, just above the skirting board. He unscrewed it and found network wiring installed when the village was built but superseded by Wi-Fi broadband. Jeff found the right cable in cardboard boxes in the computer room and connected the lunchbox computer to the socket. He got a connection—not to the internet, but to the village main

254

computer server.

Using the backdoors and passwords, he was inside the server and the CCTV network. Now he started running through the video archives, following Don's footsteps. He hoped the two weeks stored video would be enough. People follow tight patterns.

Don with Mariah. 3:30 pm, three days ago. They never kissed on entry or exit. Never embraced. No curtains pulled. Jeff was reassured, and a little relieved. 4:29pm; Don stops in with Steele Larsen.

Four days ago Don passed Junada at 9:32 am, leading out his jogging gaggle from the day room. Don says something. Junada stops and encourages Don to join them. Don gestures at the fatigued runners. Junada shakes his head firmly and flails his arms. Don shrugs and walks away.

Don met Gerald, Mark Hollis Avenue. 11:45 am, five days ago. They shook hands. Don slotted the shaken hand into a pocket. Don was with Mariah for the afternoon.

Six days ago, Don passed Usinae, Gabrielle Grove. 11:46 pm, on his way to Mariah. They nodded. Nothing more. He eats a late meagre lunch with Cobbles, who spoke constantly while eating a cooked main and dessert.

Don sitting with the exhausted jogging lady, 9:23 am, seven days ago. He sits with her a while on the pavement where she has sat, drained of energy. She smiles and pecks his cheek. On his way home, he meets Gerald. They shake hands. Don deposits a hand in his pocket. 10:26 am: He visits Larsen again.

Don is cornered in the TV room at 1:29 pm, eight

255

days ago, just as the Coven gathers to watch TV. There seems to be an argument. He escapes. 1:46 pm: Don passes Gabrille. They high five. 2:17 pm: Don checks in with Larsen for a few minutes.

Jeff shook his head after a few hours of scanning video. He made himself blackcurrant cordial. Lisa phoned.

'Amanda died today.'

'Don't know her.'

'Lovely lady. Blonde, blue eyes. Wore patterned dresses a lot.'

'Nah, sorry.'

'She had the hots for Junada. Was running with him.'

'Oh, she had the nineties running gear?'

'That's her. She had a heart attack, or stroke. So soon after Don…Coincidence?'

'Around here that's correlation. Not causation.'

There was silence.

'She was a fitness nut?'

'She kept trying, but it wasn't good for her.'

'Why did she do it?'

'She was afraid of how Junada would respond if she dropped out. He's quite intense. Don tried it for a bit, but didn't get on with Junada.'

'Lisa, did you know Don was doing drugs?' Jeff asked.

'I didn't ask. He didn't say anything. But after all these years, you just know anyway'

'Did the drugs and mood problems start about the same time?'

'Correlation, not causation, Jeff.

'Yeah, but hard street drugs can stress the heart.'

'How do *you* know he was using drugs?'

'Gerald deals. I've seen him handing out packages—to Don as well.'

'Gerald came around here a lot. I thought maybe he had a

256

crush on me.'

'That would be understandable.'

Lisa didn't respond.

'You're…you know…well, did you know Don was seeing Mariah?'

'That was my idea. She was into some new age mystic stuff. I thought Don should try it.'

'Did he describe what they did?'

'Only that it was a new way of thinking about death. It involved a kind abstinence.'

'From what…?'

'Food, alcohol, sex…'

'All the good stuff. Lisa, I'm going to check a bit more. Amanda and Don both knew Junada. We need to find out who else they had in common—like Gerald or Mariah.'

'What do you mean?

'If the running is too much for people, then Junada must be asked to calm down. Maybe some of Gerald's drugs are too much for older people, or he had a bad batch. We can get him to change. Maybe the mystic stuff is dangerous, and Mariah needs to chill out as well.'

Jeff ate ham slices and prunes for dinner, then sat down at the lunchbox computer. He brought up the video archive and started looking for Amanda.

He watched hours more video at double-speed. Amanda never connected with Gerald or Mariah in the previous two weeks.

It had grown dark outside, and the window now reflected the room's phosphorescence. Jeff sighed and pressed pause on the playback. Amanda didn't do drugs and didn't do mystic rituals. He felt deflated at the death of his most interesting hypothesis.

He was left with old people stressing their hearts with a fitness regime and wondered whether Junada was doing it deliberately. Running old people to their death was an intriguing method of serial killing, but ultimately, it was pathetic one. Either way, it was worth reporting to the village administration. But they'd just chat with Junada and get him to chill.

We're all on some sort of drug, and we're all dying anyway.

The video playback was showing the camera over the village square, and the picture was paused. Steele Larsen stood outside her clinic, leaning on the door frame causally, arms folded so she held her biceps.

Jeff nudged the keyboard and the video jagged with an electric fizz and started playing.

Larsen swaying her shoulders side to side, pivoting her spine against the doorjamb. Her black hair of finger-tight curls was pulled back from her face, with a tight elastic hair tie. It was an impassive working face. The lips were narrowly parted.

When someone approached, the face moved into another mode. The eyebrows lifted, the eyes widened, the pinched ends of the mouth curled up, and teeth laughed. When they passed, the working face returned.

As Jeff watched, Amanda approached Larsen. The face swung into action and the arms unfolded to grasp Amanda warmly and direct her into the clinic.

Jeff switched to the waiting-room camera. Larsen had one hand firmly on Amanda's shoulder, and the other in front of her, palm up and fingers grasping air. Amanda placed a white vial in Larsen's hand and they entered the consulting room. The door closed behind them.

With his bottom lip pushed out, Jeff squared his shoulders and tapped out a short sequence on the keyboard. Video came alive on a second monitor. It was from a camera placed outside the pharmacy. Jeff wound it back a few minutes before Amanda had met Larsen. The pharmacy was busy. People chatted in pairs. Some wandered down aisles, aimlessly lifting pieces of toiletry. At the rear of the store, Jeff could just make out Debbie Wong serving a short line of customers. He switched to the counter camera, in the corner behind Debbie. Amanda was next in the queue. When Amanda left the store, she was carrying a white plastic bottle—the bottle she gave to Larsen.

Jeff hunched over the keyboard and clacked out some new instructions. He took all the cameras back to the same day and time a week earlier. Amanda took pills from Debbie, dropped the bag in the bin, walked to see Larsen, where she handed over the pills, and went into the consulting room.

Jeff rang Lisa back late that evening. She answered, a little drowsy.

'Sorry, Jeff. I've just taken a sleeping pill.'

'Oh, okay. I'll be quick. One question—why was Don seeing Larsen?'

'To get his mind right?'

'Did he talk about it?'

'He said Steele was trying hypnotherapy.'

'Did it work?'

'He thought so. Some sort of modern regime.'

'Of what?'

'He didn't explain…apart from saying it was about removing bad influences.'

'Why is the secret to life always stopping something?'

'Larsen told Don to stop his medicines.'

'Did he?'

'I told him not to.'

'I've talked to Larsen only once. It didn't go well. Have you?

'Well yes, today. She checked in. I said you and I had been chatting. She said that was nice. She said we should book in some hypnotherapy. I said maybe.'

'Is that what she does?'

'Yes. She came around after Don died. She wanted to use hypnotherapy on me so I wouldn't feel so bad. I told her I preferred grief. She was irritated by that. She thought everyone should avoid pain.'

259

'I'm going to report this to Tom Doyle.'

'What are you going to tell him?'

'Larsen's trying some funny stuff on residents—and two of them just died.'

'He's gonna say death is what happens in a retirement village.'

Jeff was stumped. 'I'm gonna call anyway.'

Doyle's response was exactly as Lisa expected. 'People die in retirement villages.'

'But Don and Amanda were both her patients.'

'Should I investigate Dr Nightly as well—all her patients in the village also die?'

'But she's not trying out weird stuff. Larsen's taking their medication.'

'She's a counsellor. She works in tandem with Dr Nightly. If anything like that happened, it would be planned.'

'Do you think Nightly knows about the hypnosis? Lisa said Larsen wanted to use it on her to...'

'Lisa Draver? Are you bothering her?

'It's none of your business.'

'It is if you're worming yourself into a new widow by besmirching staff.'

'That's a stupid thing to say. Just take a look at Steele, will you.'

'I don't need a convicted hacker to tell me how to do my job.'

'I'm still good at mine. It's about time you got good at yours.' Jeff jabbed angrily at the off button.

Lisa brought dinner around that night—a fish pie. 'Thanks for calling Doyle. But maybe he's right. Dr Nightly is a good person. She'll be working with Larsen. All that hypnosis stuff is just what they do these days.'

'Taking pills from patients is what counsellors do?'

'But what evidence do we have? All we know is that she talked about it with Don, and then with me.'

260

Jeff took a deep breath. 'Lisa, I saw Amanda hand her pills to Larsen.'

'How?'

'I watched it on the village CCTV. I'm a computer hacker. I was in prison for it once.'

Lisa seemed to take the news in her stride. 'Is this on video? Just show it to Tom.'

'Yes, it's recorded. But I can't admit it. I've hacked the whole system—everything and everyone here. I haven't stolen anything or hurt anyone, but that won't matter. I'll go to jail again.'

Lisa stood up from the dinner table and took their plates to the kitchen sink. She stood with her back to Jeff. 'So, it was you who reported Don's death? You saw it on the camera?'

'I saw him on the footpath, after he'd died. I couldn't call 111 because they would find out about me. So I sent the message.'

'It's a strange world where we see real people dead on a screen, then write about it on a screen.'

'It has been like that for a while now.'

'I prefer the world you can touch.' Jeff suddenly felt very embarrassed. He stared at his stubby fingernails. Lisa rinsed the plates for a long time before facing him again. Her taut jaw tightened her cheeks.

'Okay. We must find evidence Tom Doyle can't ignore. Real proof.'

'Sure, like what?

'Something in Larsen's consultation room. Maybe Don or Amanda's unused medicine bottles.'

'She would have ditched them.'

'You don't know people very well.'

'What do you mean?'

'She will just toss them in the rubbish if she doesn't think she's doing anything wrong. If she is deliberately killing them, she will dispose of them instantly and secretly, or...she'll hide

261

them as a twisted record of what she's done.'

'How do we find out?'

'We go over there—we search the clinic.'

'Really? That sounds dicey. What if she finds us?'

'Someone always does the hard physical work of the dirty people behind the computers.' Lisa bent over and patted Jeff's leg cast. 'You're the guy behind the computer. I'm the gal doing the hard work.'

The mission started the next evening. Jeff sat at his computer, watching and recording. He panned the village square camera and found Lisa standing at the village notice board. The moon was out, and light from the day room, where night owls hunched watching TV, cast into the square. Lisa checked her watch.

Jeff's fingers patted at the keyboard and accessed the village security system. He unlocked the magnetic latch on the clinic door, found lighting control, and flicked on the clinic lights.

That was Lisa's cue. She checked for people in the square, then walked straight to the clinic door.

Jeff switched to the reception room camera. Lisa entered and closed the door behind her. She walked boldly into Larsen's office and out of camera view.

Try the waste bin first.

Jeff waited, slotting fingernails together. If Larsen was serious about her hypnosis, Lisa will find the medicine bottles quickly. But Lisa didn't appear at the doorway.

Try her desk drawers.

Jeff rocked his head and shoulders quickly back and forth, silently urging Lisa on.

Try the cupboards.

Light from the office doorway shifted in strength as Lisa's figure moved about. Jeff pinched at the skin between his eyebrows.

Jeff startled himself. He'd forgotten to check the other cameras. He clacked at the function keys and cycled through

262

the day room, the pharmacy, the square. Nothing.

No, wait!

There was someone in the shadows. Jeff held his breath and panned the camera. The person was standing still, a dark shadow against the day-room lights. A spot of intense light glowed briefly, lighting the puffy face. It was Cobbles, having a sly ciggy.

Jeff flicked back to the clinic reception camera and waited. Lisa appeared in the doorway. She walked towards the camera, holding up medicine bottles in her hands.

The reception door opened, and Lisa spun around. Larsen walked into the room. Her face snapped into that practised smile.

Jeff gasps.

Lisa started talking, but Larsen noticed the things in her hands and her face dropped instantly into suspicion.

Get out of there, Lisa!

Larsen stepped quickly toward Lisa and grabbed a hand, wrenching a plastic bottle free.

Lisa, don't wait. Leave now!

Larsen looked at the vial and held it up to Lisa—and appeared to ask about it.

Lisa's face grew angry. She remonstrated with Larsen. Pointing to the vials and to herself.

Larsen lashed out with a hand, slapping Lisa, who stepped backward with the force of the blow.

Oh my God, Lisa!

Larsen followed up, slapping again, then grabbing Lisa by the shoulders. Lisa looked away and up toward the camera. Jeff could see her face clearly, the vivid whites of her eyes round and frightened. He lurched out of his seat, and to his feet, in tears.

Larsen pushed Lisa's shoulders. She fell back against the reception desk. Her head hit the laminate top edge and her bright eyes snapped shut. Her body folded and drifted to the

263

floor, inert.

Jeff whimpered.

Lisa...

Larsen picked the fallen bottles from the floor and stood in the middle of the room, not moving.

Tears now flooded Jeff's mouth.

Move...get help...phone Doyle!

Larsen's head turned, slowly. The monitor screen glitched.

Larsen looked straight at the camera. Straight into Jeff's eyes—staring at him like he was right in front of her.

Jeff staggered back on his broken leg. He twisted to land on all fours. Sobbing from his stomach, he grasped his chair to pull himself up. He steadied himself in front of the monitor. Lisa lay on the floor in a broken bundle. Larsen was gone.

He slapped desperately at the function keys, cycling through the cameras. It was dark and there were shadows everywhere.

He found her, walking quickly, on Camera 9—Lange Lane, an access way to the gas and electrical service rooms.

He punched in Camera 10, then 11, then 12. Larsen was on Sherry Street, near the main parking lot. Jeff frowned and tapped into Camera 15 on a hunch. Larsen came into view—out of shadows and into a street light. She was glancing around furiously. Then she found what she was looking for—Camera 15. She stared straight into it and mouthed something to Jeff.

Jeff stood up, panicked.

She's guessed...and she's coming here.

Jeff switched to Camera 19. Larsen's figure is moving in the half-light. He figured he's got a few minutes until she arrives. A security light flicked on. She looked into the security camera again. Jeff hit the screen grab button to record the image. He logged into the village chat and opened a direct message box to Tom Doyle's account.

He punched out, 'Larsen coming to kill me. Help. Jeff.' He attached the screen image and clicked *send*.

Releasing a whimper under his breath, he wobbled over to

264

the work desk. An old CRT screen sat with its cover off, the grey picture tube exposed. Jeff plunged his hands desperately in a cardboard box under the bench. He cursed at the tangle of wires and plugs. His old fingers tried to unfold a wire from many others. He yelped as it came free. Jeff connected it to the glass and wire bulb at the back of the tube, and then to the knob of the closed door.

The front door opened

Shit, I shoulda locked it.

Someone moved down the hallway.

He plugged in the power lead of the exposed computer screen and switched it on. The screen crackled and fizzed as electricity and heat contacted dust. He remembered why he had started working on it.

The person in the hall walked past the computer room door toward the lounge.

The screen started emitting a high frequency whine outside of the range of Jeff's aged hearing.

The person in the hall heard it and turned back toward the door. They touched the knob and then screeched with surprise as the CRT delivered a mild electric shock. The person moved into the lounge whining. 'You old bastard!'

They came back up the hall and the door was thudded with something heavy. It held.

Jeff grabbed a crutch and hefted it in his hands like a weapon.

The door handle was hit with a heavy object that flicked the latch back. The door slipped slightly ajar, then was kicked and swung open. Larsen was standing in the hallway, one hand tucked under an armpit. She stepped into the room.

'Hello Jeff. Want to talk?'

Jeff slumped into his computer chair, but held the crutch out in front of him, pointing it at Larsen.

'You're still hacking, aren't you?

Jeff kicked the chair back into a corner of the room, between shelves of monitors.

'And sent Lisa to do your dirty work?'

Jeff waved the crutch about. The tip hit a shelf and rebounded to the floor. Jeff fumbled with the handle, lost hold of it...then caught it before it tumbled from his lap.

'Honestly, you crusty shits really are a waste of space.'

Larsen advanced along the wall of shelves, to the tip of the crutch, hands up, ready to tear it from him.

But Jeff swung it away from her, at a CRT screen near her. The vacuum tube imploded, showering Larsen with glass that peppered her raised forearms. A cloud of powder choked her and made her eyes water. Jeff coughed in the spill-over.

Larsen's face emerged from behind her arms. She growled and lurched forward.

Jeff swung the crutch again, catching a larger CRT screen full-on. It imploded right next to Larsen's face, spraying tiny shards. She slipped to the floor and he pummelled the back of her exposed head, bending the crutch and making her release a hideous screech.

Jeff's arms hurt from the effort but he sucked air into his shallow lungs and raised the crutch. He struck her head again and she slumped flat to the floor. He tried to raise the crutch yet again but couldn't gather enough strength.

Tom Doyle's voice called from the hallway.

'Jeff, you here?'

Doyle came to the door and grasped the frame in disbelief.

'My God, what the hell have you done?'

Jeff held a palm up at Doyle, stopping him at the door.

Doyle said, 'It will all be on camera.'

Jeff sprawled toward the computer keyboard and tapped at some keys.

'Not anymore. You're going to have to do some proper detective work, Doyle—like in the old days.'

Vault

Andy Rausch

Nobody in the bank paid any attention to the men. There were five of them, and they managed to blend in with the crowd of customers. The only thing that was different about them was that they were wearing long coats, despite it being too warm for such attire. It was still fairly early on this Monday morning, the bank having just opened, so nobody was all that alert. Nobody except the bank robbers. The lobby was crowded, and the robbers spread themselves strategically around the room. There was one—a blonde man with a beard—standing away from the crowd, back near the entrance. The other four men— two with brown hair, one with black, and another who was bald—had sawed-off shotguns under their coats.

A single guard, a stocky older man, stood against the wall between the two entrance doors. He looked over and noticed the blonde man standing a short distance from him. Having been robbed only once in his thirty-three years as the bank's security guard, he didn't think anything of it. In fact, he considered whether or not he should nod and smile if the man turned and looked his way. Like the rest of the employees, the guard was still half-asleep, perhaps even more so since he was nursing a hangover. After briefly studying the blonde man, the guard returned to eyeballing the curves of the female customers.

Five tellers were manning their positions, and each of them had a good-sized line of customers standing before them. In the front of the middle line, a fifty-something man wearing a construction helmet was becoming increasingly angry, and his voice was starting to rise above the everyday sounds of the bank lobby.

'We're married!' the man growled. 'We've got the same last name! You've seen us together in here a dozen times. I *know* you have because you've waited on us. It's not like I'm trying to cheat anybody. I'm just trying to deposit my wife's check. She woulda done it herself, but she had to work this morning, and I've gotta pay the rent.'

Becka, the pretty young blonde teller, looked nervous. 'I understand, Mr. Jennings, but it's the bank's policy. Your wife has to be on the account for you to deposit her check.'

Even though a good number of customers and bank employees were now watching, the man tried to convince the teller to let him deposit the check anyway. 'Look,' he said, 'nobody's gonna know. It's signed over to me, and I ain't even trying to cash it. I just wanna deposit it. I assure you, this is on the up and up. And I won't tell nobody.' He held up his hand to show the teller his wedding ring. 'Here's the proof that she's my wife.'

'I understand, Mr. Jennings, but—'

'No, I don't think you do,' he said. 'I don't think you understand at all. Me and my wife live all the way across the city, and it's hard for us to get over here to get to the bank. And this place closes at five, which is when my wife gets off work. There's no way she can get here in time to take care of this, and I don't think she should have to take a day off from work just so she can deposit her check.'

'I'm sorry, but like I told you—'

'I want my money!' the man said, slamming his fist down hard onto the counter. The teller shrunk back in fear. Seeing this, the security guard started moving towards the crowd. The tellers rarely needed his assistance, but he wanted to be there if she did.

As the guard made his way into the crowd, the blonde bank

robber moved to one of the entrance doors and locked it with a zip-tie. He looked around to make sure no one saw him do this. Confident they didn't, he went to the other door and locked it, too.

'This isn't fair!' the angry customer at the counter yelled.

The teller looked frightened. She was still trying to calm the customer. 'Look, mister—'

The security guard was nearing the front of the crowd, his fingers hovering over his holstered pistol. His concentration snapped when he heard the shotgun rack. 'Where do you think you're going?' asked the robber holding the shotgun. The guard turned just in time to see the gun explode in his face.

The angry man at the front of the line, and everyone else for that matter, stopped what they were doing. There was a collective gasp, some murmuring, and a couple of screams. The crowd started moving to disperse, but a voice from the far right yelled out, *'This is a robbery! Everybody better do what you're told, or you'll join that security guard out in the graveyard!'*

Everyone looked to the robber making the announcement. He was raising a shotgun of his own.

To keep the customers on their toes, the robber on the opposite side of the room fired a shot into the ceiling. One of the robbers made his way past the one who'd shot the guard. When he got to the front counter, he climbed up onto it. He stood there with his shotgun up in front of him, looking down at the tellers. 'I want you all to start stuffing bills into bags. I don't want the bills off the bottom of the drawers. And I don't want any dye packs. If I get one—let's just say this, if one goes off and I turn blue, I'll be coming back to make you turn red!'

'Ninety seconds!' the blonde robber near the entrance called out to remind his colleagues that they had to wrap up quickly.

Now the robber on the far left climbed up onto the counter. As he was climbing up, the robber standing over the middle station hopped down behind the counter. *'So help me God, if one of you hits the silent alarm, you'll all die!'*

The tellers were visibly frightened.

'Do what I say, and you won't get hurt!' the robber on the counter barked.

The robber who had gone over the counter charged directly at the bank manager, Mr. Avery, a skinny, weasel-faced man with perfectly-groomed white hair. Having done his homework, the robber recognized him as the boss. Mr. Avery stood against the wall behind the tellers when the robber rushed at him, shoving the shotgun barrel into his mouth and pinning him against the wall.

'Open the vault, or your head becomes a memory,' the robber demanded. 'You don't know me, but if I say something, I keep my word. And I *promise* you, I will blow your head off if you don't open that vault *now*.'

Mr. Avery looked at the robber with big eyes. He nodded but couldn't do it very well with the gun barrel in his mouth.

'Good,' the robber said. 'Snap to it.'

The robber pulled the barrel out of Mr. Avery's mouth, allowing him to take the dozen or so steps to the vault. Mr. Avery looked down at the vault's keypad, considered it, and then looked at the robber again. It was clear that he was considering feeding the robber some lie to keep from opening the vault, but when he looked at the shotgun again, he said, 'This'll take a minute.' When Mr. Avery turned to push some buttons, the robber jabbed him in the back with the shotgun and warned, 'You'd better not hit any buttons you're not supposed to hit. If the cops show up here, I'll turn this place into a bloodbath.' Mr. Avery's hands were shaking, but he entered the code. The vault made a loud clicking sound, letting them know it was unlocked, and Mr. Avery stepped back.

'Open it up!' the bank robber ordered. Mr. Avery turned the handle and pulled the vault door open.

As this was happening, a thirty-something guy in a Phillies cap, lying on the floor on the other side of the counter, grabbed

270

the dead security guard's pistol and turned it on the robber who'd killed the old man. The robber looked down, saw the gun pointed up at him, tried to say something, tried to swivel his shotgun, but caught a bullet in the throat. The loud crack of the gunshot startled everyone, and all eyes turned to the robber, who dropped his shotgun, clutched his throat, and fell forward onto the dead security guard.

The guy in the Phillies cap sat up with the pistol trained on the fallen robber. He was about to squeeze the trigger again when the robber on his left cried out, *'You're gonna die for that!'* The robber came running toward him, hopping over customers on the floor as he did. When the robber was about ten feet away from the man with the Phillies cap, Phillies Cap let off a shot that went wide and zinged off the wall. The robber kept coming at top speed. Phillies Cap tried to reposition the pistol and get his aim just right, but the robber had his shotgun up now, and he pulled the trigger, catching Phillies Cap in the chest and causing him to flop back onto the floor.

There were more screams.

The robber who had made Mr. Avery open the vault turned toward the tellers. He pointed at them with the shotgun. *'You!'* he yelled. 'I want you all to come get in the vault!'

Two of the tellers started moving, but the other three looked confused, causing the robber to scream frantically, *'I said get over here! You get over here, or you all die!'*

The tellers were starting to move toward the vault.

'See those bags of cash back there?' the robber said. 'Grab those and bring them out to me!'

The tellers went into the vault. The robber stood outside with his shotgun aimed in their direction. Mr. Avery just stood and watched all this. There was nothing else he could do.

The tellers carried out the five big, heavy burlap bags and sat them at the robber's feet. The robber still standing on the counter hopped down and hurried toward the vault to join his colleague.

Now the robber on the far right side of the room was coming over the counter, too, leaving crowd control to the two robbers still in the lobby. As he moved toward the vault, he turned and looked down at several bank employees lying on the floor. He kicked one of them—a man named Arthur—in the side and yelled, *'Get up! All of you! Get up and get in the vault!'*

The employees stood up and started making their way into the vault, joining the tellers inside. The robber who had forced Mr. Avery to open the vault turned his shotgun on the bank manager. Mr. Avery saw it coming, and his eyes grew big just before the robber fired, blasting him in the chest and knocking him off his feet. The robber racked his shotgun.

'You're a coward!' David, a bank employee, yelled from inside the vault.

This act of disobedience angered the robber, who turned and looked at him for a moment before charging towards him. *'What did you say?!'* The moment the robber stepped inside the vault, Michael, another bank employee, rushed at him, smashing him into the wall and knocking him out. The robber's shotgun went off in the collision with a deafening roar, firing wildly. The unconscious robber dropped to the floor, and the gun clattered beside him.

'Shut the door!' one of the robbers yelled.

Before anyone inside the vault knew what was happening, the heavy door closed, and they could hear its lock pop into place.

There were now seven employees—Becka, Carol, Arthur, Clive, David, Floyce, and Michael—as well as the unconscious robber, locked inside the vault. There were dim lights, and the inside of the vault was warm.

Everyone stood in silence for a moment, looking at one another.

Michael, who had knocked out the robber, asked no one in particular, 'What's going on out there?'

'How would we know?' Floyce asked. 'We know as much as you do.'

'That's not true,' Clive grumbled. 'I know a lot more than that idiot.'

Michael rounded on Clive. 'Who are you calling an idiot?'

Clive stood his ground. 'If you don't know, then you just proved my point.'

Carol, who, at sixty-three, was the oldest person in the vault, said, 'Would you two knock it off? In case you haven't noticed, several people were killed just now; people we *worked* with.'

'Jesus,' Arthur said, cupping his face in his hands. 'Did you see how that man put the shotgun right up to Ernie's face and shot him? Ernie was close to retirement. He'd been working here, what? Thirty years?'

'A long time,' Clive said.

Arthur nodded. 'Thirty years working here is a *long* time.'

Michael pointed down at the unconscious robber. 'And it was all because of this piece of trash.'

Everyone turned their gaze toward the unconscious man.

'We should kill him,' Becka suggested nonchalantly.

'I don't know that we should kill him,' Arthur said. 'But someone needs to grab that gun before he wakes up.'

Michael approached the unconscious robber's shotgun.

'We need to check and see if he's got any other weapons,' Floyce suggested.

Michael stopped, considered this, and turned to look at his co-workers. 'I'll grab the shotgun and keep it trained on him while one of you searches him for weapons. That way, he can't wake up and hurt anyone.'

'Real tough guy, aren't you?' Clive said. 'You're too scared to do it yourself.'

'Are you kidding me?' Michael asked. 'In case you didn't notice, I'm the one who knocked him out in the first place.'

'Will you two stop?' Becka said.

Michael looked at her for a long moment, saying nothing.

He then turned and reached down, picking up the shotgun. He stepped away from the robber and held up the shotgun, examining it. 'This is a nice gun,' he observed.

'Yeah, real nice,' Clive said. 'Let's not forget that's the gun that just killed Mr. Avery.'

Still looking at the gun, Michael managed, 'Yeah.'

'Good riddance,' said Carol, now sitting on the floor.

Everyone turned and looked at her, but no one said a word. Although they were shocked to hear the remark, none of them had liked Mr. Avery.

'Do you think they're still out there?' David asked, speaking for the first time since they'd been locked in.

Michael walked to the door and cocked his head, trying to hear.

'Do you hear anything?' Floyce asked.

'Not a thing.'

'They're probably gone by now,' Carol said.

'What makes you say that?' asked Becka.

'They were counting down the seconds they had to get finished,' Carol said. 'The man said ninety seconds. That was a while ago.'

Becka nodded, satisfied. Then she asked, 'How long do you think we'll be in here?'

David started chuckling.

'What's so funny?' Clive asked.

'Her asking how long we're gonna be here,' David said. 'What a stupid question. How could any of us possibly know that?'

Clive's face turned red, and he said, 'Hey, there's no need to insult Becka.'

David grinned. 'Why? Because she's your girlfriend?'

'She's not my girlfriend,' Clive said indignantly. 'We're engaged.'

David laughed at this.

Seemingly oblivious, Floyce asked, 'Does anyone know

274

how long we can survive in here without fresh air?'

Everyone stopped to consider this for the first time.

'They pump oxygen in,' Becka said.

'No, they don't!' David growled.

Clive stepped forward and pointed his finger at him. *'I'm warning you!'*

David grinned and shrugged. 'Her being your fiance doesn't make her stupid observations any less stupid.'

'He's right,' Carol said, looking at Becka. 'If you don't know something, you don't need to speak or make things up just to hear your own voice.'

Becka just glared at the older woman.

Michael, holding the shotgun, was in front of the door with his back turned to the others. 'Oh no,' he said.

'What's wrong?' Carol asked.

Michael stepped back to point at the emergency phone, destroyed by the earlier shotgun blast. 'We can't call out for help.'

The robber awakened as this was happening and grabbed a snub-nosed .38 from inside his coat. He raised it, aiming at the center of the group.

'Why don't you all just shut up?' he snapped.

Still holding the shotgun, Michael turned around to look at the robber. When he swiveled, the barrel of the shotgun swung around, pointing at the robber. Seeing this, the robber fired a shot, shooting Michael in the face. Because of the vault's acoustics, the gunshot sounded like an M-80 exploding in a coffee can. Becka and Clive both screamed, and Floyce started to gag.

'You didn't have to do that!' David said.

The robber pointed the pistol at David. 'Oh yeah?'

David said nothing and shrunk from the confrontation.

For a moment, no one spoke. The robber reached into his pocket and produced a pack of smokes. He skillfully extracted a cigarette and put it to his lips using only one hand. Then he reached into the same pocket and fished out a lighter.

'You can't smoke that in here,' Carol said. 'You'll kill us all.'

The robber sat staring at her, the lighter's flame in front of his face.

'There isn't enough air for all of us to breathe very long anyway,' David said.

'Please,' Floyce said, hoping to appeal to the robber's humanity.

The robber said nothing. He lit the cigarette and puffed on it, keeping it tucked into the corner of his mouth. 'I'm gonna die anyway,' he said around the cigarette. 'You know what they say—misery loves company.'

Seeing the metal drawers lining the walls, the robber asked, 'What's in those drawers? Do they all have money in them?'

'Of course they do,' Clive said. 'What do you think they got in 'em? Lollipops?'

Before the robber could respond, Becka asked him a question. 'Why'd you do it?'

He looked at her. 'Do what? Rob the bank?'

Becka nodded. 'Yeah.'

The robber started laughing hard, and his dangling cigarette jiggled, threatening to fall, but it didn't. The laughter caused him to cough. The coughing continued, and the longer he coughed, the harder his coughs became.

Attempting to take advantage of the robber's momentary vulnerability, Clive, who had been squatting, sprung forward toward the robber in an attempt to take the pistol. The robber saw him coming. Still coughing, nearly choking, the robber fired, shooting the airborne Clive in the stomach, and Clive crashed hard onto the floor.

'*Clive!*' Becka screamed as she rushed to her lover's side.

The robber considered shooting her, too but decided against it. She was the only attractive woman here. If he was going to go to prison and get the chair, he wanted to savor the little bit of a time he had in the presence of a pretty woman. Becka squatted down over Clive, who was lying face down, whimpering. Becka's tears came immediately, and they streamed down her cheeks.

She looked up at the robber. 'Can I at least turn him over?'

The smoking robber shrugged. 'Do whatever you need to do, sweetheart. He's a dead man anyway.'

Becka's co-workers watched her roll Clive onto his back.

Floyce glared at the robber. *'You're a killer!'*

The robber chuckled. 'That's pretty astute. You must have gotten straight A's in high school.'

'This state has the death penalty,' Carol said. 'You're going to die for this.'

The robber grinned. 'I've been thinking about that,' he said. 'They can't kill me twice. So tell me, what's to stop me from shooting all of you? I'll get the same sentence either way.'

'There's one thing stopping you,' David said.

The robber looked at him. 'What's that?'

'You don't have enough bullets.'

The robber considered this. 'This is true. I've got four bullets, and there are five of you. Still, those are pretty good odds.'

'You'd better not miss,' David said.

'What?' the robber asked. 'Do you want to be the next to get shot?'

'What about the shotgun?' Carol asked.

'I forgot all about that,' the robber said.

'But what if one of *us* gets ahold of it instead of you?'

The robber looked at the shotgun lying beside Michael's body. Then he looked back at Carol. 'If any of you feel froggy, feel free to jump. Just try and get that gun and find out what happens.' He looked at the bank employees. 'Any takers?'

No one moved.

Becka glared at him. 'What if we all rushed you at the same time?'

277

The robber's eyes lit up. 'That could be fun,' he said, nodding slightly. 'I think I could pop at least a couple of you before you get me. And if you kill me, who cares? Like the old broad said, I'm going to die anyway.' He chuckled again, but this time he didn't choke.

Becka looked down at Clive and saw that his eyes were staring off at endless nothingness, and he was no longer breathing.

'Clive?' she asked frantically. *'Clive, baby?!'*

She pounded on his chest with her fists.

She looked up, meeting the robber's gaze through blurry tear-filled eyes. 'If I get free, so help me god, I'll kill you.'

'I've got a bullet with your name on it, too, honey. Go ahead and try me.'

'Becka,' David said. 'Why are you so upset about Clive anyway?'

Everyone turned to look at David.

'It's not like you were loyal to him,' David said. 'How many guys did you cheat on him with?'

She glared at him with fire in her eyes.

'How can you say something like that?' Carol asked.

David smiled and gave a half-shrug. 'It's not hard.' He looked at Becka. 'Go ahead, Beck, you tell them. Tell them about how me and you spent those nights at the Shady Elm Motel when you were supposed to be visiting your mother.'

'Shut up!' Becka snapped.

David chuckled. 'There's no way I was the only one.'

The robber spat out his cigarette, which had burned down to the filter. He looked at Becka and said, 'If you want, now that your boyfriend's gone, you can come over here and sit on my lap and—'

Becka stood, wavering, and glared at the robber. 'I'll make you pay for this.'

'No, you won't,' the robber said as he fired a round into Becka's heart, killing her instantly. As she toppled to the floor,

Floyce screamed.

Carol stared at the robber with the most intense glare she could muster. *'You killed a woman!'*

The robber grinned. 'Women are always screaming about how they want equality. So I gave her equality. What's the difference anyway? You think killing the men was somehow more justified than shooting her?'

Carol said nothing, and the room was silent for a while.

Finally, Floyce said, 'Why do you think it's taking so long for them to come and get us out of here?'

'Maybe all the cops are busy eating apple fritters,' Arthur said.

'It's kind of weird,' the robber said. Thinking of something, he asked, 'Do any of you have cell phones?'

'You don't have one?' Carol asked.

'I left it at home,' the robber said. 'I figured, why would I need it? I'm robbing a bank.'

'You didn't bring your phone, but you brought cigarettes?' Arthur asked.

The robber looked at him like he was stupid. 'You're not a smoker, are you?'

The exchange reminded the robber that he hadn't smoked a cigarette in a while, and he went to work using his free hand to get another cigarette. He looked at the bank employees. 'None of you have cell phones?'

The bank employees shook their heads.

'That was Mr. Avery's bright idea,' Floyce said. 'We're not allowed to have our phones while we're at work.'

'Except for Becka,' Carol said nastily. 'She did whatever she wanted to.'

'I always wondered how she got away with that,' Floyce said.

'I didn't,' David said. 'I think she was having an affair with Mr. Avery, too.'

'Really?' Carol asked.

David shrugged. 'I wouldn't put it past her.' Still looking at Carol, he said, 'You're probably the only person in here she wasn't sleeping with.'

The robber interjected. 'Who's Mr. Avery?'

'The bank manager,' Carol said. 'He was the white-haired jerk you shotgunned.'

'You don't sound too broken up about it,' the robber said.

Carol shrugged, and David said, 'He was something else. The man thought he was Mussolini ruling the bank with an iron fist. Nobody liked him.' He looked down at the dead girl. 'Well, maybe Becka, but I doubt she liked him, even if she was fooling around with him.'

The robber lit the cigarette in his mouth and started puffing.

'You're going to kill us all,' Carol said. 'Seriously, you should put that out.'

Floyce coughed. 'I can't breathe.'

'You'll live,' the robber said.

Now he looked at the shotgun lying on the floor a few feet away.

'You,' he said, pointing at Floyce with his pistol. 'Pick up that shotgun and bring it over here.'

Floyce stared at him, saying nothing.

The robber repositioned his pistol, aiming it at the middle-aged woman's face to make a point. *'I said get me that gun!'*

Floyce looked at Carol and David, unsure what to do.

'Do what he says,' Carol advised.

Floyce raised herself from the floor and moved slowly toward the shotgun, her eyes locked on the robber. 'Please,' she said, her voice wavering. 'Please don't shoot me.'

The robber grinned. 'I won't shoot,' he said. 'Not if you do what I tell you to do.'

Floyce made her way to the shotgun. She was trembling. She leaned down to pick it up, showing her profile to the robber as she did.

'That's it,' the robber said. 'You're doing just fine.'

Floyce picked up the shotgun. She turned towards the robber and brought the shotgun barrel up, aiming it at his face. The robber's eyes got big, and he started to move, his lit cigarette falling from his mouth and onto his lap. Floyce pulled the trigger and heard a loud metallic *click!*

The robber laughed. 'You've got to rack it first.'

Floyce looked at him with equal parts fear and stupidity.

'Go ahead,' the robber said. 'Rack it.'

Floyce, confused, looked down at the shotgun. The robber raised his pistol and shot her in the face, dropping her like a sack of potatoes. He giggled like a schoolboy.

'You killed her!' Carol said.

The robber sat there, giggling hard with tears sprouting up in the corners of his eyes, and he said, 'Yes, yes I did. I shot her deader than a Kennedy.'

David, sitting against the vault's back wall, shook his head but said nothing. Carol was sitting criss-cross applesauce about four feet from the robber. Arthur was in the middle of the vault, chewing his fingernails. They all sat in silence for fifteen minutes or so.

David eventually broke the pause. 'I can't believe nobody has let us out yet.'

The robber asked, 'Do either of you know how long you can survive inside a vault before you run out of oxygen?'

'One person can stay alive locked inside the vault for about fifteen hours,' Carol said. 'But with multiple people, that fifteen hours becomes a lot less.'

'Then maybe you should thank me,' the robber said.

'Why on earth would we thank you?' Arthur asked.

'I killed these four idiots. That should preserve the oxygen a little bit longer.'

Arthur stared at him and nodded, recognizing the truth in the statement.

'I'd live even longer if the three of you were dead,' the robber said, saying it as the thought came to him. He looked at

David, sitting against the back wall. 'I've got two bullets left, and the next one is for you.'

David's eyes got big. '*Me?* Why *me?*' He looked at Carol. 'Why not *her?*'

Carol said, 'That's real chivalrous, David. Thanks.'

'No, I mean it,' David said, pleading. 'Why me and not her?'

The robber grinned at Carol and then looked David's way and raised the pistol. 'Because she's a woman, and you're not. Today is gonna be my last chance to be with a woman. So yeah, it's gotta be you.'

Carol was horrified hearing this.

Arthur asked, 'Does that mean you're going to kill me, too?'

Without acknowledging this, the robber swiveled his pistol towards Arthur, shooting him in the chest. The robber then swiveled the gun back towards David, shooting him center mass as well.

The bank robber grinned as he looked at Carol. 'It's just you and me now.'

Carol sighed.

'So how do you want to do this?' the robber asked. 'We can do it the easy way, or we can do it hard. I really don't care which.'

Carol decided to do what she had to do. She looked at him, batting her eyes now, attempting to act seductive. Seeing this, the bank robber grinned.

'Do you think we've got time?' Carol purred.

'I sure do.'

Carol smiled at him, still feigning a look of interest.

The robber patted the floor beside him. 'Why don't you come over here and get a little bit closer so we can become friends and snuggle.'

Carol didn't want to sit beside him, but she went along with it, playing her role in this game. She scooted towards him. When Carol was next to him, the robber put his arm around her.

She was repulsed, but she didn't let him know.

She looked at him, batting her eyes again. 'Do you mind if I take my shoes off?'

'You can take off anything you feel like taking off.'

'Why don't you take your coat off,' she suggested.

'Good idea,' the robber said. As he started taking off his coat, Carol removed her high-heeled shoes. The other tellers had made fun of her for wearing high-heels at her age, but, as it turned out, Carol had been right. As the robber worked to remove the coat, she tightened her grip on the shoe she was clutching. He was completely distracted when Carol brought the shoe around hard, burying its heel deep in his eye socket.

He screamed and thrashed wildly like a wounded animal. Carol stood up and got the shotgun. She looked down at the thrashing robber, racked the shotgun, and said, 'And then there was one.'

Author Biographies

Josh Pachter was the 2020 recipient of the Short Mystery Fiction Society's Golden Derringer Award for Lifetime Achievement. His stories appear in *Ellery Queen's Mystery Magazine, Alfred Hitchcock's Mystery Magazine, Black Cat Mystery Magazine, Mystery Magazine, Mystery Tribune*, and elsewhere. He edits anthologies (including Anthony Award finalist *The Beat of Black Wings: Crime Fiction Inspired by the Songs of Joni Mitchell*) and translates fiction and nonfiction from multiple languages, mainly Dutch, into English. *joshpachter.com*

Rebecca A. Demarest is an award-winning author, playwright, book designer, and writing instructor living in Seattle, WA, with her husband and two muppets. When not being held hostage by words, you can find her at her day job (working the people side of unbelievably awesome tech) tending to her indoor jungle (now with real frogs and lizards!), crafting, sewing, running Dungeons and Dragons as a professional Dungeon Master, and failing to teach her dogs new tricks. For more information on her work, please visit *rebeccademarest.com*

Joseph S. Walker lives in Indiana and teaches college literature and composition courses. His short fiction has appeared in *Alfred Hitchcock's Mystery Magazine, Ellery Queen's Mystery Magazine, Mystery Weekly, Tough*, and a number of other magazines and anthologies. He has been nominated for the Edgar Award and the Derringer Award and has won the Bill Crider Prize for Short Fiction. He also won the Al Blanchard Award in 2019 and 2021. *jsw47408.wixsite.com/website*

Paulene Turner is a writer of short stories, short plays, and novels. A former journalist, she is currently editing her 6-book YA time travel series. Her short stories have appeared in anthologies and magazines including *Luna Station Quarterly*, *The London Reader*, *Specul8*, *Jayhenge Publishing* and *Black Beacon Books*. As well as writing short plays, she also directs them for *Short and Sweet, Sydney*, the biggest little play festival in the world. She lives in Sydney with her husband, twin daughters and twin pugs, Holmes and Watson.

Jason Fischer is a writer, reader, and lifelong Alfred Hitchcock fan. His library is overflowing with everything and anything suspense, from horror to crime, dedicating many of the bookshelves to the anthologies from the Master of Suspense himself. When not writing, you can find Jason biking the trails around his home, playing with his nephews, adding to his VHS collection, or on the deck feeding the deer and enjoying nature. He lives in the far south suburbs of Chicago with his wife. *jasonfischerauthor.com*

Elizabeth Elwood spent many years performing with Lower Mainland music and theatre groups and singing in the Vancouver Opera chorus. Having turned her talents to writing and design, she created twenty marionette musicals for Elwoodettes Marionettes and has written four plays that have entertained audiences in both Canada and the United States. A Derringer Award nominee, she is the author of six books in the Beary Mystery Series, and her stand-alone short stories have been featured in many mystery magazines and anthologies. Elizabeth was the winner of Best Short Story in the Crime Writers of Canada Awards of Excellence in 2022 for her story, "Number 10 Marlborough Place", published in *Ellery Queen Mystery Magazine*. Visit her website at *elihuentertainment.com*

Cameron Trost is an author of mystery and suspense fiction best known for his puzzles featuring Oscar Tremont, Investigator of the Strange and Inexplicable. He has written two novels, *Letterbox* and *The Tunnel Runner*, and two collections, *Hoffman's Creeper and Other Disturbing Tales* and *The Animal Inside*. Originally from Brisbane, Australia, Cameron lives with his wife and two sons near Guérande in southern Brittany, between the rugged coast and treacherous marshlands. He runs Black Beacon Books and is a member of the Australian Crime Writers Association. *camerontrost.com*

The idea of Hitchcock filming a movie in a zombie apocalypse bunker literally came to **David Carroll** in a dream, but it took a lot more research to get the details down. When not dreaming, David is a computer programmer and gamer. He has written for role-playing games and on the history of horror, as well as various published short stories. His first novel, *Prismatic* (co-written as Edwina Grey), won an Aurealis Award for best Horror Novel and has been rereleased this year. He lives with author Kyla Lee Ward and a pair of cats.

Roger Johns is a former corporate attorney, a retired college professor, and the author of the *Wallace Hartman Mysteries*, *Dark River Rising*, and *River of Secrets* from St. Martin's Press. He is the 2018 Georgia Author of the Year (Detective·Mystery Category), a two-time finalist for Killer Nashville's Silver Falchion Award, and runner-up for the 2019 Frank Yerby Fiction Award. His short fiction has been, or will soon be, published by *Saturday Evening Post*, *Alfred Hitchcock's Mystery Magazine*, *Mystery Weekly Magazine*, *Dark City Crime & Mystery Magazine*, *After Dinner Conversation*, and *JOURN-E: The Journal of Imaginative Literature*. Roger's articles and interviews about writing and career management for new authors appear in *Southern Literary Review*, *Writer Unboxed*, *Career Authors*, and *Southern Writers Magazine*. *rogerjohnsbooks.com*

H.K. Stubbs is an Australian writer, journalist, and creative producer who loves following stories and paths—both her own, and others'—for the discoveries along the way and the surprise at the end of the journey. Stubbs's stories have been published in *Apex Magazine*, *Kaleidotrope*, *Midnight Echo*, and anthologies by Black Beacon Books, IFWG Publishing, GSFG, Knightwatch, and more. Her non-fiction appears in *We Are Gold Coast* and *Nevertheless*. She is happiest rock-climbing in the mountains of South-East Queensland. *helenstubbs.wordpress.com*

Mark Blackham writes about ordinary people in extraordinary circumstances not too different from these, in ordinary times not far from now, and in ordinary places not far from here. His first novella, *A Sky of Wretched Shells*, is available in paperback or ebook format. He lives in Wellington, New Zealand, with his wife and an alternating number of their four adult children. In his spare time, he goes kayaking. He's founder of the New Zealand Natural Burials Association and he is a boxing official (referee and judge). *markblackham.com*

Andy Rausch is a Rondo Hatton Award-nominated film journalist, celebrity interviewer, screenwriter, and author of more than fifty books. His novels include *Layla's Score*, *American Trash*, and *Savage Brooklyn*. His short fiction appears in more than twenty anthologies. He also writes for numerous publications and has a regular column in *Screem* magazine. Additionally, he is a web editor at *Diabolique* magazine. He has worked on numerous films and co-wrote the motion picture, *Dahmer vs. Gacy*. He has written nonfiction books about such notable people as Stephen King, Elmore Leonard, Quentin Tarantino, Martin Scorsese, and Orson Welles. He is a heart transplant recipient, a disability rights activist, and lives in Independence, Kansas, with his wife and two of his children.

For news, reviews, competitions, author interviews, and exclusive excerpts

Visit our website
blackbeaconbooks.com

Like us on Facebook
facebook.com/BlackBeaconBooks

Join us on Twitter
@BlackBeacons

Find us on Instagram
instagram.com/blackbeaconbooks

Subscribe on Patreon
patreon.com/blackbeaconbooks

Made in the USA
Monee, IL
12 December 2022

21144077R00173